THREE QUEERDOS AND A BABY

NINA PACKEBUSH

Three Queerdos and a Baby

YESYES BOOKS *Portland*

Cover & Interior Design: Alban Fischer

ISBN 978-1-936919-90-1
Printed in the United States of America

Published by YesYes Books
1631 NE Broadway St #121
Portland, OR 97232
yesyesbooks.com

KMA Sullivan, Publisher
Brandon Courtney, Senior Editor, Operations
Alban Fischer, Graphic Designer
A. Tony Jerome, Assistant Editor
Karah Kemmerly, Assistant Editor
Jill Kolongowski, Manuscript Copy Editor
James Sullivan, Assistant Editor, Audio Books
Gale Marie Thompson, Senior Editor, Book Development

To my feral family

When your heart is broken, you plant seeds in the cracks and pray for rain.

—ANDREA GIBSON

Chapter 1

Pain tore through me like a tornado, starting slow and then swirling faster and faster, sucking me into a vise grip of pain.

I tried to breathe through it as my round belly grew hard. I glanced over at the monitor. The numbers on the screen rose with the pain. The jagged lines on the thin strip of paper emerging from the machine began to form another little mountain. I closed my eyes and squeezed Lou's hand, trying to somehow match the clenching agony of my belly with my grip on his hand.

"You're doing great," he said, but his dark eyes were wide with fear. I think he regretted saying he'd be here for this. Sweat beaded on his forehead. "Don't forget to breathe," he said and then made a breathy *hee hee hee* sound to remind me of how we had practiced. He had stopped shaving his head and instead he was letting it grow out, styling it into an afro. Between contractions he nervously ran his hands through his hair until it stood straight up on the top of his head. It was a good look for him, but at this moment all the *hee hee hee breathe* talk made me want to punch him in the face.

Lou and I had sat in my dingy bedroom most nights for the past two weeks watching YouTube videos on Lamaze breathing. My doctor, Alice, had given me information on a birthing class at the hospital, but I thought that two queer teenagers—one white and one black—might not fit in so well with all the grown-up mommies and daddies. "How does breathing like that possibly help with the pain?" Lou had asked.

I can now say that it doesn't. At best it sort of distracts you so you don't fall into a well of panic, that's about it.

A short, chubby nurse dressed in pastel green scrubs splattered with pink and blue teddy bears walked in. She smiled as she glanced at the monitor. "Oh, that's a big one. You're getting closer." Her words held just a hint of an Indian accent.

She reached for my wrist to take my pulse, but I jerked it away.

"Who are you?" I gasped.

"I'm Olivia, your afternoon nurse," she smiled again. "Doctor Fraser will be in to check on you soon. We can wait until this one passes before I take your vitals." She stood back and watched the numbers on the screen before taking the paper that was being fed out of the machine. She examined the mountainous landscape of my labor laid out above the jagged road of the baby's heartbeat.

"It's looking better," she said.

I squeezed my eyes shut and clenched my teeth against the pain as the contraction reached its peak, trying hard to remember to breathe. Finally, the pain began to ease, and I released Lou's sweaty hand.

"Who's Doctor Fraser? Where's Alice?" I asked.

"Alice?"

"Doctor McCanne. Alice," I said, my eyes still shut tight.

"Oh, Doctor McCanne is off today. Doctor Fraser will be taking care of you. He's great. You'll love him."

"I want Alice," I said opening my eyes to glare at her.

"I'm sorry kiddo, Doctor McCanne is off today."

"Alice promised me she'd be here. She promised me. And I don't want a male doctor." I felt the tears building.

Lou reached over to take my hand again. I shoved it away. He looked hurt. "I'm going to go find your mom," he said, getting up.

"Are you Daddy?" the nurse asked.

Lou began to stammer, "Um, well . . . I . . . ah . . ."

"Yes," I said, smiling to myself, thinking about the confusion that would spread across Olivia's face if she knew that not so long ago, Lou had been Pru, or the horror that would flash in her eyes if she knew that the two of us had both been residents of the third floor—the psych ward—not so long ago. "He's the dad."

Lou turned and practically ran from the room.

I wasn't completely sure why I said that. I think it was part active-labor-angry mixed up with some wishing it were true, but as soon as the words were out of my mouth, I regretted them. I had been working real hard these past couple of weeks to not think about my baby's other parent, Gray. As this day got closer, I knew that I needed to block the origin story of this pregnancy from my mind with all my might. If I let my mind wander too far back in time, if I let myself fall into those old sweet memories of me and Gray or think about that terrible day when they made that terrible choice to walk onto the freeway, I start to shrink inside.

Going crazy and ending up in the mental ward is something I never want to experience again and so I try my best to keep the memories locked up tight in my brain and only take them out in tiny doses and when it feels safe. Anna, my counselor, taught me how to walk through my memories. She taught me that I can feel them without letting them stick to me and suck me under. It's like staying in the shallow part of a river and just letting the memories run over my bare toes, rather than diving into the current of them. But sometimes I miss Gray so hard. Knowing that they will never know their baby feels impossible.

Nurse Olivia turned back to me, "Okay kiddo, time for your vitals and a little poking and prodding."

I wondered if she called non-teenage mothers kiddo. Or just us children. She took my wrist, feeling for my pulse, and then started poking at my belly. "You're doing great," she said, with way too much cheery enthusiasm. "Just remember that we need you to stay in bed. Your baby's heart rate is doing just fine right now, but no getting up, okay kiddo?"

My birth plan had stated that I would get to walk around during labor, maybe stand in the shower, or lay over the big rubber birthing ball, but my baby's heart kept slowing down every time I got up, so now I was ordered to stay in this stupid bed and I would have to give birth to Gracie this way. I had heard that being on your back makes delivery more difficult than squatting or standing but seeing Baby Gracie's heart slow down like it might stop almost made my own heart stop. Of course, I wasn't going to get up and walk around. Nurse Olivia was treating me like a child.

I wanted Alice.

After I got released from the psych unit three months ago, Mom had taken me straight to see an obstetrician. Before that we, meaning me and Mom and my sister, had all been in denial about my pregnancy, but after I went crazy, reality slapped us right across the face. The staff psychiatrist at the hospital had tried to force me to take meds and kept threatening to have the baby taken away from us after she was born. Mom had rushed out the day I got released and found me a counselor and an obstetrician. We got super lucky with the obstetrician. Alice turned out to be a totally gay former teen mom and Alice promised me that she would be the one delivering my baby.

I wanted Alice.

I needed Alice.

I couldn't do this without her. I didn't want some dumb man putting his face down there and barking orders at me. I didn't want some nurse secretly feeling sorry for my baby and treating me like I was four years old. I didn't want to have to explain Lou or about Gray and how Gray wasn't really a boy or a girl or how they were Gracie's real parent. I didn't want to explain about the semi-truck. I didn't want anyone finding out about my stay on the third floor and asking questions or suddenly thinking that I was too crazy to raise Gracie. Alice knew my story and I trusted Alice.

My heart sped up and my hands were wet with sweat. The air in the room was too thick. My lungs couldn't take in enough air. I reached over and grabbed the bed remote. I needed to raise the head of the bed up higher. Maybe I wouldn't feel so helpless if I was sitting straight up, but just then I felt the familiar grip start at my belly button and begin to spread. The numbers on the monitor began to climb. As the pain took hold, I realized that I couldn't do this. None of it. I couldn't keep going through this pain. I couldn't push a baby out of me. I couldn't be a mom. I wanted them to cut her out of me and then find that gay couple that I had chosen to adopt her and tell them they could have her after all. I began to gasp for air, gulping it like a fish out of water.

"I can't do this. I can't. I can't do this," I cried, swinging my head side to side on the pillow. My body slowly glazed with sweat as my mouth filled with saliva. I was going to puke. I shoved the tears away with the back of my hand.

Nurse Olivia came over to me and put her hand on my forehead. "Breathe, kiddo. Hee hee hee puff, hee hee hee puff. Remember, shallow breaths."

"No!" I gasped. "I can't breathe! I don't want to do this. I want a C-section. Now. Take the baby out of me. And stop calling me kiddo!"

I could feel my chest closing up as the pain continued to roll across my belly like a giant fist squeezing harder and harder. I wanted out of this.

"You're doing just fine," Olivia crooned, completely ignoring my words.

Just then, Mom, Lou, my sister Sam, and her kid, Henry, burst through the doors. I closed my eyes and gripped the sides of the bed willing myself not to vomit.

Mom glanced at the monitor, "How're you doing, honey?"

I kept my eyes shut as a low moan rose from deep in my throat.

"Breathe, baby, breathe. You can do this," Mom commanded.

Thank God she didn't start hee hee heeing at me.

I opened my eyes and glared at her and then leaned over the bed. The vomit hit the floor with a hard splat. Nurse Olivia rushed over to me. Mom told her she would take care of it.

A look of relief washed over Olivia's face. "Okay, if you're sure. I'll be back shortly," she said, heading for the door.

As the vise grip began to loosen and the room came back into focus, I realized that tears were streaming down my face. Mom quietly began sopping up the vomit with paper towels.

I felt a small hand slide over mine. I turned my head to see little Henry staring at me. "Hey French Fry," I said, trying to smile.

"Are you okay, Banj? Is the baby okay? Do you want me to go see if they have any popsicles in the caferteria?" At nine years old he still couldn't say the word cafeteria properly and it made me smile. There were a lot of words that Henry couldn't say properly, probably because we all thought it was so cute that nobody corrected him. One advantage of Henry being unschooled rather than in public school is that he was able to keep his innocence a bit longer. He was both mature for his age and also very innocent. He took his free hand and shoved his scraggy bangs out of his dark eyes, which were huge with worry.

I squeezed his hand. "I'm okay. It just hurts."

"Is the baby okay?"

"Yeah, she's fine. You'll get to meet her soon. Are you excited?"

His face relaxed a little but remained serious, "I'm epically excited." Lately Henry has been experimenting with cool kid talk he picked up from the neighborhood kids. It was as adorable as his mispronunciations. I wondered if my baby would be as cute as Hen.

I looked past him to Mom as she carried the gross paper towels to the trash. "They told me that Alice has the day off so some man doctor is going to deliver my baby. Alice promised me, Mom. I don't want a man doctor." I felt the panic start to rise in my chest again.

"I've already sent her a text and she's on her way," Mom said.

"Really?"

"She said it would be about a half an hour before she got here, but she'll be here. Don't worry."

"What if Gracie comes before that?"

"Honey, you have a way to go yet."

I wondered how long *a way to go* was. I couldn't imagine lasting much longer.

Sam stepped forward, "You look great, Banj. Can I get you anything?"

"They told me I can't have anything but ice chips. I'm so thirsty."

Mom let out a loud sigh. "What is this, the 1970s? Wait until Alice gets here and then we'll get you some water or juice to sip."

"Or a popsicle," said Henry seriously.

"A popsicle is a great idea, Henry," said Mom.

"C'mon Hen, let's go get Banjo some ice chips," said Sam.

"Is James coming?" I asked Mom. James was my big brother. We weren't especially close, yet for some reason I wanted him to be here.

"He'll be here right after work," said Mom.

"Okay."

Lou slouched against the far wall by the door. "You don't have to stay," I said.

"Don't you want me to stay?" he asked, the hurt wild in his eyes.

"I just don't want you to feel obligated."

"I want to be here," he said. "I just don't know what I'm supposed to do."

"Just be here. That's all you need to do," said Mom.

He smiled. "Hey, did anyone text Dylan?"

Dylan was the other crazy homo kid we met when we were residents of the third floor. Dylan lived in a halfway house now. His fundamentalist parents kicked him out when they discovered gay porn on his computer. Once he was released from the psych ward he was sent to a group home until they could find a foster home for him. He turned eighteen before they found a family, so he transitioned into a young adult halfway house for homeless gay kids.

"He'd want to be here," Lou added.

Dylan had come over every day that he was free from house chores or work or school to help me and Lou practice breathing. Gay Dylan with his fluff of frizzy red hair and his big soft body sat on the floor with us concentrating on his hee hee hee breathing and learning all about dilation and contractions and episiotomies. He even sat with us as we watched a video of a woman actually giving birth. Poor Dylan's face was on fire the entire time. He never looked away or said a word, though his stuttering was much worse after the video than it had been before the video.

"Text him," I said.

When I was making my birth plan I didn't want anyone in the room except maybe my mom and Sam. I couldn't imagine being naked in front of Lou or Dylan. Mom and Sam and Alice kept telling me that once you go into labor you don't care if the world sees you naked. When my sister had Henry, I remember her ripping her gown right off and throwing it on the floor. She gave birth totally naked. I couldn't imagine ever doing something like that. Not only did the thought of being naked to the world sound like the worst idea in the world, but the thought of Lou seeing me naked for the very first time when I was pushing a kid out of my vagina sounded about as much fun as, well, as pushing a kid out of my vagina.

Now I was starting to understand. Maybe I would even let Lou stay for the actual birth. Maybe even Dylan. Maybe by the end of this I would be naked and not even care.

Lou pulled his phone out of the back pocket of his jeans, relieved to have something to do. A couple minutes later his phone chimed. Lou smiled at the phone, "He says, *O.M.G. O.M.G. O.M.G. I'm going to faint and pass out and oh my god oh my god oh my god. I'm on my way. I'll ask them to excuse me from curfew tonight. And tell Banjo I made her a playlist.*"

"You should be proud, Banj, you've made the born again take the Lord's name in vain," Lou laughed.

"Hmmm I wonder what kind of birthing playlist a former born again Christian gay boy will create?" I said.

"I guess we're about to find out," said Lou, smiling. "But please oh lord who art in heaven don't let there be any Vampire Weekend on it."

This made me laugh. Dylan had some weird crush on the gay guy in Vampire Weekend and as a result he managed to find a way to work one of their songs into every playlist he had created since we met him. Lou and I were both over it. Dylan was a total hipster when it came to music.

"No kidding. I thought gay guys were supposed to be into disco or something," I teased.

"Actually, he's been expanding lately. I even heard him playing rap the other day. And I think his new crush is everyone in The Neighborhood. Oh, and Vance Joy. If I have to listen to Rip Tide one more time I might explode," said Lou.

"Thank God, sometimes all that mopey music of his makes me totally want to kill myself." The minute the words were out of my mouth I wanted them back. I'm so stupid sometimes. The room fell into an awkward silence.

Just then, Sam and Henry returned with a cup of ice chips, saving me from my own stupidity. And right behind them came Alice. The sight of her caused me to burst into tears.

"None of that, young lady. None of that," scolded Alice as she swept into the room. Her mop of white hair was sticking up as if she had just crawled out of bed, but I knew she hadn't. Alice's hair was always a mess. "This is a happy day, remember? Now let's take a look at what I've missed." She patted my knee as she made her way around my bed to the machine. She adjusted her thick-rimmed, black plastic glasses as she examined the strip of paper showing the history of my labor and my baby's heartbeat. "Oh this looks just lovely. You're coming along just fine, Banjo. We need to keep an eye on little Gracie's heart rate, but right now things look just fine."

"Thank you for coming," I sobbed.

"Are you kidding me? I wouldn't miss this for the world. Now stop those tears, okay?" She surveyed the room and then ruffled Henry's already ruffled hair, "You about ready to meet that baby, Sir Henry?"

"I'm so so so so excited!" he said.

"So am I," she said. She turned to Mom, "Jane, how are you holding up?"

"Well, I just mopped up a nice bit of vomit." She laughed. "I'm so glad you're here Alice. This means so much to all of us."

Sam nodded in agreement.

"Like I said, I wouldn't miss it for the world. Looks like the whole family is here. Good good."

"Almost everyone. We're waiting on James and Dylan," said Mom.

Alice turned to Lou. "Mr. Anderson, I'm so glad you made it." She winked at him. "Now if you all will excuse me, I need to go put on my official baby delivering clothes. They're pretty strict about that sort of thing around here, so I'll see you all in a bit. And don't worry. By the look of things we have some time."

As she turned to go I felt the tightness start up again. This time I tried hard to breathe.

"Lou?"

He jumped up, "Yeah, what do you need?"

I glanced at the monitor and back at him. "Will you help me breathe?"

Chapter 2

My contractions were coming minutes apart and lasting nearly as long. With each contraction unbearable pain ripped through my belly and my back. I had rejected the epidural and was seriously regretting it. What had I been thinking?

They had removed the bottom of the birthing bed in preparation for the delivery. The lower two feet of a birthing bed folds down and slides under so that when it's time to deliver the doctor has full access. My butt was about a foot from the edge and my knees were bent and spread wide. I wanted the option of squatting or using a birthing ball, but I knew that was not possible. Everything felt like it was spinning out of control. Lou and Mom were on either side of me. Sam, Henry, and Dylan—who had arrived just as I began to push—stood off to the side cheering me on.

I had a moment of relief before another contraction slammed into me.

Alice announced that it was time to push again. I had been pushing through each contraction for what felt like hours. I wasn't sure if I could go on.

Another contraction hit and Alice almost yelled, "Push. Come on, Banjo, push. That's it. That's it. You're doing great. Okay, relax and breathe." Alice looked up from between my legs, "Deep breaths now. You're almost there. A little bit of poo slipped out. Totally normal. I'm just going to clean you up a bit."

I had shit myself.

Mom, Sam, Henry, Lou, and Dylan were all in the room, I was naked from the waist down, and I shit myself in front of everyone. I barely cared.

Lou pushed my damp bangs out of my face. "You're doing great," he whispered.

I opened my eyes and flashed him a weak smile before the next contraction swept through me.

"Okay sweetie, look in the mirror." There was a mirror placed in such a way that I could actually watch my baby come out of me. "Do you see the top of little Gracie's head? You're almost there. She's almost here, but she needs to come out now. This time I need you to push as hard as you can, okay?" Alice's voice sounded more serious than it had before.

I nodded.

I leaned forward, grabbing my knees, and at Alice's direction I pushed with all my might. I could feel the ring of fire—that burning feeling of my vagina being stretched far past the point that I could imagine possible.

"That's it. Keep pushing. Keep pushing. Keep pushing. That's it. That's it. That's it. Okay now relax."

The contraction eased, but the pain in my vagina and the terrible pressure didn't. I was shivering.

"Banjo, sweetie, Gracie needs to come out now. Do you understand me? Her heart rate is dropping too low with each contraction. We need to get her out now." She turned her attention to Nurse Olivia. "Olivia, please go tell Doctor Fraser to prepare for an emergency C-section right now." Alice's voice was just this side of shouting.

Olivia rushed from the room. Mom took my hand. I heard Henry start to cry and Sam's voice soothing him. This was all happening too fast. She can't die, I thought. She can't die. Please Gray, wherever you are, please keep Gracie safe. Please.

Just then I felt another contraction sweep across my belly and slam into my lower back. "Okay Banjo, this is it. Push this baby out. Push. Push. Push."

Mom put her hand on my forehead, "Banjo, you can do this. Push now. Baby, push now."

I gripped my knees, bending myself in half and pushed with every bit of strength I had left. It felt as if all the veins of my face might explode. "Okay, relax," said Alice.

Just then Olivia came rushing back in.

"Banjo, I'm afraid we are going to have to do an episiotomy. We need to get Gracie out right now." Alice turned her voice to Olivia, "Olivia please bring me the tray."

"No," I said. Nothing was going the way I had planned. I didn't want them to cut me. I didn't want any of this. This wasn't how it was supposed to be.

"Sweetie," Alice soothed. "We need to get Gracie out right now. Do you hear me? Right now. Doctor Fraser is preparing for a C-section, but I'm not sure we have the time for that. I'm just going to make a small cut, just enough to help Gracie's head slide though. Okay?"

I nodded as tears sprang from my eyes. I just need this to be over with. Lou squeezed my hand. I heard Dylan start to pray across the room.

"Hen, come on. Let's go get a snack, okay?" Sam said with a shaking voice.

"No!" he yelled. "I'm staying here."

"Come on, Buddy. We can wait just outside the door," Sam said as she guided Henry from the room. I could hear his muffled sobs through the door.

"Okay," said Alice, "just a quick pinch of the needle."

The pain down there was already so intense that I couldn't imagine it getting any worse.

"Okay, now you may feel a mild tugging sensation. There shouldn't be any pain," Alice said as I heard a strange popping sound and realized it was my skin being cut.

I felt my belly begin to tighten again.

"Lou, Jane, can you each hold one of her knees please? We need to get this done and done now." Mom and Lou both let go of my hands and grabbed my knees spreading my legs even farther apart. "Okay Banjo, here it comes. When I tell you to push, I want you to push with everything you have. Let's get her out of there. Here we go. Push. Push. Push. Push. That's it. You got this," Alice was cheerleading from between my legs.

Lou held my knee as he watched what was happening between my legs, "Dude, you're doing it. You're doing it. I can see her head coming out!"

"Come on, sweetie, push. You can do it." Mom joined in while holding my other knee.

I leaned forward with my hands on Lou's and Mom's hands. I squeezed my eyes shut and pushed down with every bit of strength I had left. I felt the most intense pain and then suddenly the pressure was gone, and I felt my baby slide out of me.

I opened my eyes and saw panic on Mom's face. Alice pulled Gracie away with the umbilical cord still connecting her to me. She was blue-gray and limp. Olivia rushed forward. Gracie was silent. She wasn't moving. I saw tears erupt from Mom's eyes. No. No. No. This can't happen. Please Gray, please save our baby. Wherever you are, please, please don't let her join you. Send her back. I need her here. Please, Gray, send her back to me.

I heard screaming. Who was screaming? Make her shut up. Make her shut up. Make her shut up. Lou grabbed me and pulled my face into his chest and the screaming became muffled. I realized it was me. My baby was dead. How could this happen? How could she be alive inside of me just minutes ago and now be dead? I lost Gray, I couldn't lose Gracie. I just couldn't. I clung to Lou, my teeth chattering. I was vaguely aware of other people in the room—more doctors and nurses. The energy in the room felt dangerous and chaotic. There was so much noise. Voices. Clattering. The sound of fast-moving feet and beeping equipment. I started to feel suffocated.

Someone laid a heated blanket over me.

I heard a baby whimper and then cry.

"That's it. That's what we want to hear," cheered Alice.

I pulled away from Lou and looked towards Alice. She was holding Gracie and I saw Gracie literally turn from blue-gray to pink before my eyes. She screamed her little head off.

Mom burst into tears as she leaned in to take Lou and I into her arms. "She's okay. She's perfect. Oh Banjo, she's perfect."

I could still hear Dylan mumbling a prayer. I guess the former born-again still had some God left in him after all.

Mom and Lou let go of me. Alice clipped and cut the cord, then she came forward and placed the Gracie on my chest. She was smeared in blood, white globs of goop and slime. She was the most beautiful thing I had ever seen in my life. I tucked her under the warm blanket and watched her little mouth open and close and her tiny eyes blink at the light. She looked just like Gray.

"She's beautiful," Lou whispered, taking her tiny hand in his. Tears ran down his face.

Dylan came up behind him. "C-c-can I touch her?"

"Of course."

He reached out and put his hand on her head. "I-I-I was so a-a-afraid. I even p-p-prayed," he laughed. He could barely control his stuttering.

I looked for Mom, but she had vanished. "Where's Mom?" Just then she came back in with Sam and Henry. Henry ran to the opposite side of the bed from Dylan and Lou. I felt a little weird having Henry in the room. Alice was back between my legs inspecting things. I was having cramps, so maybe the placenta was coming out. Henry didn't seem to notice what was going on down there.

"Gracie," he whispered. He reached forward and touched her back. "I love her."

I don't know why, but this made the tears start back up again.

Mom came up behind Henry, "Oh sweetie, she's gorgeous. She looks like Gray."

"She does," I said. "Just like Gray."

I didn't say it out loud, but I knew that Gray had saved Gracie. Gracie had died inside of me. I knew that. And Gray had sent her back to me. It was like the dream I had when I was pregnant. In that dream Gray had come and taken her from me. That dream resulted in me ending up on the third-floor psych ward. In that dream Gray came back from the dead and demanded that I hand Gracie over to them. In that dream Gray wanted Gracie to live in the place that they and their mom lived. Maybe that had actually been more of a premonition than a dream. I think Gray just needed to meet her for a minute, hold her in their arms, maybe show her to their mom, and then Gray sent her back to me.

They sent her back to me and Lou.

Olivia came forward with a tiny white hat with pink and blue stripes. "Let's put this on her head," she said. I saw her glance from Gracie to Lou. It was clear that she was trying to figure out how Lou had produced such a white baby.

"Can we come in?" It was my brother James and his girlfriend Megan.

"Yeah," Henry answered for me.

Thankfully the placenta was out and Alice was all done sewing me up.

James came forward with the strangest smile on his face and holding three mylar balloons. One was in the shape of a rainbow, one said *it's a girl*, and one had a silly cartoon baby on it. "Hey little sis, how're you doing?" He was clearly uncomfortable and maybe even a little embarrassed by the bouquet he held in his hands.

"I'm okay."

"Here," he said, shoving the balloons at me.

Mom came up and took them from him. "I'll put them over here," she said, giving him a little kiss on the cheek.

Megan came forward and laid her hand on Gracie. "She's beautiful, Banjo. So beautiful." She turned to James, "We need one."

"We can talk about it," he said, clearly flustered.

"You're such a dude," chided Sam.

I looked around the room. Mom, Sam, Lou, Dylan, Henry, James, Megan, and even Alice. Everyone I loved was gathered around me and Gracie. For a minute I felt like maybe Gracie was the luckiest baby in the world. Maybe I could be enough for her after all. Maybe we could all be enough. I looked down at my baby. It was just so weird. I had a baby. I was a mom.

Olivia came back in several minutes later, with a diaper which she set on the edge of the bed. "Let's get her weighed."

I gently lifted Gracie and handed her over. Olivia took her over to the scale, which looked like a Rubbermaid tub of some sort, took off her hat, and placed her inside. Gracie began to scream. Her entire body began to quiver.

"Seven pounds, six ounces," she announced. "Now let's see how long this little girl is."

Olivia seemed immune to my child's suffering. I suddenly had an almost uncontrollable urge to slap her, grab my baby, and flee.

Mom immediately cupped Gracie's head and like she had hit a switch, Gracie became quiet. Olivia then measured her chest. Somehow Mom kept her hand in place even as Olivia lifted the baby to get the tape around her.

"Thirty-three centimeters," she said as she laid Gracie back down. Mom's hand never moved.

Next Olivia placed one end of the measuring tape at the tip of Gracie's head. She glanced at Mom. "Would you mind holding that in place?"

Olivia ran the tape down Gracie's body as she gently straightened her leg. Despite Mom's calming hand Gracie began to scream again. I hated this.

"It's okay, little one," Olivia cooed. Then, "Nineteen inches on the dot," she announced. "Or forty-eight point two-six centimeters. You have yourself a nice healthy baby. Let me just get these eye drops in and we're done."

"Does she have to have the eye drops?"

"You can opt out, but they're important in preventing any possible bacterial infections that can occur at birth."

I glanced at Mom. She nodded.

"Okay," I said.

The drops took a second, and then, without asking permission, Mom lifted the still-screaming Gracie out of the plastic tub and returned her to me. I wondered if I would ever have the kind of confidence that Mom had.

Gracie's eyes were a little greasy looking from the drops and the sludge on her body was beginning to dry, making her skin sticky. My poor baby. I tucked her back under my blanket and against my bare skin. Gracie became quiet again. She stared up at me and I felt waves of love wash over me.

"Let's think about getting a diaper on this little one. I can show you how to put it on properly without disturbing the umbilical cord clamp," said Olivia.

"I know how," I said. And I did. I learned how when Henry was an infant. Not only did Mom believe in attachment parenting, she also believed in letting older children care for younger ones. *It's how the Goddess intended it to be*, she would say. This was during her Pagan stage. She gave up on the Goddess at some point, but she still believed in natural parenting. I wondered if I believed this too.

Olivia started to protest, but Alice stepped forward taking the diaper from her and handing it to me. "It's important to respect a mother's choices," she said, giving Olivia a wide smile.

Olivia's face remained neutral as she nodded and then turned to go. "I'll be back to check on you a little later," she said, without turning around.

"Can you help me?" I asked Mom as I attempted to adjust my gown so I wasn't exposed to the world. Now that the intensity of labor and delivery was over, I wasn't so thrilled with the idea of being buck naked in front of my family and friends. James turned around, pretending to be really interested in looking at the monitors that were still in the room. I laid Gracie down while Mom helped me readjust my gown. I lifted my baby again. It was hard to remember that Henry was ever this tiny. She felt so breakable. Diapering her suddenly seemed scary. I was afraid I would hurt her somehow. Why hadn't I felt like this when I used to care for Henry?

Mom hovered. I slid the tiny diaper under Gracie's little butt and then pulled the front up. I folded down the top so it sat below her gooey umbilical stump with its plastic clip. I fastened it with the little tabs. She began to fuss. "It's okay, don't cry," I said, feeling like everyone in the room was watching me.

"Do you want to wrap her up now? Or maybe you want to eat first? Mom asked. I was famished, but I was also worried that Gracie was cold.

"I want to swaddle her first."

Mom pulled from my bag one of the ten thousand receiving blankets that I had brought and handed it to me. She chose a sunflower yellow blanket covered in tiny lime-green alligators. I lifted Gracie to my chest and then tried to lay the blanket down with one hand. Mom wasted no time jumping in to help me. "Mom, I got it," I said.

She backed off. "Sorry."

"It's okay. I didn't mean to snap. Will you just hold her a second?"

Mom took her from me.

I laid the blanket down on my lap so one corner was pointing towards me and the other away. I folded the top triangle of the blanket down about six inches and then Mom laid Gracie down so her neck was at the straight line of the fold. I brought one side over her and tucked it under her little back. Then I brought the bottom up and hesitated, forgetting exactly where it should go. Mom started to reach for it and then backed off. Her control issues were front and center. I looked up at her, giving her permission to tell me what to do next.

Mom brought the bottom part of the blanket towards Gracie's head and tucked the corner over her right shoulder. I took the other side of the blanket and brought it across Gracie, around her back, and tucked it into the top of the blanket.

"There," I said proudly.

"Not bad," said Sam.

"Why d-d-do you do that?" asked Dylan.

"Because newborn babies are used to being all smooshed up in the uterus, so swaddling makes them feel secure," Lou answered before I could.

I looked up at him and smiled.

He flushed. "I've been studying up on this baby caring business," he said, avoiding my eyes.

"How does someone get food around here?" I said, saving him from his embarrassment. I was so hungry I felt like I could eat my own arm.

"Coming right up," he said. "C'mon Dyl, let's go get this woman a cheeseburger. She needs dinner!"

"And a coke. No, two cokes and an ice water," I demanded, as they disappeared out the door.

Chapter 3

"**H**ey sis." I opened my eyes to see Sam standing next to the bed. "Looks like they brought your lunch in while you were sleeping. Hungry?"

"In a minute," I said, yawning. I glanced at the clock on the wall. I had been a mom for over sixteen hours already. "What did they bring me?"

Sam lifted the lid on the tray. "Not bad actually. Turkey sandwich with lettuce and tomato, a fruit cup, chips, and a slice of cake."

My stomach growled.

"Knock knock." The door to my room opened and a woman in her mid-forties with a side ponytail stuck her head through the door.

"Oh good, you're awake. I'm Cecelia, the lactation consultant. You must be Amanda," she said, extending her hand towards me.

"I go by Banjo," I said, taking her hand. "This is my sister, Sam."

Cecelia took Sam's hand for a brief moment. "Nice to meet you, Sam."

Sam nodded. "You too."

Cecelia turned back to me. "So Banjo, if this is a good time I'd like to answer any questions you may have about breastfeeding. And I'd like to say that I'm just so happy to see that you've chosen to breastfeed your baby."

I wonder if she announced to older moms how happy she was to see them breastfeeding. Sam must have had the exact same thought.

"Happy?" asked Sam.

Cecelia smiled big, not catching the sarcasm in Sam's tone. "Of course, breastmilk is always the best choice and it's just so nice to see such a young mother willing to give it a try."

Sam and I glanced at each other. Sam rolled her eyes.

"So Banjo, can I answer any questions for you?"

I shook my head. "Nope." I decided right then that I did not like this woman and even if I did have questions, I had no desire to go to her for answers.

"Okay well, what I generally like to do is observe the baby and mother, so would you mind waking her up and seeing if we can get her to nurse a bit? Are you comfortable having Sam in here?"

"She's been nursing fine. My mom and Sam both helped me. Thanks anyway."

Cecelia looked from me to Sam and back to me, unsure of what to do.

"We got this," said Sam, smiling a sugar-sweet smile.

"Of course. It's always nice to have mothers and older sisters around to help out, but I'd love to just do a quick observation in case—"

Sam cut her off. "Seriously, we've got this." The sugar was gone from her voice.

Cecelia stiffened. She turned her body so that she was facing me, but had her back to Sam. "I'm very happy to hear that the baby seems to be doing well with her feeding, but we've found that strong support at the beginning of the mother and baby breastfeeding relationship is the key to long term success. You want your baby to have the very best start in life, don't you? I know that sometimes when things are going well it may be hard to look into the future and imagine that something may go wrong. It does happen though. Even to us older moms. I have a lot of tricks up my sleeve." With that she smiled big.

I looked past her to Sam. Sam took my cue and went around to the other side of my bed to offer reinforcement.

"I have my mom and my sister to help and I watched a lot of YouTube videos before she was born, plus I read a lot. I think I'm fine."

"Oh honey, YouTube videos are great for the basics, but nothing beats hands-on help. And let me tell you, those breast pumps are tricky business sometimes. At least let me help you get acquainted with the pump." She turned to grab the breast pump that we had arranged to rent from the hospital.

"I have my mom and my sister and—"

Sam cut me off. "Look, women have been feeding their babies since the beginning of time. I think lactation consultants are wonderful—I really do—but my sister said she doesn't want any help right now. Maybe she will later or if a problem does come up, but right now she doesn't. My mom breastfed three kids and I breastfed one, we have seriously got this. Both my mom and I know how to use a breast pump. Thank you for your offer to help."

Just then, Mom came through the door.

"Oh look, my two favorite daughters are here," she said. She extended her hand to Cecelia. "I'm Jane, Banjo's mom."

"Nice to meet you, Jane. My name is Cecelia. I'm the lactation consultant and I was just explaining to Banjo the importance of having a session with me to ensure her breastfeeding success and—"

Sam cut her off. "And we were just telling her that Banj feels like she's got this and has you and me to help if she runs into any problems. Cecelia is concerned that because of Banjo's age she may not grasp the complexities of long-term breastfeeding."

Cecelia ignored Sam, keeping her eyes on Mom, sure that Mom would take her side. "Sometimes younger parents just don't realize how hard it can be. What's that saying, move out now while you still know everything?" She laughed. "I know how my teenagers are. Maybe you could have a word with Banjo?"

Mom raised one eyebrow and I had to fight the urge to smile. This was going to be good. I shot a look at Sam and she turned away fast in an effort to keep from laughing.

"Banjo, you don't want a consultation with Cecelia?" asked Mom.

I shook my head.

"You think you have this down?"

I nodded.

"Okay then. Banjo feels confident that she will be fine without a consultation at this time. I'm so glad I was able to help clear this up." Mom flashed a smile that seemed to be made up of pure sarcasm. "I do understand what you say about these very young moms thinking they know what's best for themselves and their babies though. Funny how that works. I mean who would think that a mother would know what's best for her child? Am I right?"

Cecelia stared at Mom. She didn't seem to grasp what Mom was saying.

Mom went on. "Sam here was a teen mom and so was I. Teen parenthood is our family tradition and we take it very seriously. We are so excited that in sixteen short years our little Gracie will be able to continue the tradition. Every family should have a tradition, don't you think?"

Cecelia clutched her folder to her chest and practically ran from the room.

"Nice meeting you," Mom called after her.

As the door swung shut we all burst into laughter. "Holy shit Mom, that was beautiful," said Sam.

"I agree," I said. "And that part about it being our family tradition.

Oh my god, did you see her face?"

As if on cue Gracie began to wail.

"Kid is hungry. Being that you're so young you may not understand the cues. When a baby cries they are often hungry. When the kid is hungry that's when you have her nurse," Sam's voice dripped syrup.

"Thank you so much, Sam. Whatever would I do without you?" I slid Gracie into the football hold and brought her up to my breast. With my free hand I directed the nipple into her mouth and she latched on right away.

"She really is a good nurser, Banjo. I feel so sorry for all the other teen moms who may be struggling with breastfeeding or who may have a baby who isn't so eager. People like Cecelia can really undermine the confidence of a new mom. Trust me, I know.

"I only breastfed your brother for three months because everyone acted as if it were some sort of miracle that an eighteen-year-old, unmarried mother would actually breastfeed her baby. Things were different back then. I mean, breastfeeding wasn't the norm and I didn't have a lactation consultant, only a nurse to help out that first day, but everyone acted shocked that I would even try."

"I got lucky with my lactation lady" said Sam. "She was the best. Henry refused to nurse and I was so afraid that he would die that I even tried the bottle, but he wouldn't take that either. She saved me."

"I had forgotten about that," said Mom. "She was great. I don't remember her ever mentioning your age or doubting you."

"Nope. Not like old Cecelia."

"If you do want a consult, we can ask Alice to send someone else," said Mom.

"I don't think I need one."

"I don't either," agreed Mom.

There was a knock at the door.

"Come in," I said.

It was Alice. "Well, well, well, I hear the three of you gave Cecelia a run for her money. She came to me distraught. You should have seen that women's face when I told her I had also been a teenage mother. It was a hoot."

"Maybe it's the oxytocin talking, but I love you guys," I said.

"Group hug," cheered Sam.

Mom, Sam, and Alice wrapped me in an awkward hug while trying not to dislodge Gracie from her lunch.

"Team Teen Mamas represent!" cheered Alice.

Chapter 4

I was dozing with Gracie on my chest when the nurse came in to announce that I'd be able to leave in just a few hours. Normally when you give birth you get to go home the next day, but because of Gracie's difficult birth, Alice insisted they keep us another day. Although it had only been two nights, it felt like forever.

"Before you go, don't forget to fill out the forms," she said tapping the stack of papers on the table near the rocking chair.

I had been dreading this moment for months. How do I fill out a birth certificate when the other parent is dead, not to mention technically the father. But not at all a father?

"Okay. Will Alice be in to see me before I go?"

"Alice? Oh, you mean Doctor McCanne. I think she comes in at one, so I'm sure she'll be here shortly." She grabbed my crusty breakfast plate that had been sitting there for the last couple of hours and vanished without another word.

I figured Alice would be able to tell me what to do. It felt wrong not to put Gray's name on the birth certificate, but I was worried that somehow their dad would find out about Gracie, and if there was proof that Gracie was Gray's, then maybe he could take her away from me. Or at least sue to see her or something. Part of me knew this could never happen, but what if?

I traced my finger over the top of Gracie's fuzzy head. Her wispy hair was so blond it was almost invisible. She reminded me so much of Gray. I was happy she looked like them, and at the same time it was so hard to see Gray each time I looked into her little face. I wished I had some baby pictures of Gray so I could compare the two of them.

"We get to go home today," I whispered. The thought of taking her home made my head hurt. Was I really going to take this baby home and be a mom and do mom things? What if I screwed up? What if I dropped her or forgot about her in a hot car or buckled her car seat wrong and we got in an accident? What if she got sick and I didn't take her to the doctor in time or I fell asleep with her in my bed and rolled on top of her and suffocated her? What if I hated being a mom?

I lifted Gracie from my chest, careful not to wake her, and laid her in the clear plastic bassinet that they had parked next to my bed. I picked up the form and began to fill in the blanks. Where it said Mother's Name I wrote: *Banjo Logan* and then scribbled it out and wrote in my legal name: *Amanda Logan*.

I skipped over the Father's Name part.

"You get to go home today." Alice appeared in the doorway smiling. She crossed the room and leaned over Gracie who was still sleeping soundly in her plastic box. "She's gorgeous, Banjo. You did good."

"How do I fill this out? I mean with Gray being, um . . ." I still couldn't say the word dead out loud.

"Honey, you can just leave it blank or you can write deceased."

"Blank? Won't they want to know who the other parent is?"

"The state may ask for more information later, especially if you end up getting any assistance like food stamps or child care. Unfortunately, you can't put the name of someone who's deceased unless you were married."

"But Gray is Gracie's other parent." Suddenly I needed Gray's name on this piece of paper. "Isn't there any way I can put their name down?"

"I'm afraid not, sugar. There are ways to get their name on there, but you'll need a copy of Gray's death certificate and other information that you just don't have right now. You may be able to fix this later. I'm sorry, Banjo."

Getting a death certificate seemed impossible. I don't even know what happened to Gray's body after they died and I can't imagine that their dad would even talk to me. Poor Gracie. And poor Gray. Gray deserved to take some credit for our baby.

I felt my face get hot, a sure sign that I wouldn't be able to stop the tears. "So I really can't put Gray's name?"

"I'm sorry sweetheart. If you weren't married it gets complicated."

The tears broke loose.

"Oh Banjo, I'm so sorry." Alice sat down next to me on the bed and pulled me towards her. I buried my face in her chest and sobbed.

"Let it out, sweetheart. It's okay. It will be okay. Let it out." She laid her face down on the top of my head. "You don't need a piece of paper to know that Gray helped to make this beautiful child, okay?"

I pulled away and reached for a tissue. "Thank you, Alice."

"Thank you?"

"You know, for being my friend. For being so nice to me and Gracie." I suddenly felt embarrassed. "I don't know what I would have done without you."

"Oh Banjo, please don't thank me. It's an honor for me to know you and your family. I'm the one who should be thanking you. You're the first teen mom I've had the pleasure of working with, and that means so much to me."

Gracie squirmed awake and began to fuss. "I think the peanut needs a nip," said Alice.

She lifted Gracie from her plastic bed and handed her over.

I took my baby from Alice and settled her onto my breast.

"You're an expert at that," she said, as Gracie slurped away.

"It's my one skill."

Alice glanced up at the wall clock. "Your lunch should have been here by now. I'm going to go see what's holding it up. You're due to be discharged at 3:00. Hold off on that paperwork until after you eat, okay?"

I nodded. "Alice?"

"Yes, sweetie?"

"Will I still, like, be able to see you after we leave? I mean, since I won't be your patient any longer?"

Alice frowned. "I damn well hope so," she said. "As soon as you stop being my patient I plan to tear down every last professional boundary these grouchy hospital types are so uptight about. We teen moms have to stick together, right? As a matter of fact, why wait until you're no longer my patient, what's for dinner tonight?"

"Crab legs, steak, salad, sourdough bread, and chocolate cake for dessert. We have a birthing day to celebrate," said Mom from the doorway. "Be there at 7:00 and bring some good beer, will you?"

I looked from Alice to Mom and then back to Alice. "Wait. What? You're coming to dinner?"

"Of course, she's coming to dinner," said Mom, as if I were an idiot to even question it. "We're having a party to celebrate Gracie's very first days on earth and you think we aren't going to invite the woman who helped her land here safely?"

Alice nodded, "A Birthing Day celebration. That sounds lovely. Wouldn't miss it for the world. Nor would I turn down fresh crab and beer. For now though I'm going to see what's taking your lunch so long. The service around this place sucks." She glanced at Mom and when she did I noticed a look. Maybe I was imagining it, but I swear something passed between them. Were Mom and Alice crushing on each other? I wasn't sure how I felt about that.

Alice stopped at the door, "Banjo, has the pediatrician been in to see Gracie today?"

"No."

Alice let out an exasperated sigh. "This place. Okay, let me see if I can round someone up. You can't go home until Gracie's been examined and officially discharged." And with that she disappeared out the door.

"You don't mind that I invited Alice, do you?" Mom asked after Alice had left the room.

"No. No, of course not. It just surprised me, that's all." I noticed Mom wasn't really looking at me. She was definitely crushing on Alice.

"I invited Anna too," she said quickly changing the subject away from Alice.

"Is she coming?" I asked.

"Yep. She said she can't wait to meet Gracie."

Anna was my counselor. Years ago, she and Mom had casually dated for a while. I was pretty young and don't really remember. After I lost it and ended up on the third floor, Mom had asked Anna to take me on as a patient, or client, or whatever it is they call you when you see a counselor. Technically Anna said it was against the rules, but Anna is a total old hippie and said if we didn't care, she didn't care, and so she became my counselor. She ran her business out of her house, so her cat, Gyles, and her border collie, Betsy, were always hanging around as unofficial therapy animals.

"Thanks, Mom."

"No need to thank me. You look exhausted. Why don't you try to nap a bit? I'm going to go run some errands. I'll be back in plenty of time to pick you up." She leaned over and kissed the top of my head, took a quick peek at Gracie, who had fallen back asleep in my arms, and then she was gone.

Chapter 5

I sat in the rocking chair nursing Gracie and staring out the window at the water on the edge of the city. The hospital sat on a hill and the rooms that faced west overlooked the Salish Sea. I could see the distant San Juan Islands and beyond that the Olympic Mountain range. Puffy white clouds drifted across the brilliant blue sky. A steel-gray barge chugged slowly across the gray-green water.

There were no views like this on the third-floor juvenile psych ward. The barred windows of the psychiatric unit faced the eastern landscape of clogged city streets and drab buildings. If you looked north, you could see the edge of a homeless encampment with its scattered tents and trash.

This view only created more anxiety for those of us behind the barred windows. When you find yourself in a psych ward you can't help but wonder if you're destined to be one of the forgotten. Having a bird's eye view of your potential future life isn't a motivator to help you move forward, instead it's a terrifying reminder of just how far you've fallen. And have yet to fall.

It was hard for me to wrap my brain around the fact that this building where I sat rocking my beautiful and perfect new baby was the same place where just months ago I sat trapped in fear and uncertainty with my psychiatrist, Doctor Jack, threatening to take her away. A shiver ran through me.

I looked down at my baby. She looked so much like Gray. Loss swelled in me. I missed Gray so much. I traced Gracie's face with my finger. "I wish you had known your other parent." I whispered. The word parent sounded so formal. I wonder what Gray would have wanted to be called. Suddenly the word Gaga popped into my head. I don't know why, but something inside of me told me that Gaga was what Gray would have wanted. "Your Gaga would have adored you," I whispered.

I let myself drift into sweet memories of Gray, something I had been avoiding these past couple of months. I closed my eyes and thought about those nights in Gray's old apartment, sprawled on their saggy bed, drinking bad coffee and just talking. that's what I miss the most: just talking. And laughing. I miss how we used to laugh and I miss who I was back then, before life got so complicated. Things seemed hard then but looking back now, it seems like it was so easy. I was so innocent.

I miss me and Gray walking Rags late at night. I miss watching the sunset over the water from the park we liked to go to. I miss scrounging for change and then walking to the store for snacks. I miss walking home together, sharing a bag of chips and a single bottle of Coke.

I began to hum Bob Marley's "Three Little Birds" to my sleeping baby. Gray's mom used to sing it to Gray every morning to wake them up. When I found out I was pregnant I made a vow to sing this song to my child in honor of her other Grandma.

"Hello there."

I jumped. I had been so lost in thought that I hadn't heard the man enter my room. I felt annoyed that he had interrupted my moment with Gracie. Had he been standing in the doorway watching me? He was very tall and wore his silver hair close-cropped. A pale blue and white striped button-down shirt was tucked neatly into his khaki pants. He had a tan that told me he spent a lot of time on vacation to places I would never see. If it weren't for the doctor badge clipped to the front of his shirt and the cart stacked with baby exam stuff, I might have mistaken him for a forty-year-old new dad who had accidently walked into the wrong room.

"Oh, I'm sorry. Didn't mean to scare you. My name is Doctor Benton. I'm the pediatrician on staff today. I'm here to take a look at your baby and give her the okay to go home this afternoon."

He offered me his hand. It was warm and dry and too smooth, just like Doctor Jack's had been. His hands told me he hired people like me to mow his lawn and scrub his toilets, just like Doctor Jack.

"Hi, I'm ah Banjo Logan."

"Banjo? Paperwork says Amanda, is that correct?"

"Oh yeah, that's my legal name. I go by Banjo."

"Okay no worries," he said, as if giving me permission to go by my name of choice.

"If you can bring her over here and undress her, we can get this over with," he said, smiling, and like Doctor Jack his smile didn't reach his eyes.

I brought Gracie over to the little plastic bed that sat on the scale and laid her down. I undressed her. "Diaper too?" I asked.

"Yes please."

I removed her diaper and then stood off to the side. He didn't tell me my baby was cute or say hi to her. He didn't ask her name. He just wrapped a measuring tape around her head and then asked me to hold her leg extended while he measured the length of her body. She began to scream. He didn't react. Instead he recorded the measurements and then took her weight. I stepped forward and put my hand on her little head like Mom had done yesterday, "It's okay, baby."

"I'll need you to step back. She's fine. It's good to hear she has nice strong lungs."

It seemed wrong to me that a baby who hadn't even been on this planet for two full days should be left naked and screaming, especially my baby, but I stepped back. Doctor Benton was too much like Doctor Jack and it scared me.

"Seven pounds four ounces," he said, without looking up.

"Is that okay? I mean, that she lost weight. She lost two ounces."

"It's perfectly normal for her to lose up to ten percent of her birth weight the first week. We just want to keep an eye on her. Make sure she's eating regularly and urinating. You'll have to make an appointment with your regular pediatrician for one week from today. If you haven't already chosen a pediatrician, you'll need to do that right away. Do you have a pediatrician yet?"

"No, but Alice said she'd refer me to one."

"Alice?"

"Doctor McCanne."

"Oh right. That's fine. Just make sure you make that appointment."

I nodded.

He listened to her heart and lungs. He picked her up and ran his hand over the soft spot on her head, her clavicle, arms, and down her body. Her little body began to turn red and her lower lip quivered as she howled. He pressed on the spots where her thighs met her torso and then bent her legs in this weird way. "Testing her muscle tone," he said.

He turned her over and ran his fingers down her spine and butt and then laid her back down. It was all very clinical. There was no warmth to his touch or his voice. I wanted him gone.

"Everything looks good. We just need to do a quick heel prick and then you can go ahead and get her dressed."

"Heel prick?'

"PKU test. Nothing to worry about. It's a rare disorder, but it is important right away," he said, as he poked her heel with a tiny needle and then shoved a little card against her foot to collect the tiny drops of blood. Gracie shrieked and then went silent.

"What's wrong with her?" I froze in terror.

"She's fine. Sometimes infants hold their breath when they cry." With that he handed her back to me.

My heart felt like it was going to explode. As soon as I placed her against my body she took a deep breath and screamed even harder than before.

"Shhhh shhhh, it's okay. You're okay. Mama's here. Mama's here." I realized that I was crying. I hated this man.

"I assume you're breastfeeding. Put her to your breast," he stated with no emotion whatsoever.

I did as I was told. She became a frantic animal searching for the nipple. Once she found it she calmed immediately. I hated that he was right.

She nursed for a couple of minutes—letting out tiny hiccup sobs now and then—while Doctor Benton typed away on his laptop. When she had finished nursing I laid her back down in the plastic bed so I could put her diaper and clothes back on, being extra careful to fold the top of the diaper down so it didn't cover her umbilical cord stump. I didn't want him making any comments. I noticed that my hands were shaking. I slid her into her orange fox sleeper, lifted her from the bed, and pulled her to my chest. She snuggled into me, sucking furiously on her tiny fist.

"Go ahead and have a seat if you'd like. I'd just like to go over a few things."

I went back to the rocking chair.

"So going over her chart I see that there were some complications at birth, however she seems to be just fine now, so no need to worry about that. It happens sometimes. You're breastfeeding exclusively? No formula supplementation?"

"Yes. I mean yes, I'm breastfeeding exclusively."

"Good. Do you have any questions or concerns?"

I shook my head. This guy made me so nervous and I didn't even know why.

"How old are you?" he asked.

"I'm seventeen." I wondered if he asked adult parents this question. Like if someone was twenty-six or thirty-four would it matter how old they were?

"Do you have a plan for birth control?"

So now it was clear why he was asking my age. Since when does a pediatrician counsel new moms on birth control?

"No."

"Well Banjo, it's pretty important that you do what you can to delay another pregnancy for as long as possible for your health and for the health of your baby."

My gut twisted and heat surged through my body.

"Don't worry about it. I'm gay," I said quietly.

"Well you may be gay, but it seems that you managed to get pregnant once, so let's not let it happen again. This baby deserves a shot at life and having another child will only make it harder for the both of you. Give yourself some time to grow up a little before making her a big sister, okay?" That smile that wasn't a smile spread across his mouth.

I looked down at my perfect baby. She was not a mistake. She was not a regret. And I would give my life to make sure she had the best life any baby could have. I wanted to say something to this guy. I wanted to scream at him or at least fight back, but my words were like wisps of smoke that I couldn't get a hold of. I kept my eyes on Gracie and my mouth shut.

"Look, I'm not trying to pick on you. I just want your baby to have the very best chance in life. And you too, for that matter. I'm a pediatrician and that means my job is to look out for the health and wellbeing of children, of which you are one. Don't you find it interesting that you and your baby could both be my patients?"

I kept my eyes on Gracie. I wish Mom and Sam were here. Or even Alice. I felt tears building, but there was no way I was going to let this jerk see even one slip out.

"Okay, well let's move on. Do you have any questions about caring for your baby?"

"No."

I could feel his eyes on me.

"Knock. Knock." Lou and Dylan came through the open door to my room. They saw Doctor Benton and stopped. "Oh sorry. Should we wait outside?" asked Lou.

"No, please stay." I was so damn glad to see them.

Doctor Benton looked at the two of them and then stepped forward. "I'm Doctor Benton. Nice to meet you," he said, offering his hand to Dylan and then to Lou.

"So is it safe to assume that you're Dad?" he said to Dylan.

The look on Dylan's face was priceless. "N-n-no," he said.

"Oh pardon me, I just assumed that—"

"I told you I'm queer," I interrupted. "Are we done?"

He looked from Dylan to Lou and then to me. I would have liked to be a fly on the wall of his brain as he tried to make sense of the three of us.

"We're done. I'll send a nurse in to get her vaccinations out of the way. It was nice meeting you all," he said as he headed towards the door. Then he hesitated and turned back towards me. "Think about what I said about birth control." And then he was gone.

"Who was that?" asked Lou.

"The pediatrician."

"He re-re-reminds me of Doctor Jack," said Dylan.

"Totally Doctor Jack." Lou agreed.

"Word. He was awful. He kept telling me to get on birth control before I ruined Gracie's life any more than I already have by being her mom."

"Ugh. I'm sorry. Pretty damn hilarious that he thought our boy Dylan was Gracie's dad though."

Dylan rolled his eyes.

"So, is she okay?" Lou asked.

"Yeah, he released her to go home today."

A nurse, dressed head to toe in scrubs covered in pastel baby bottles, appeared in the doorway. She had the most amazing dreadlocks piled up on top of her head. Tiny red, orange, and yellow ribbons were wrapped around a few of the locs. She carried a small white tray with a tiny vial and needle and a clipboard under her arm.

"Hello there, my name is Neela. I'm here to give that little peach her vaccination." She had a distinct Ethiopian accent. I glanced at Lou. He looked at me, raising one eyebrow.

Neela handed me the clipboard. "I'll need you to sign these forms giving us permission to vaccinate your baby. What's her name?"

"Gracie."

"Oh I love that. So beautiful. The first sheet is an information sheet about the hepatitis B vaccine. You get to keep that one, and then the second page is the waiver form. Just sign where I've highlighted."

"Does she have to have her shot today?" I asked.

"No of course not. It's up to you if and when you vaccinate. I do think it's best to do it today. Your call though." She smiled and it went all the way up to her eyes. "Take your time and read through that information sheet."

I read over the page learning about the dangers of hepatitis B and the risks of my baby contracting it. I felt like if I had to watch my baby be poked and prodded again I would fall apart completely.

"Could I wait until her first real doctor appointment? She's supposed to go in a week or so."

"Is anyone in your home or does anyone who may come in contact with Gracie, known to have hepatitis?"

"No, not at all."

"Then I think it's okay to wait a bit. I would get it soon though, if I were you."

"Okay, thanks. I would just sort of like to wait. I mean, if you're sure it's okay."

"No problem. Just check the box that says you're declining it today and then sign where I highlighted."

"Um excuse me. Ah can I ask you a personal question?" Lou interrupted.

"You can ask, but I may not answer," said Neela, smiling.

"Are you, um, from Ethiopia?"

"I am, actually."

"Me too," Lou practically shouted. "I was adopted and came here when I was six"

"I'm also an adoptee," she smiled.

"I'm jealous that you still have your accent," said Lou. I noticed that his hands were shaking slightly.

"My adoptive mom really went out of her way to keep me connected to the local Ethiopian community. I was pretty lucky in that way."

"I wish my parents—adoptive parents I mean—were like that."

"My adoption was actually pretty shady. Shortly after I came here my adoptive parents found out that my mom had been coerced into giving me up, so every couple of years my adoptive mom took me back to Ethiopia to see my family. They weren't able to undo the adoption or send me back, so they tried to mitigate the damage for everyone. My first mom died when I was sixteen. My adoptive mom made sure I was able to be with her when she died," said Neela.

"Wow, you're so lucky. I mean, not that your mom died. I'm sorry . . ." Lou trailed off, clearly embarrassed for his poor choice of words.

Neela smiled. "It's okay. I knew what you meant, sweetheart."

Lou hesitated a moment and then went on. "My parents suck. They changed my name and won't tell me anything about my birth family. My adoption was shady too. I remember my mom. They thought I was four when they adopted me, but I was actually six." He was rambling.

"Oh sweetie, I'm sorry. I am one of the lucky ones in that I landed with adoptive parents who really wanted to do right. Have you been able to connect up with any other Ethiopian adoptees?" asked Neela.

"No, are there like groups or something?"

"Yes actually. There are support groups as well as organizations who are trying to put a stop to the trafficking of babies and kids. Do you know what a searcher is?"

"Yeah, I have a list of people to call, I just haven't done it yet," said Lou.

"You know what? How about I give you my number? Is that okay?"

"Oh my God, please. Thank you so much."

Neela stood there looking at Lou. Lou looked back at her blankly. "Um do you have a phone on you, or would you like me to write it down?" asked Neela.

"Oh yeah," said Lou. He was flustered and fumbled to pull his phone out of his back pocket.

"I didn't catch your name," said Neela.

"Oh sorry, I'm Lou. Thanks so much. Really."

"No problem." She recited her number to Lou and he read it back to her. "Okay, why don't you send me a text and then I'll have your number. There's a group that meets once a month at a church here in Everett. I'll send you the information."

I could tell that Lou was fighting back tears. He nodded. "Thank you."

"You're very welcome, young man." Neela turned to me, "Okay then, you make sure to get your sweet peach in for her vaccination in the next week or two. She's a beauty, that one." She turned and left.

"I'm going to find my mom," said Lou, finally letting the tears loose.

Chapter 6

I sat in the backseat of Mom's grungy Subaru with Gracie, holding her little hand and making sure her head didn't flop over in the car seat. Gravel crunched under the tires as Mom turned into our driveway. We lived in a grimy working-class city, but our house sat quite a ways off the street. Mom planted fruit trees and bamboo all along both sides of our property so coming home always feels like arriving at some little house way out in the country. The gravel and dirt driveway cut right through the center of the yard where masses of wildflowers grew. In the winter the yard was mostly just a mud pit, but in the summer it's beautiful.

Mom pulled up in front of the house and killed the engine. Sam's car wasn't there. I wondered where she was. I could see Rags—the dog I had inherited from Gray—in the smeary window, standing on the back of the couch barking her head off. This was it. We were home and I was officially on my own with a brand-new baby. It's so weird how less than seventy-two hours ago I was just a teenager—okay, I was a pregnant teenager and that's pretty huge—still, I was just a teenager, and now here I was somebody's mom. I leaned over and unclipped Gracie from her car seat. I lifted her slowly and then tried to scooch out of the car. Pain rose from my episiotomy wound and from my belly. I readjusted myself as best I could, trying to ignore the pain. My heart was pounding in my chest. I wasn't sure I was ready for this, but I guess there was no turning back.

Mom grabbed my backpack off the front seat, came around, unclipped the car seat, and carried it up onto the sagging porch. I looked at the peeling paint and realized we would have to take care of that before Gracie got mobile. What if there was lead in that old paint?

Mom unlocked the door and pushed it open. Rags flew out of the house, ecstatic to have me home. "Rags, down," I yelled. She ignored me. "Rags goddamn it, down now!"

"Easy there, Banj. She's just happy to see you."

"She's going to hurt Gracie."

"Why don't you kneel down and let her see, Baby" offered Mom.

She was right of course. I squatted down. "I'm sorry, Ragsy. Look, it's your new baby."

Rags sniffed all over Gracie's face and head, her tail wagging in wild circles, and then she gave her a big fat lick right on the mouth. "Rags!"

Mom laughed. "Simmer down. A little dog spit never killed anyone. You've had your fair share."

"But she got her right in the mouth. That's so gross. What if she gives her worms or something?" I said, standing up. "C'mon Rags. You can come in and look, just don't touch her again." Rags ignored me and ran out into the yard to pee.

"Don't be dramatic. Rags doesn't have worms. Just don't let Gracie lick her butt."

"Seriously Mom?" Sometimes my mom's immaturity amazed me.

Just inside the door was a huge bouquet of balloons in all colors as well as the bouquet that James and Megan gave me. A paper banner that read *Welcome Home* was tacked up on the wall over the couch. Below the banner Mom had cut out a cartoon speech bubble and tacked it up so it looked like the giant Ani DiFranco poster was saying, "Hi Gracie!" My mom was a total stereotypical lesbian when it came to her love of Ani DiFranco.

Gracie and I settled onto the couch underneath Ani, while Mom went back out to get the diaper bag. I wasn't really sure what to do. What do moms do when they come home with a brand-new life? Like it seemed weird to just go lounge on my bed and scroll through my phone or go take a shower or turn on the T.V. It felt like I should be doing something momish. Gracie began to fuss and root around on my arm, so I guess that answered the question of what I should be doing.

I lifted my shirt and slid her mouth onto my nipple. I winced in pain. My nipples were so sore. Mom and Sam assured me they'd toughen up fast. "Don't worry, Banj, before you know it you'll have some nice nipple calluses and won't feel it at all," Sam had said. The idea of nipple calluses did not exactly excite me. Who even knew there was such a thing?

Mom came back in with the diaper bag. Rags was at her heels. She jumped up on the couch and once again began to sniff all over Gracie. "Git down, Rags." She flopped down next to me and began chewing on her feet.

"Have you showered?" Mom asked.

"No. Do I stink?"

"No, but you should shower. When she's done, I'll take her and then why don't you go shower before everyone gets here for dinner."

"Who all is coming?"

"Well, Sam and Henry, Lou, Dylan, Alice, James, Megan, and Anna."

"Is that still okay with you that I invited Anna and Alice?" asked Mom.

I nodded my head and slid my finger between Gracie's gums and my boob to break her suction so I could stick her on the other boob for a while. Mom and Sam and the YouTube videos all say you need to drain both boobs equally. As I pulled her off, thick yellow milk dripped from my nipple. I guess it's not technically milk, it's colostrum—which is like some sort of super milk that lasts about three or four days before your regular milk comes in. I watched the thick milk drip out of my nipple and it didn't even seem weird. And it didn't seem weird to be sitting here talking to my mom with my leaky boob hanging out. I just kept tripping out on all the strange things that my body was doing and how it all felt so normal.

Gracie's face crumpled and she let out a scream of protest as I unlatched her from my boob.

"Easy there, kid. You won't starve," I said as I tried to center her screaming mouth onto my left breast. She missed my nipple and latched right onto the areola. Pain shot through me. "Ow! Jesus, Gracie." I tried to re-center her mouth and this time she latched onto my nipple. She smacked and sucked and made all sorts of cute little sounds.

"It's a good idea to try to burp her between boobs," said Mom.

"Okay."

"Since you're busy feeding her I'm going to run to the store for a few last-minute things. When I get back I'll watch her while you shower. Nobody should be here until around seven, so after you shower you can nap if you want."

"Wait. You're leaving me here alone?"

"I'm just running to the store, honey. You'll be just fine."

I wanted to beg her to stay, but I kept my mouth shut. Did older moms panic at the idea of being left alone with their baby for the first time? Probably not. Or maybe they do. I don't even know. What if this is the first sign that I'm really not capable of raising this kid? What kind of parent is afraid to be alone with her own baby?

Being home all alone with Gracie felt dangerous. What if I tripped and fell and hit my head? Or what if I tripped and fell with her in my arms? What if there was an earthquake? Or a fire?

"Please don't go, Mom."

"Sweetheart, you're going to be fine. I'll only be gone half an hour. If she falls asleep nursing then take a little cat nap while I'm gone. Sleep when the baby sleeps is your motto for the next several months. I'm going to make you a cup of that Mother's Milk tea before I go. I want you to drink the whole thing, okay? It's important to stay hydrated and that tea really helps your milk production." She turned and went into our tiny kitchen to make me a cup of her hippie tea. I heard her fill the kettle and set it on the stove.

I stared down at my baby. She was starting to drift off to sleep. She'd close her eyes, her mouth would go slack, and then just as the nipple would start to fall out of her mouth she'd latch back on. It might be the cutest thing that I had ever seen in my life.

A few minutes later Mom came in with a mug of tea. She grabbed a T.V. tray from the corner and set down the cup of tea.

"Need anything else?"

"Could you grab my phone out of my backpack please?"

Mom handed me my phone and left me on my own. I reached for the tea, then thought better of it. What if I spilled it on Gracie? I'd let it cool down a while. It was way too hot out to be drinking steaming tea anyway. Gracie was full on asleep now. I pulled my shirt down and then with one hand I unlocked my phone.

I sent a group text to Lou and Dylan. *What time will you guys be here?* Minutes passed with no reply. An image of Lou and Dylan in a terrible car accident flashed through my mind. I thought about texting them again, but what if I sent a text and Lou glanced down at his phone and that caused the crash? My skin tingled and goosebumps spread across my arms. What was wrong with me? Why was I so paranoid? Is this what motherhood is? Just an endless panic attack? Is this why mom and Sam seem so damn crazy all the time?

My phone dinged. *Hey, dude. Dylan is with me. We should be there in a couple hours.* My phone dinged again. It was a little red heart emoji. I smiled at the phone. Suddenly I was so tired. I gently adjusted Gracie so that she was on my chest, leaned back against the arm of the couch, pressed my feet up against Rags' hairy body, and let sleep wash over me.

The front door opening woke me up. "Hey sleepy head, I'm glad you got a little nap in." Mom came in with three grocery bags—reusable of course—loaded with crap.

I took my finger and fiddled with Gracie's bottom lip, causing her to pout and squinch up her face. I needed to make sure she was still alive.

I yawned. "I thought you were just going to get a few things? That's not a few things, Mom." Mom must have blown this month's food budget out of the water with this party.

"Well, I decided we needed a salad and they had crab on sale, so I got more. A couple bottles of wine, some sparkling water, and that bread you like." She headed into the kitchen. "I'm going to put this stuff away and then I'll take Gracie and you can shower."

Chapter 7

fter Mom finished putting all the groceries away I handed sleeping Gracie off to her. "Please don't let Rags lick her," I said.

Mom waved me away.

I walked down the hall to my room. The last time I had been in my room I was just a pregnant teenager, now I walked in a mom. I was thankful that I had cleaned things up before I went into labor. I had read that in the last week or two of pregnancy pregnant people go into a nesting phase and it turned out to be totally true. A few days before Gracie was born I got this uncontrollable urge to clean my room top to bottom. I organized, rearranged, threw away, put away, and scrubbed. I had begged Mom to let me paint it, but she was firm in her no. "You can't be breathing paint fumes, and it's not safe to be climbing ladders and stretching like that when you're this close," she had said. She promised me that after Gracie was born we would paint my room, maybe even the whole house. Mom always has to take things to the next level.

She did buy me a large blue throw rug though, which was nice because my carpet was matted and gross. Definitely not fit for a brand-new baby. Mom also splurged on a new down alternative comforter. No geese were harmed in the making of my blanket. The comforter was in different shades of 1970s oranges and yellows, browns and blues, and I loved it. It's not often Mom buys things new and I appreciated the effort.

There was a rocking chair in one corner of my room, and a baby swing in the other. It was cramped, but with the new rug and comforter it felt cozy.

It was good to be home.

I pulled open my dresser drawers and tried to figure out what I should wear. My belly still looked like I was at least five months pregnant. I decided on a pair of dark green, loose basketball shorts that stretched to accommodate my post-baby belly and a loose-fitting white t-shirt with a sparkly green narwhal on the front.

I grabbed a clean towel out of the hall closet and resisted the urge to go check on Gracie one last time. I pulled the bathroom door shut behind me, opened the rusty mirrored medicine cabinet and read over the collection of essential oils. I wanted something that smelled clean. I chose mint. I filled the diffuser with water, shook in a few drops of mint oil, and turned it on. A stream of minty steam rose from the top of the diffuser. I peeled off my clothes and checked the thick menstrual pad to see if I was still bleeding. I was, but just a little. My vag was still wicked sore from the episiotomy stitches. I thought about taking a mirror and checking it out, then decided that I really didn't want to see.

I turned the water on and slid under the lukewarm spray. The barely warm water felt good on this blistering day. I grabbed a lump of Mom's handmade soup and lathered up. I used my bare hand to scrub my body. I used to trip out on my pregnant body, but this mom body was almost more surreal. My boobs had grown at least two sizes. Mom and Sam said, "Just wait until your real milk comes in." Apparently when that happens they're going to turn into giant, veiny boulders for a few weeks. I was not looking forward to that. I touched my breasts and the strange new finger-like nipples.

I ran my hands over my belly. I heard people compare an after-baby belly to bread dough, and that's about the best description. It takes awhile for the uterus to shrink back down and for your belly to go back to normal or at least normalish. I traced my fingers over the thick pink stretch marks that covered my belly, hips, boobs, and thighs. When I was pregnant I worried so much about what my body would be like after Gracie was born. I was terrified of droopy, stretch-marked boobs and a sagging belly, but standing here looking at my boobs and belly, I kind of liked it. This body of mine made a baby, a perfect baby, and now my body was making food to grow this kid. What was that Ani line about stretchmarks? *See how I've grown.* It was true.

I wondered what Lou would think of this body. He didn't know me with a pre-pregnancy stomach and boobs. Gray did though. I wondered what Gray would have thought about this new body of mine.

Shit.

Oh my God.

Today was the nine-month anniversary of Gray's death. How did I not realize that? I was so thankful that Gracie didn't arrive on Gray's death date. All this time it never occurred to me that if I got pregnant on the day Gray ended their life that I might also give birth on that day nine months later. Thank God I didn't. But here it was my first day home with our child, and it was the same day nine short months ago that my entire world collapsed. For the past nine months I'd measured my life by Before Gray and After Gray. It was like Gray was the measuring stick for my entire existence. Gray's choice transformed me into an entirely new person and I was powerless over that transformation. I had no say in any of it. And now I had Gracie. I made the choice to have her and now, for the rest of my life, I think I will also measure my life by Before Gracie and After Gracie.

I turned up the hot water a bit.

If Gray were alive would they be here today at Gracie's welcome home dinner? Would they be out on the couch right now snuggling her? If Gray were alive would we have named Gracie after Gray's mom? I bet we would have. I said the name out loud. Jolie. Maybe I should make that Gracie's middle name. Gracie Jolie. It doesn't really flow. Gracie Jo? Yeah, I like that. Gracie Jo Logan. When Alice gets here I'm going to ask her how to change the birth certificate to add Jo as Gracie's middle name. And I think I'll spell it J O E rather than J O. Gray was both girl and boy, it might be cool to have Gracie's name reflect that.

I poured way too much shampoo into my hand and lathered up my hair. The sharp smell of tea tree mixed in with the steamy mint. I imagined that tea tree is what the desert smells like. Maybe like tea tree and sage. I've never been to the desert, any desert, and I decided right then that I would take Gracie to the desert one day. We'll camp under the open sky and hike through canyons and watch shooting stars light up the night sky. The first thing I'm going to buy when I finally get a job is a tent. I'm going to give Gracie all the things that Gray's mom couldn't give them: adventure, travel, and safety.

Why did you do it, Gray? Why?

What kind of weight will this be on Gracie as she grows up? Both her other parent—her Gaga—and her other grandma dying by suicide? What kind of legacy is that for a child? I'm going to have to be such a good mom. Every single thing I do from now on will be for Gracie. She's my entire reason for living. I will fill up the holes that Gray and their mom left.

I will be the best mother that any kid could want.

I turned up the hot water a little bit more. I needed to feel the burn. I rinsed the shampoo from my hair and then smeared the matching conditioner through it. I sat on the floor of the tub, letting the conditioner do its work and watched my skin turn red.

What was I doing at this time nine months ago? Nine months ago today Rags and I would have been at our spot by the freeway. I closed my eyes and traveled backwards. Rags and I sat in the grass overlooking the freeway and I began to convince myself that I had made the whole thing up in my head. I actually started to believe that Gray had just gone to get us donuts. I had convinced myself that I was delusional, and they had not really walked out onto the freeway and been hit by a truck. And then I had caught a glimpse of something in the grass glimmering in the sun. It turned out to be the snow globe that Gray's mom had given them when they were a kid.

Each night when Jolie tucked Gray into bed she would shake the little snow globe and as the flakes gently fell onto the tiny snowman Jolie would whisper to Gray that one day the two of them would leave their shitty Florida town and the heavy fists of Gray's dad and together they would be free. She promised little Gray that one day they would live in a place with seasons and snow and safety, but they never did escape. Or I guess they did, just not in the way that either of them had planned.

The moment I found that snow globe was the moment I knew that Gray really was gone forever. I wasn't delusional. I wasn't making it all up in my head. Gray had not gone out to get donuts.

I rinsed the conditioner from my hair.

I tried to imagine myself in Jolie's position. I'd like to think that I would take Gracie and run. Run to a women's shelter. Run to a homeless shelter. Run to the woods. But would I? In the end would I make the same choice as Jolie? Would I make the choice to walk in front of that train and leave Gracie behind the way Jolie left Gray behind?

Gray once confessed to me that sometimes they thought that maybe their dad had actually killed their mom and made it look like suicide. That seemed a little hard to believe given the fact that Jolie was found on the train tracks, but in a way Gray's dad did kill Jolie. He convinced her that she was such a horrible human being that she didn't deserve to live. He must have said things to her that day that finally broke the last thread of hope and she was no longer able to hold on.

My thoughts were interrupted by a knock on the door.

"You okay in there?" It was Mom.

I realized that I was crying.

"Yeah, I'll be out soon," I yelled over the sound of the water.

"Banjo, are you crying?"

"No Mom. I'm okay."

Mom hesitated. She wasn't fooled by my reassurance. "Okay honey, just checking," she said.

I lay down flat in the tub and let the spray bounce off my brand-new belly. I closed my eyes and tried to bring an image of Gray into my mind. Without a picture to look at, it was hard. Death yanks a person from your life like yanking a bandage off a cut. It hurts like hell and then you're just left with a scar where that person used to be and you cling to that scar as if your life depends on it, because sometimes it does. Then despite your best efforts, death slowly and subtly erases that person from your brain and softens the scar. It steals their voice, their image, their smell, until all you have left are photos and fuzzy memories. And even the memories become tainted because as time passes you add and subtract things and eventually you have no way of knowing if what's left is authentic or just another made up story that you've told yourself. I was glad I had Gracie to help me remember.

I sat up, turned off the water, and toweled off. I pulled on my boxer briefs, tucked a pad in the crotch, slid into my shorts, strapped myself into my new nursing bra, and pulled on the fresh t-shirt. I rubbed some coconut oil through my hair and then added a squirt of sculpting cream. My hair was a mess but oh well. Maybe Sam could cut it for me later.

Mom was in the kitchen chopping veggies for the salad. Gracie was strapped into her bouncy seat which was sitting on the table. She looked way too small to be in that seat.

"Are you sure that's safe?" I asked Mom.

"Of course it's safe, sweetie. She's in the center of the table. There's no way she can fall off."

"Are you sure she's big enough to be in that seat?"

Mom smiled without looking up from the carrots she was slicing. "Wow, you sure wasted no time in become a full-blown mom, eh? All worry, all the time."

"Mom?"

"Yeah, sweetie?"

"You know how when Gracie was born she came out all limp and blue?"

"I honestly thought we had lost her," she said. "Are you okay?"

"Yeah, yeah I'm okay. I walked over and looked down at my baby. "Do you think that it's possible? I mean, do you think that maybe she came out that way because she was like . . . with Gray?" I instantly regretted asking this. "I know it sounds crazy. It's a dumb thought. Forget I said anything."

"I do. You're not crazy."

I turned to look at her. She was drying her hands on a kitchen towel and looking straight at me.

"I thought the same thing when she came out lifeless and then returned to us so easily. You know Banjo, I'm not a religious person and I'm only slightly woo-woo, but what happened two days ago . . . I don't know. Sam and I talked about it that night. She was actually the first one to say the words. I don't know if I believe there's anything after this life. I guess I do believe all living beings have an energy. How that manifests, I don't know. I guess it's my turn to sound crazy, but I felt

Gray there. In the room. I felt them. I think they came to meet Gracie. Maybe Gray's mom was there too. I don't know."

I stared at Mom. My guts twisted and a boulder rose in my throat at Mom's words. Gray had been there that day. Gray didn't abandon me. Gray got to hold their baby.

Mom pulled me into a hug, her hands rubbing my back. Tears came slow and quiet.

"Do you think she'll remember?" I asked. "I mean, do you think Gracie will remember meeting Gray?"

"She will. In her dreams, she will."

"Today is nine months since Gray left." I said.

"I know," said Mom. "It's a good day to be surrounded by people who love you and who love Gracie."

"I love you, Mom."

"I love you too, Banjo. So much."

We stood holding each other and crying. She ran her fingers through my damp, tangled hair as she rocked me side to side, her arms tight around me.

"Mom, do you think that it's messed up that I'm like sort of seeing Lou? I mean, so soon after Gray? Gray was only . . . I mean they had only been . . ." I was unable to say the word dead and struggled to find the right word. "I met Lou only a few months after it happened. Do you think I'm awful? Do you think Gray hates me?"

"Honey, you did nothing wrong. There is no timeline for these kinds of things. You didn't go out looking for Lou. You and Lou found each other, and I think you needed each other."

"But is it disrespectful? Do you think one day Gracie will hate me?"

"You loved Gray and Gray loved you. Gray did something that blew your life up and you didn't ask for that. Being pregnant and losing someone you loved to suicide—losing the other parent of your child to suicide—honey, that's huge. Gray would want you to do whatever you need to do to make it through. And Banjo, I know with all of my heart that Gray would want someone like Lou to be there for Gracie. Lou is a lovely person and we are all lucky to have him in our lives. I think Gray was there the day Gracie was born and I think they brought her back to you and to Lou both. Gray couldn't stay here with us on this side. They needed to go and be with their mom. I think Gray wanted Gracie to be here with you and Lou and that's why they brought her back. That's what I think. Maybe I'm crazy. Hell, we all know I probably am, but I think that's what happened.

"And sweetheart, you have to live your life. You have to find happiness. You haven't forgotten about Gray and every single day that you live and every single day that you care for that little baby, you honor Gray. I'm proud of you."

"Why do you think Gray did it? Why didn't they tell me they were thinking of leaving?"

"Oh honey."

"Why would they be with me like that on the night we made Gracie and then walk out the door and choose to die? Do you know that was the first time we even kissed? I thought . . . I thought . . ." Sobs swallowed my words. Mom pulled me into a hug. She didn't say a word. She just held me running her hands up and down my back.

I couldn't understand how Gray could be so tender with me and then turn around and walk onto that freeway. Why hadn't they said something? Why would they do that knowing they were leaving that night? What if I had gone back to their apartment like I had wanted to? Would they still be alive? Would they be here celebrating our child and our life together? Why didn't I go back? Why did they do it? I just couldn't wrap my brain around it. I guess I just wasn't enough for them. I wasn't enough to save them from the grief of losing their mom.

After a long time Mom pulled back. "Banjo, do you want me to postpone the dinner? Everyone will understand."

I wiped my eyes. "No. No, I want to see everyone."

Mom wiped away her own tears. "I wish I could tell you why they did it. I think Gray was just in too much pain and they saw no way out. Their choices that night, from being with you to walking out that door, make no real sense and probably never will. I can tell you what I do know. I know that Gray loved you deeply. And they love Gracie deeply. You have to believe that, honey. They didn't do it to hurt you."

"It's so hard," I whispered.

"I know. I know, baby." She kissed my cheek. "Okay, now we have a party to get ready for. We have a life to celebrate today and in celebrating Gracie we are honoring Gray, so go splash some cold water on your face, okay?"

I nodded.

"Mom?"

"Yes, Banjo?"

"I love you so much, Mom. I'm sorry I was so crazy."

Mom smiled. "Don't you dare apologize. Crazy runs in this family, am I right? Now go splash some cold water on your face, I think I heard a car pull up. And Banjo, if you want to talk more about this I'm here for you. Anytime you need me. Do you understand that?"

I nodded. "Mom?"

"Hmm?"

"You have rivers of mascara running down your cheeks."

"That'll teach me to try being femme," she said, smiling through her tears.

Chapter 8

There was a knock on the door and Henry ran to answer it. Anna flounced in wearing a loose-fitting, purple peasant dress that looked beautiful against her dark skin and black hair. Around her neck hung a green crystal the size of Gracie's fist. And, of course, she wore Birkenstocks. No socks today due to the heat, but Anna always wore Birkenstocks. She had her giant hemp purse slung over her shoulder.

"Good afternoon, Henry," she said.

"Hi Anna. Did you bring Betsy?"

"Not today. She can get a little rambunctious, especially with a lot of people around. You should come visit her some time," she said. She turned to me and Mom smiling. "Banjo, I'm so happy to be here. Where is the guest of honor? I can't wait to meet her." She pulled me into a hug. "You've been crying," she whispered into my ear. "Let me know if you need to talk."

"I will," I said.

Mom lifted the sleeping Gracie from her bassinet. "Thank you so much for coming, Anna," Mom said, walking towards her with my baby. I felt a twinge of irritation that Mom had taken over. I should be the one handing over Gracie. I swallowed it down. I knew she meant well, but still.

I think Anna sensed my discomfort.

"Oh Banjo, she's simply perfect. It's alright if I hold her?"

"Yeah, yeah of course. Um, would you mind washing your hands first?" I said, feeling embarrassed to be asking that. Anna pretty much saved my life after I got out of the hospital and I was happy she wanted to be here for me. It made me feel special, like I was more than just a client. I just wished I had been the one to offer Gracie to her.

She went into the kitchen and scrubbed her hands. When she returned she took Gracie from Mom and settled her into the crook of her arm. I saw her eyes well up with tears.

"Oh Banjo, ella es tan hermosa. She's just beautiful. You did good. I'm so proud of you." Anna leaned down and put her nose into Gracie's fuzzy little head. "Nothing smells better than baby head."

"I couldn't agree more." We all turned to see Alice standing in the door holding a potted purple hydrangea and a six-pack of fancy beer. I ran to her and she pulled me into a bear hug without setting down the flowers or the beer.

"I'm so glad you're here," I said.

"Pishaw, of course I'm here. Where else would I be?"

"Hi Alice," said Henry.

"Hey, dude," she said, letting me go. "Hi Jane. And can I assume that you're Anna? I've heard so much about you," she said.

"I am. And you must be the famous Doctor Alice."

"Well, can't say that I'm famous, but I am a doctor and I am named Alice. Good to meet you," she said, handing the six pack of beer to Mom and extending her free hand to Anna. Anna took her hand awkwardly as she cradled Gracie.

"May I?" asked Alice, motioning towards Gracie.

"Of course," said Anna, "Banjo asked that we wash our hands first."

Alice smiled wide and winked at me. She vanished into the kitchen just as Lou and Dylan appeared.

Henry ran across the room and jumped into Dylan's arms. Dylan caught him and held him upside down for a second before handing him off to Lou. Lou held him by his knees and pretended to sniff his feet. "Woah boy, those are some stinky paws," he said as he lowered the giggling Henry to the floor.

Mom stepped forward. "Anna, this is Lou and this is Dylan. Dylan and Lou, this is Anna."

Anna reached out to shake their hands. "I've heard so much about you two—all good of course. So wonderful to meet you."

"You too," they said in unison.

When Rags heard Lou's voice she bounded out of my room and ran to Lou with her tail wagging.

"Hey Ragsy," Lou said, scruffing her ears.

Alice returned. "Mr. Moretti and Mr. Anderson, I'm so happy to see you both again," said Alice. She took the sleeping baby from Anna.

We heard a loud rumble out in the driveway.

"Uncle James," yelled Henry, running outside to greet him.

My brother's car was pretty much held together by baling wire and duct tape and it sounded like it. He killed the engine and the car continued to thunk and rumble for a solid two minutes before giving one final shake and then going quiet.

Megan came in wiping sweat from her forehead with a ratty old bandana. "I swear if his next car doesn't have air conditioning, I'm leaving him," she said.

Megan didn't drive. She preferred to get around on a ridiculously expensive titanium bicycle. She and my brother were complete opposites, but somehow it worked. She hugged Lou, Dylan, Mom, and me and then said hi to Alice and introduced herself to Anna.

"Where's Sam?" she asked.

"She'll be here soon," said Mom.

My brother came to the door carrying Henry on his shoulders. Henry was too big for that. James didn't seem to notice and neither did Henry.

James crouched down so Henry could jump off before he was beheaded by the door frame and then handed me a package wrapped up in a Target bag. "Didn't have time to wrap it," he mumbled.

"More like, didn't bother to wrap it," quipped Megan. "I bought paper, I swear. But I left him in charge of wrapping. My bad."

James rolled his eyes.

I opened the bag to find the most amazing infant unicorn hoodie I've ever seen. It had a rainbow mane and was a size six-months.

"It should fit her by the time it gets cold, assuming it ever gets cold again," said Megan. By now she was holding Gracie and Anna was digging around in her enormous purse. I had a moment of panic realizing that I wasn't sure if Megan had washed her hands, but I swallowed it down. Anna pulled a large wooden salad bowl from her bag and handed it to Mom. "I made a Waldorf salad. It should probably go in the fridge," she said.

And then she dove back into the purse. I swear her purse was like a clown car. I expected her to pull a couch or something out of it. Finally, she pulled out two small boxes wrapped in gold foil. She handed one to me. I unwrapped the box and opened it to find a beautiful black onyx elephant necklace.

"Anna this is beautiful," I said. I didn't normally wear jewelry, but the tiny black elephant was so pretty.

"Black onyx is all about emotional and physical strength. It's powerful medicine for those dealing with grief. And of course, elephants are matriarchal, which I thought was a pretty good fit for this family."

She handed me the second box. Again, I unwrapped it and opened it. Inside was a pink crystal on a chain.

"That's rose quartz. It's known as a heart stone and will help open

Gracie's heart to love. Hang that near where Gracie sleeps."

"Oh Anna, thank you so much." Tears ran down my face.

"Hey, no more crying," she said. "Well unless you want to of course, in which case I totally support you." She winked and hugged me again.

"Oh, that reminds me," said Alice. "This is for you." She handed me the potted hydrangea that she had set on the floor by the couch. "I thought you could plant this in honor of Gracie. You kept the placenta, right? It's good luck to bury the placenta and plant a tree on it. I thought a pretty flower would be better than a tree, of course you don't have to. You can just plant it in Gracie's honor sans placenta."

I had kept the placenta. Mom and Sam talked me into it. We had a small Japanese Maple out back that grew on Henry's placenta. He liked to sit out back near it and read his graphic novels. The idea of Gracie one day being able to pick a bouquet of flowers that had a tiny bit of me and a tiny bit of her in them made me smile through the still-flowing tears.

"Thank you, Alice."

"You're very welcome," she said pulling me into another hug.

"Well since it's present time, me and Dyl got you something too," said Lou.

He slid off his backpack and pulled out a grocery bag. He handed it to Dylan. "You can do the honors," he said, looking shy.

Dylan reached into the bag and handed me something wrapped in tissue paper. I unwrapped it to find a framed picture of Lou, Dylan, Me, and Gracie that was taken on the day Gracie was born. I barely remembered this being taken. It was in a custom-made ceramic frame that said *queerdo* across the top and *family* along the bottom. More tears. I couldn't look at them for fear of completely losing it.

"Thank you," I managed to say.

Dyl pulled another tissue paper package from the bag and handed it to me. I unwrapped it. It was a velvety soft lavender baby blanket with two hand-made patches hand-sewn onto the corners; one a little white and rainbow unicorn and the other a pink and green narwhal.

The tears continued.

Last, Dylan handed me a CD case. I opened it to find a CD decorated in metallic sharpie. It said *Teen Parents Rock*. There was a little paper insert that had information about each song.

"All the s-s-songs on there are by teen parents or p-p-people born to t-t-teen parents. And I wrote d-d-down who was a teen parent and who was b-b-born to a teen parent on the insert. I made a d-d-digital version, of course, but I thought it would be c-c-cool to have an old school CD that you could give to G-G-Gracie some day," said Dylan shyly.

I couldn't speak. I just fell into the both of them for a long group hug.

"Dyl spent hours on that thing," said Lou.

"W-w-we never got to l-l-listen to it when you w-w-were in labor," he said.

"Thank you," I managed to say.

The door opened.

"Mama!" yelled Henry.

"Sorry I'm late," she said, almost out of breath. "I got caught up at work. Damn protesters were there again." Sam worked at Planned Parenthood in the next town over. She was taking classes two nights a week and working at Planned Parenthood during the day doing intake.

"I'm going to set out the food and then let's eat," said Mom, disappearing into the kitchen. Alice followed, carrying Anna's Waldorf salad.

I made everyone go into the bathroom and wash their hands and then they all took turns holding Gracie. I excused myself to the bathroom to try to get ahold of my emotions. I closed the bathroom door and stared into the mirror. My eyes were swollen from crying and my cheeks were blotchy. I ran the cold water, soaked a hand towel, and then laid it on my face. It felt good. I read somewhere, or maybe Anna told me, that when you're having an anxiety attack, sometimes if you plunge your face into cold water it can stop it or at least keep it from getting out of control. Something about shocking your system or whatever.

I was lucky to have so many people who loved me. It also made me feel guilty. I wouldn't have any of these people—other than my immediate family—if Gray hadn't died. Anna, Alice, Lou, and Dylan were all in my life because Gray left my life. How can I ever reconcile that? Maybe I can't. I guess I need to talk to Anna about that at my next appointment, when I see her as a patient rather than a friend.

I dried my face, attempted to tame my too-long, too-scraggly, too-lopsided hair with water and a few squirts of hair cream, and then I returned to the party. Everyone was in the kitchen gathered around the amazing spread on the kitchen table: piles and piles of crab legs, a plate heaped with strips of cold steak, Anna's Waldorf salad, a green salad with vegetables from Mom's garden, crusty French bread, sliced melon, bowls of melted butter, lemon slices, all sorts of salad dressings, and a beautiful chocolate cake. In the corner sat a cooler of ice filled with fancy beer, wine, and sparkling water.

"She's here. Let's eat!" yelled Henry.

Alice held Gracie in her arms. "Mind if I put her into her car seat so we can eat?" she asked.

"Sure," I said, feeling the tears build again. Who was I to deserve these people?

Dylan was fumbling with Mom's old CD player that sat on the kitchen counter. Suddenly "MMMBop" filled the kitchen.

"I thought you said this was all teen parents," said Sam.

"The m-m-middle Hanson br-br-brother was a teen dad," he replied.

"Seriously?" asked Sam.

"Yep, I d-d-did my research."

"The Hanson brother was homeschooled and a teen parent? You're amazing Dyl," said Sam.

Everyone murmured in agreement. Dylan blushed.

"I have A-A-Aretha Franklin, Justin Bieber even though he's a total jerk, Lil Wayne, Solange Knowles, Selena Gomez, Dr Dre, 50 Cent, Tupac, and Fantasia Barrino. Everyone was ei-ei-either a teen parent or had teen p-p-parents."

Mom, Alice, and Anna began busting out dance moves. The three danced around the kitchen, holding their plates, bumping hips, and doing ridiculous moves. I noticed that Mom and Alice kept looking at each other in this way that was different from how they looked at the rest of us. I let the thought go. I had enough emotions roiling in my brain at that moment. A few seconds later Lou, Sam, Megan, and Henry joined them. Dylan was too shy. I was too emotional. James excused himself to go have a cigarette.

MMMBop ended and "Respect" began to play. *Just a little respect,* Aretha sang. I felt an incredible urge to tell them all how much I loved them, but I knew if I opened my mouth all that would come out would be a sob, so instead I grabbed a chipped plate from the pile of mismatched thrift store plates on the table and began to dish up while all the people I loved had a dance party in my baby's honor.

Chapter 9

Gracie and I were sprawled on our saggy couch binge watching that reality T.V. show, *Unexpected*. It was another broiling day. I hoped that we could escape this year without wildfires. The idea of another summer of smoke-filled skies was scary, but the idea of Gracie breathing that smoke was downright terrifying.

I closed the curtains to try to keep the sun out and turned on all the fans. It wasn't working. It was still a thousand degrees in our house, though the dark room at least gave an illusion that it was a little cooler inside than it was outside. Gracie dozed on my lap wearing just a diaper and even that seemed to be making her sweat. I had stripped down to my boxers and an old t-shirt with no bra.

During the commercials I flipped through the parenting magazine that I got free for having a baby. It turns out the hospital gives out goodie bags when you have a baby. Sort of like when you're little and go to the doctor or dentist and get a sticker or a crappy plastic toy for being good.

My goodie bag had some coupons for things like butt cream, baby food, and diapers. It also included a paper growth chart shaped like a giraffe, a small bottle of Pedialyte, and a free issue of *Parents* magazine, as well as a free one-year subscription. I had never even heard of *Parents* magazine until my first obstetrics appointment with Alice. I had picked it up and became instantly overcome by shame. Magazines like this weren't made for girls like me. I vowed then that I would never pick up another one, but here I was flipping through the pages that showed me just how far away from the ideal mom I really was. I mean, I'm pretty sure the ideal mom doesn't lay around in her underwear all day in a dark room watching trash T.V. I didn't care. Having a baby at seventeen ruins any chance you can ever be anyone's idea of an ideal mom.

The front door swung open, filling the room with sunlight. It hurt my eyes. I squinted against the brightness to see if the silhouette was Mom or Sam coming to invade my T.V. time.

"Hi honey."

It was Mom.

"You should open the curtains and let some light in here, not to mention some air. It's stuffy in here."

"It's a scientific fact that it stays cooler with the windows and curtains closed," I said.

"Not if there's a breeze outside and there's a breeze," she said, pulling the curtains open and sliding the window wide.

"I like it dark," I complained.

"It's not good for you to sit in the dark all day. And it's not good for Gracie either," she said, as she moved one of the fans up to the window sill.

She turned back to me. "See isn't that better?"

I didn't want to admit it, but it was better.

She glanced down at the magazine that I had balanced on top of the sleeping Gracie. "Why are you reading that thing? Those magazines are designed to make you feel like crap and to sell you crap."

"How will I ever learn how to make Gracie kale popsicles or find out how dining out changes after you have kids if I don't read this magazine? And how will I ever be able to plan a mommy and daddy date night?"

"If you need to know how to make kale popsicles I got you covered. I used to sneak sweet potatoes into your apple juice popsicles all the time!"

"You did?"

"Why do you think I let you eat popsicles for breakfast? I never thought to try kale, but let's see . . . I used squash, sweet potato, carrots, even did spinach once. You got suspicious on that one."

"I remember that. You tried to tell me it was kiwi."

Mom laughed. "Okay yeah, I did. Anyway, where did you get that magazine anyway?"

"It came in my hospital goodie bag. And I get a whole year's subscription of Let Us Show You All the Ways You Suck as a Parent Magazine just for having a baby. I've been studying up on this phenomenon called Loser Teen Mom. I'm using this magazine as sort of a compare and contrast of Regular Adult Parenting to that of Loser Teen Mom parenting.

"Anyway, my show's back on." I paused it to give Mom time to leave me alone. I didn't want to miss anything.

Mom looked at the T.V. "Oh Lord Banjo, what the hell are you watching?"

"Unexpected. It's the new teen mom reality show. I need to get some pointers. I'm new at this whole thing. It's very informative."

"Turn that garbage off right now."

"Okay. Okay. I will. Just let me finish this episode, okay?" I said as I hit play again.

Mom shook her head and let out one of her famous sighs that said, I give up, but Mom only gives up for moments at a time and then she's right back at it.

"Banjo, I'm worried about you. I think you're depressed. You can't just spend your days in a dark house watching crappy T.V. It's not good for you and it's not good for the baby."

She was right of course. It probably wasn't good for me or for Gracie. Since Gracie's birth I'd felt myself sort of sliding into this place where I had a hard time feeling anything. Well, anything other than exhaustion, with occasional sprinkles of rage or shame. But I was also really invested in this dumb show. "Mom, I'm trying to watch this show. I'll turn it off right after this episode, I promise."

"Banjo, now."

"Mom, you can't tell me what to do any more. I have a kid of my own and I get to decide what's good for her and what's not. She's almost two months old. I don't think some reality T.V. is going to rot her mind."

I paused the show again, waiting for her to leave me alone.

"I agree. It won't rot her mind, however it will send you even deeper into depression. Watching this garbage isn't good for you and neither is being cooped up all day in this house."

"Mom, I homeschool. This is education. File it under anthropology. I'm studying this unique culture known as Loser Teen Mom. I have decided to go and live among them and so must be fully prepared. Hell, I do live among them. Speaking of that, this show is about teen moms born to teen moms. You might like it."

"Wait, what?"

"All of the teen moms on this show are the daughters of teen moms and even some of the teen dads have teen moms. One family even has three generations of teen moms."

"Really?" asked Mom as she pushed my legs aside to make room for herself on the couch.

"Yeah." I hit play again.

"Is it awful?"

"It's awful in the very best way."

"Okay maybe I'll watch just a teensy bit. I should tell Alice about this show," said Mom.

I looked at her. "Mom, do you talk to Alice a lot?" I was seriously starting to suspect there was something between them.

Her face went red, but just then Sam came through the front door, saving her from having to answer me.

"Man, I'm beat. Works sucks. I have to tell you guys about my day..."

"Shhh," Mom and I said in unison.

Mom patted the empty spot on the couch beside her. "Sit down."

"What are you guys watching?"

"*Unexpected*. It's a reality T.V. show about teen moms who are the children of teen moms," I said. "It's like a show about our family."

"Oh for God's sake. You aren't serious?"

I stopped the show again and then brought up the first episode.

"Okay, I will admit that it's pretty bad and exploitive and all of that, but it's also so good. C'mon Sam, Mom's willing to give it a try. Let's have a family T.V. hour. I promise you won't regret this."

"You all are serious right now?" Sam looked at Mom in disbelief.

Mom patted the couch again.

"Alright. Alright. Let me go grab a beer. You all want anything?"

"Beer please," said Mom.

"Iced tea for me please," I said.

Sam disappeared into the kitchen and returned a few minutes later balancing our drinks, a mixing bowl of leftover pasta salad, and three forks. "Dinner," she said, handing mom her beer and me my glass of iced tea. She put the giant bowl of salad on Mom's lap since she was between us, and settled in. Henry was spending the night at the neighbor's house, so we didn't need to worry about rotting his impressionable mind.

I hit play again.

It felt nice to be sitting on the couch with my teen mom family watching this teen mom show. The show follows the lives of four pregnant teenagers through their pregnancies and the birth of their babies.

I had already watched the first few episodes, but didn't mind starting the show over for Mom and Sam. It was sort of amazing to me how young the pregnant girls seemed even though they were about my age. Was I that young just a month and a half ago? I think in some ways I was. I feel like the minute Gracie was laid in my arms I transformed. I sure as hell didn't feel like a kid any longer. I actually could barely remember life before Gracie.

"We should have applied to be on this show," said Sam. "We could have used the cash."

"Something tells me they wouldn't be so down with the gay," said Mom.

"I don't know, we do have a pretty good story line in this family," said Sam.

"Maybe we should start a YouTube channel and make our own show," I offered. "I hear you can get rich on YouTube."

"You can only get rich if you're a straight, white misogynist asshole dude under the age of twenty-four," said Sam.

"Maybe," I said. She was probably right.

"Girls, quiet down." Mom was really getting into this show.

Sam leaned across Mom and looked at me. "What have you done with my mother?" she asked.

"Oh stop," Mom gave her a little shove.

Four hours and four episodes later Mom announced that she was going to bed.

"I have to admit I'm hooked," she said. "We can watch more tomorrow."

"I told you, didn't I?"

"You did."

"What time is it?" Sam asked.

Mom looked at her phone. "Ten fifteen," she said as she leaned down to kiss Gracie.

"Alright, see you all in the morning." She walked down the hall to her room.

Sam yawned. "I'm heading to bed too. I'm so glad Henry isn't here. It will be so nice to have the room to myself without all of his sleep talking."

"Okay."

"And hey, don't watch any more without me and Mom. This was nice."

Something occurred to me. "You guys aren't watching this just for my sake, are you? I mean, is this some sort of trick or something?"

"Hells to the no. This dumb show totally sucked me in. I need to find out what happens especially with that guy Shayden," said Sam.

"Oh man, I so hope she dumps that guy."

"Me too. 'Night sis. I'm beat."

"Goodnight, Sam."

Sam followed Mom down the hall and disappeared into the room she shared with Henry.

Gracie did not look like she was in the mood to sleep, so I strapped her into her bouncy seat and carried her into the kitchen. I set the bouncy seat in the center of the table and poured myself a bowl of hippie organic cereal, dumped in two giant scoops of raw sugar, and then drowned the whole thing in sweetened, vanilla soy milk.

Sitting alone in the quiet house with Gracie I could feel the anxiety begin to seep in around the edges of my brain. I would be responsible for this kid for eighteen more years. You can make a lot of mistakes in eighteen years and when you're a mom your mistakes are no longer your own. Your mistakes can become scars on your kid. I was starting to think parenting was nothing more than trying to make sure your mistakes did the least damage possible. Like how much TV should she watch? Should I send her to regular school or homeschool her like me and Henry? What if I don't read to her enough? I mean, maybe I should already be reading to her. Am I already behind? Will it ruin her if I take her to McDonald's for a Happy Meal? What about when she's a teenager? Will I notice if she's on drugs or depressed?

What if I make a mistake I can't undo? What if the fact that her other parent died by suicide has already formed a scar that will never heal? How will I tell her about Gray? What if I let her get attached to Lou and Lou leaves?

I watched Gracie stare transfixed at the ceiling fan spinning above her. She was so beautiful. So perfect. I didn't deserve this kid. She wasn't even two months old and already her life was complicated. Her Gaga was dead by their own hand and her mama was seventeen and a giant mess.

"I love you, Gracie. I love you so much."

Her gaze broke from the fan and she looked right at me and I knew, at least for that moment, that I could do this.

Chapter 10

Exhaustion filled my body like sand, weighing me down and making it hard to even lift my arms. I felt like I could sleep for a year. Mom and Sam kept insisting that I let them take Gracie for a night, let them bottle feed her some of my stashed milk. No way. I refused to be one of those teenage moms who couldn't handle it. I refused to be what everyone thinks teen moms are: lazy and incapable. I just had to try harder. It's just not that hard, right?

I glanced at the clock on my bedside table. 12:14 am.

"Please Gracie. Please just sleep. Okay? Do it for your mama. Please go to sleep."

I had spent the past two hours nursing her or pacing around jiggling her and patting her little butt or rocking her in the rocking chair. Anything to keep her quiet and try to lull her into sleep, but every time her eyes closed the slightest change in movement sent them flying open. If I stopped patting her or jiggling her or pacing or nursing or rocking she sprung awake and screamed. I could feel frustration seeping into the sands of exhaustion. I never knew a human being could feel this completely worn out.

Mom and Sam's words popped into my head. *You don't have to be perfect.* Maybe they were right.

I patted and jiggled her over to the battery-operated baby swing. "Okay, if you're going to screw around all night then you're just going to have to hang out in the swing for a while. Cuz your mama needs a nap."

I lowered her into the swing, made sure her head was supported properly in the little pillow thing, and turned it up to high. I gave it a little push to start it and off it went swinging her so hard it made me feel dizzy, but that's how she likes it. By some miracle she did not start screaming the second I set her down. I flopped onto the bed, wrapped myself up in a sheet, and felt sleep begin to crawl over me.

I woke up to the room filled with light. For a minute I was so confused. Why was my light on? I glanced at the clock, 5:42 am. Oh my god! I couldn't get my mind to snap out of its fog. Where was Gracie? I started digging through the sheets and blankets, expecting to find her with a pillow over her face.

And then I remembered. The swing.

Oh my God. In that half second of terror I did the math in my head. I'd been asleep almost five hours. She never sleeps that long. I knew she was dead. I knew she had died of SIDS. What had I done?

"Mom! Mom! Oh my God, Moooooommm!"

I rolled over and practically fell out of the bed trying to get to her. I tried to remember the YouTube videos on infant CPR as I half crawled, half ran to the swing. And there was Gracie stretching and letting out a giant baby yawn. The swing had stopped swinging, probably hours ago. She wasn't dead.

I scooped her up and held her face to mine. My hands trembled as my tears soaked her face.

Mom burst through the door with Sam right on her heels, "What is it? What's wrong?"

I laughed through the sobs, "I thought . . . I thought . . . I thought she was . . . I thought she had . . ."

I couldn't make myself say the word dead or died. That word seems to have permanently vanished from my vocabulary since Gray died, and that word should never ever be a word associated with a baby, especially my baby.

Mom and Sam broke into laughter.

"Aw how adorable, you had your very first mama panic attack," said Sam. "Let me guess, SIDS?"

I nodded. "How'd you know?"

"We've all been there, honey," said Mom.

"Congratulations, you're officially a neurotic mom like the rest of us. Don't worry, it only gets worse." Sam laughed.

They both came over and sat on the edge of my bed. Mom took Gracie from me and held her so she was facing her. "Ms. Gracie, you are not allowed to do that to your mama ever again, understand?"

Mom kissed her cheek. "Gwacie? Gwacie, do you love your Gwanny so much? Do you?" Sam and I leaned in and joined in the baby talk. Suddenly Gracie's face twisted up into the most wonderful, most beautiful, most amazingly perfect smile that I'd ever seen in my entire life.

"Her first smile," we all said at once. Gracie turned her head away from us and frowned and then she turned back to us and the crooked smile returned.

My heart melted into a puddle of pure love. I started to cry again. I glanced at Mom and Sam. They had matching tears.

"Have you guys really freaked out thinking that one of us had died in our sleep?" I asked.

"Oh hell yeah," said Sam. "I used to do this thing where I always kissed Hen before putting him to bed because I was so convinced that if I didn't he would for sure die of SIDS. One night I fell asleep with him on my chest before I kissed him. I didn't mean to fall asleep. I woke up convinced he had died. I think I only had about seven thousand SIDS related panic attacks when he was a baby. Even well past when SIDS was even a possibility. Like he was probably two when I finally relaxed. I swear that's part of the reason I went crazy. I was always so worried and on edge and trying so hard to be perfect." She turned to me. "That's why I'm worried about you, Banj. You have got to ask for help."

"She's right Banjo. There's no such thing as a perfect mom, only a good enough mom," said Mom. "I did the exact same thing with each and every one of you. I had the SIDS panic attacks too many times to count. Also the they-rolled-over-and-suffocated panic attack, and the cat-got-in-and-smothered-them panic attack, and the they-choked-to-death-on-their-own-spit-up panic attack."

"Oh yeah the choking on spit up panic attack is a classic," said Sam.

"I swear I could have fifty kids and I'd still wake up in terror at least once a week," said Mom.

"I thought I was just a freak or something," I said.

"Baby, you have to start reaching out and talking to us and letting us help you. It's just not healthy for you to try to do this all on your own. Motherhood is the hardest job you'll ever have. You have to ask for and accept help." Gracie began to fuss. Mom laid her face down across her knees and then began to softly bounce her.

"She's right, Banj. You're going to crack if you don't. You can't keep this up. It's not good for you or for Gracie," said Sam. "Trust me, I know. You remember what happened to me, how I fell into psychosis and mania?"

"It's not like I could forget," I said, with more edge in my voice than I had meant. When Sam lost it when Henry was around three my life turned upside down. My childhood got pushed aside as Mom dealt with Sam and I cared for Henry.

"I'm sorry, Banjo. I wish I could go back and change things. I know none of that was fair to you. I'm just afraid you'll end up in the same place if you don't let us start helping you. I never let anyone help me. I pushed myself too hard to be perfect and then one day I wasn't perfect anymore. I just snapped. It's taken me years to even begin to regain my footing."

"I know. It's just hard. I don't want to be a loser. It seems like everyone thinks I'm just a giant loser."

"Who thinks you're a loser? We don't," said Mom, handing Gracie to me. She was on the verge of a full-on hunger meltdown. "She's hungry."

"Not you guys, but like the world. Society. Everyone else who isn't a teen mom," I said, as I slipped Gracie onto my nipple.

Mom and Sam nodded.

"Yeah, can't argue," said Sam. "But it's not true and you can't let those ignorant jerks get to you."

"Sam's right. It never goes away, Banjo. Do you know how many times I'm out with Henry and when people find out he's my grandkid they feel compelled to tell me I don't look old enough to be a grandma? I mean it feels nice in a way, but it also feels shitty because it's once again pointing out how I don't belong. I mean even now when people find out how old James is, they always have to comment. My favorite is, what were you twelve when you had him?"

"Oh God, I've had so many people say that to me too. What is with the twelve comment? It's so gross," said Sam. "I've had people ask me if I know who Henry's dad is. If I know how babies are made, so it won't happen again. As if Henry is some sort of terrible mistake or car accident or something I regret. I've even had people flat out ask me if he was the result of a teen pregnancy. Like, fuck you. Seriously, I wish I had the courage to just tell people to go fuck themselves. I never know what to say."

"Half the time I don't know what to say either. You'd think I'd be used to it by now and have some witty comebacks stashed away, but each time it happens I'm just as shocked as I was the first time it happened," said Mom.

Sam nodded her agreement.

We all sat in silence for a minute watching Gracie slurp away. She acted as if she hadn't eaten for days, or at least five hours. Her little fists were curled up on the side of her face, which was the cutest thing ever. Mom pulled out her phone. "May I?" she asked.

I nodded and Mom proceeded to take several closeups of Gracie and her fists.

"Make sure you don't show any nipple," I reminded her.

Mom shoved the phone back into the pocket of her cut-off Levis.

We sat in silence for a minute, then Mom spoke again. "You know, in the late '80s when I had James, the hospital social worker tried to convince me I should give him up. They assigned me a social worker against my wishes and even sent a nurse to our house after he was born as a sort of welfare check in disguise. They treated me almost like I was abusive because I wouldn't give him up to some rich family." Mom shuddered with the memory.

"One thing most people don't realize is that just after James was born the Republicans came out with this thing called The Contract for America. It was a policy proposal to fix the country. One of the top Republicans, Newt Gingrich, proposed that the children of unmarried teenage mothers be put into orphanages. That was in the '90s. It wasn't enacted, but a whole lot of people thought this was a legitimate proposal. Pretty much the worst thing you can be is a teenage parent.

"It's scary how many people feel completely justified treating teenage parents like garbage. Maybe that's why I shut down so much when you were thinking about giving Gracie up. I just couldn't face it. It triggered too many memories and fears." Mom's eyes filled with tears.

"I am sorry for how I let you down," she said.

"You didn't, Mom."

"I did and it's okay to admit that."

Sam put her arm around Mom.

"Did you ever think about giving Henry up?" I asked Sam.

"No, but I got a lot of pressure from the family to give him up." She looked at Mom. "Remember when Uncle Al tried to get me to give Hen to his friends who were trying to adopt that baby from Guatemala?"

"What happened?" I asked.

"Al and Clair had these rich, white friends who were trying to adopt this kid from Guatemala. At around the same time the Guatemalan government was shutting down adoptions because of the child trafficking—like what happened to Lou—and so they thought my pregnancy might be a good chance for their friends to get themselves a nice white kid without all the hassle and expense of their Guatemalan brown baby. And the worst part is that after they brought him home he was too difficult so they rehomed him on craigslist. It was totally legal."

I felt like I was going to throw up.

"Imagine sweet Henry being raised in that family. Sometimes it keeps me up at night. If things hadn't gone well for Hen we would have known about it and yet there wouldn't have been a single thing we could have done." Sam's eyes filled with tears.

"You know," said Mom, "back in the day girls had several days, sometimes several weeks to change their minds, but they were lied to and tricked so they often didn't realize that or were made to feel so much shame and guilt they became paralyzed even if they wanted their babies back. The scary thing is that these days girls have from twenty-four to seventy-two hours to change their minds, depending on what state they live in. That's it. After that they lose all rights. It's terrifying. If Sam had agreed to give up Henry, she would have lost all rights to change her mind twenty-four hours after giving birth."

Or if I had gone through with giving up Gracie, I thought. I remembered how I had been so convinced that finding a nice gay couple to raise Gracie was the right thing to do for her. I closed my eyes, trying to prevent another round of tears.

I thought about the night Mom and I watched the movie Juno together. It was the night that I realized I would not be giving Gracie up. That movie was so completely unrealistic. I saw that then, but now, after giving birth to this kid, I really saw it. No mother, including teenage mothers, just happily give up their kid and then go about their life as if nothing ever happened. On my first appointment with Alice she had suggested I watch the movie.

"I want to punch Juno in the face right now," I said.

A small laugh escaped from Mom's mouth.

"Word," said Sam.

"Though, I guess the day I watched that movie was the day I knew I wasn't giving up Gracie, so there's that. I guess I can thank Juno for that after I punch her in the face. I feel like that movie was just another kind of teenage mother shaming. Do you think Alice told me to watch the movie so I would decide on my own to raise Gracie?"

"I think she told you to watch that movie so you could have another viewpoint to base your decision on," said Mom.

"That's what I thought. Speaking of Alice, are you two dating?"

Mom and Sam stole a quick glance at each other as Mom's face flushed red. "I'm having a hot flash," she said, trying to cover up the fact that I had caught her.

"No, you aren't. I knew there was something between the two of you. It's okay, Mom. I mean, it's a little weird, but Alice is rad. She'd make a good step-mom and step-grandma. You should marry her. Four teen mamas in one house, what are the odds? Also go Mom, you snagged yourself a doctor. Does this mean we'll be rich?"

"Not so fast," laughed Mom, her face still on fire. "First of all, we are just dating, don't be marrying me off so fast. Second, Alice is not rich. As a matter of fact, after making her student loan payments she's poorer than we are. And third, are you really okay with her? I mean, the two of us together?"

"Mom, I love Alice. She's the best." I did love Alice and she was the best, but I wasn't entirely sure I was okay with she and Mom dating. In some weird way I felt like Alice was mine. I was too exhausted and fragile to think about it much.

Chapter 11

They say that four a.m. is supposed to be the most creative hour of the day. I'm not actually sure who says that or why, but I remember hearing it once on some podcast my mom was listening to. I've become quite familiar with this time of the day. It's Gracie's favorite time to be awake. She may be asleep at midnight or two a.m. or five a.m., but never four. Maybe she's an artist.

The sky at this early hour in the late summer is still deep dark blue. The stars have all faded and it begins to get light around the edges. It's a time just before the birds begin to wake and welcome the sun with their songs. It's quiet, deserted, lonely, and peaceful. The raccoons, rats, and opossums begin to head back home. When you're up at 4 a.m. it seems like everyone else in the world is asleep.

This is the time of day when I sing to Gracie. Ever since that day in the hospital when I first sang her Bob Marley's "Three Little Birds" I have managed to keep my promise to sing it to her every single morning. When I made that vow I had pictured me singing to her in the morning when she woke up, but at that time I never dreamed it would be four o'clock in the morning. I was thinking more like six or eight, maybe even ten. I was so naïve then. Still, our song time is one of my favorite times of the day. When I sing she stares directly into my eyes and watches every move I make. It feels good to honor her other grandma. Part of me hates this early morning time, and part of me loves it. It's our private time. If only my body wasn't disintegrating from the lack of sleep.

I laid in the bed, quietly singing, playing with Gracie's hands, and thinking about what kind of life we might have together. Mom said I should focus on school and not find a job until I have graduated, but what then? College? Work? Internship? Trade school? Pack a backpack and travel the world with my kid? Start my own business? And should I continue to unschool or should I do something more official like online school or Running Start or something?

I decided that maybe I needed to write down some plans. I went to my dresser and found the notebook that I had been using to work through stuff before Gracie arrived. After I had started seeing Anna, she had suggested that I begin trying to write every day. She said to write about my feelings, to record my memories, to rage, vent, dream, or just doodle and draw pictures. She explained that sometimes things get locked in our body and the act of moving hands on paper can unlock things that we didn't even know were locked up. She said that it was also helpful to write things down so over time I could see patterns emerge.

I hadn't written anything since the week before Gracie was born. I flipped through the worn pages, and then realized this was not a good idea. This notebook held too much pain. I opened up the desk drawer and pulled out another notebook. I needed to start fresh, not just a fresh chapter in my life. I needed a whole new story.

I had several unused notebooks to choose from, so I chose a graph paper composition book with a lime green plastic cover. The color felt like hope and happiness.

I gathered up Gracie, my notebook of happiness, and a purple gel pen and went out into the living room. I turned the T.V. on low for company. I opened to the first page and wrote the word GOALS at the top of the page, and then I began to brainstorm and list the things that I wanted to do with my life.

Finish high school. Either keep unschooling or maybe do formal school.

Learn to drive

Take Gracie to the desert and look at the stars at night

Buy a hiking backpack, tent, sleeping bag, etc.

Eat better

Be nicer

Take Gracie to the mountains

Teach Gracie sign language

Get a haircut

As I wrote my list Gracie lay on the couch just looking around the room. She was so beautiful.

I glanced up at the T.V. to see that the local news had come on. That meant it was already 5:30. There was a clip of a whale swimming along with something on its back. I grabbed the remote and turned up the volume.

The video showed a mother orca from the local J pod swimming around with her dead baby on her back. A lump grew in my throat. The reporter explained that the mother had given birth to her calf eight days ago. The calf had been born alive, but then died within an hour of its birth. The mother, grief stricken, had placed the baby on her back and refused to let him go. She had been swimming with her dead calf for eight straight days. They said that her family had been helping her with the dead calf, even taking him for bits of time when she needed to dive, eat, or surface.

I felt a hole begin to rip open inside of me.

A marine biologist explained that because of salmon overfishing, climate change, pollution, dams on the rivers, noise pollution in the oceans, and a million other human-caused factors, the whales were dying. This mother gave birth to a baby she loved and because of forces beyond anything she could possibly hope to control, he had died. She couldn't bear the grief. Even the scientists said this was grief. She couldn't accept that her baby was gone.

The hole inside me began to grow larger as I watched the mother whale, whose name was Tahlequah, cling to hope where none existed. What would have happened if Gracie had not come back to me? What would I do if I lost Gracie? What would I do if one day she chose the same path as her other parent and grandparent?

Grief burst from me and suddenly I was drowning in it. I could barely catch my breath. Tahlequah was me and I was her. Her baby was Gracie and Gracie was her baby. Tahlequah had been helpless in protecting her baby, just as Jolie had been helpless to protect Gray. I couldn't fool myself. I had no real control over Gracie. Whatever control I had was an illusion. I had no more control than Mom had over us or the mothers of black boys shot by police or the mothers of daughters killed by boyfriends and husbands. No more control that the mothers in Syria whose babies were claimed by war or mothers fleeing Mexico who have watched their children be locked in cages. I had no more control than the mother whose child was overdosing on fentanyl right now, or the one whose child was swallowing the handful of pills. No more control than the mother whose child was slowly starving to death in some drought-ravaged country. I had no more control than Tahlequah.

The clip ended and I shut off the television. I scooped Gracie into my arms and sobbed. I sobbed for Jolie, for Tahlequah, and for myself. I even sobbed for Lou's mom back in Ethiopia. I sobbed for all the mothers everywhere whose babies suffered as they could only stand by and watch.

I thought about taking out one of my stashed razor blades and digging it into my arm to release some of the pain; instead, I walked back to my room, opened up my nightstand drawer, and pulled out the necklace that Anna had given me. I laid Gracie on the bed and I clipped the chain around my neck. I fingered the smooth black mother elephant. Black onyx helps with grief, she had said.

I lay back down in my bed next to Gracie and watched the day grow brighter outside my window. I thought of Tahlequah as I offered my boob to Gracie. She was safe in my arms. I drifted off imagining a mother whale and her dead calf swimming through the ocean together.

I woke up in a puddle of my own drool, my clothes drenched in sweat, and Gracie still in my arms. I reached for the day-old glass of water on my nightstand and chugged it. I'm sure it was full of Rags's hair, but I didn't care. My mouth felt like it was stuffed with swamp flavored cotton. A little dog hair was no match for the cesspool that was my mouth. Crying, breastfeeding, sweating, and hormone-induced hot flashes left me feeling like a raisin.

I gently slid Gracie out of my arms and onto the mattress, rolled onto my back and willed myself get out of bed. I could hear the faint voices of Mom and Lou over the low drone of my fan. I had read that keeping a fan running at night decreased a baby's risk of SIDS, so I decided that Gracie would sleep with a fan for the rest of her life. There are a few things a mother can control, I thought.

Dylan's cat, Petunia Rhubarb, was curled up on the pillow next to me. I ran my hand down her bony back and scratched behind her ears. She was getting so old. After we all met in the psych ward Dylan had told us about being kicked out. He mentioned his old cat, how much he missed her, and how worried he was that his dad would hurt her. Right then and there Lou had devised a plan to "liberate Petunia." Without saying a word he had snuck over to Dylan's parents' house and stole the old cat right off their porch. She has lived with us ever since.

I rubbed my foot along Rags's body and wondered if Rags was still missing Gray. Seeing the heartbreak of Tahlequah's mourning made me wonder about how much dogs could comprehend about loss. Gray had left Rags to me and after they died Rags had been a nervous wreck, always looking for Gray and waiting to go home. Was Rags over it now, or was she like me? Did she carry that grief deep in her guts? Was it forever a part of her, just waiting for the right trigger to bring it right back to the surface?

"We seriously are The Land of Misfit Toys, aren't we guys?" I said to the two snoozing animals.

They both ignored me. I forced myself out of bed and stripped out of my sweat-soaked clothes. I stood in front of the fan and let the air run over my naked body before pulling on clean shorts, bra, and tank top. I gave Gracie's butt a little squeeze to see how full the diaper was and decided she could wait a while before I changed her. Diapers cost a lot so unless she pooped, I tried to avoid changing her unless the diaper was threatening to rupture.

I roused Gracie and did the hungry test by putting my fingers up to her mouth to see if she tried to latch on. She didn't. She just yawned and stretched and so we headed out to the living room.

"Hello there, sleepy head," said Mom.

"I'm so groggy," I complained.

"Up all night and then sleeping into the heat of the morning will do it every time," said Mom. "It's almost eleven. I'm glad you slept."

"Your mom and I were just talking about you. We both agree that you'd look hella cute with some sort of faux-hawk sort of haircut," said Lou.

I looked from Lou to Mom, realizing they had probably been talking about a lot more than my hair. What had they said about me? What stories had they shared?

"Oh yeah?"

"Yeah Banj, you've been saying you need a haircut. Let me cut it for you?" said Lou.

"You know how to cut hair?" I was suspicious.

"You don't trust me," he said with a giant dose of pout in his voice.

I rolled my eyes. "Trust has nothing to do with it. I trust you will do your best, I just don't trust that it will work out."

"C'mon, what do you have to lose?" he countered.

"My dignity and my pride and my self-esteem or what's left of it."

Lou looked hurt.

I sighed. "Don't look so hurt. I mean you're the one that just basically told me that I look like shit."

"That's not what I meant," he protested.

"Okay, okay. My God, whatever, cut my hair." I yawned, placed Gracie in her bouncy seat and turned on the little vibrating thing.

"Sweet," said Lou.

Mom vanished down the hall and came back a few minutes later with her hair cutting kit and a couple bath towels. She bought the kit at Costco a few weeks ago. She had gone on and on about how it was only thirty dollars and how if we all started cutting our own hair, we would save all sorts of money. It was one of Mom's never-ending schemes to be *more self-sufficient and thrifty*. I realized she was probably itching to use her new toy. This was probably less about my new hair style and more about Mom and Lou bonding over this fun new gadget.

"Go wet your hair in the sink," she said.

"You two do realize that I just woke up, right?"

"Go," said Lou.

Mom tossed me a towel. I caught it in mid-air.

I filled a mason jar with tap water and gulped it down before sticking my head under the kitchen sink faucet. What the hell was

I thinking, letting those two cut my hair? I guess it couldn't possibly turn out worse than the rusty scissor haircut I gave myself the night I found out I was pregnant, and it probably couldn't be worse than what I currently had. I hadn't had a haircut since that day and that was months ago. My hair had grown out into a scraggly, slightly fluffy, lopsided mop. It was a style somewhere between gutter punk and soccer mom.

I towel-dried my hair as I returned to the living room.

"Let's do this out on the front porch. Less mess," said Mom, as she picked up the bouncy seat with Gracie still in it and headed out the front door with Lou right behind her carrying all the fun new tools.

I followed Mom and Lou outside and flopped down on one of the green plastic chairs that sat on our saggy front porch. The hot plastic stung the back of my thighs. The late morning air wrapped around me like a wet wool blanket that just came out of the oven.

"It's so hot," I moaned.

"Getting rid of some of that hair will help," said Lou.

Mom plugged the electric clipper into the outside outlet. "All set," she said.

Lou walked around me, inspecting my shaggy mess.

"Here we go," he said.

He ran the clippers up the back of my neck and I felt a huge chunk of hair fall. This was such a bad idea. He moved around to my right side and I couldn't help but notice how the muscles on his arms flexed as he ran the razor up the side of my head. I guess things could get hotter out here.

Mom moved in to inspect my head. "Right here. You missed a spot right here," she said, pulling on a bit of hair.

"Ow, be careful. That's still attached."

"Sorry dear."

Lou ran the razor over the spot and then stood back to inspect my head.

"Nurse, please hand me the scissors," he said to Mom.

"Yes Doctor."

"I'm so glad you two are having such a blast," I said.

They ignored me. Lou clipped and snipped away with the scissors, stopped, inspected me from a variety of angles, and then resumed his work.

"Have you guys heard about that mom whale whose baby died?" I asked.

"It's heartbreaking. I was actually hoping you wouldn't hear about that," said Mom. "I mean it's just so sad and to hear that story as a new mother adds another layer of despair."

I nodded.

"Hold still," said Lou.

"Sorry," I mumbled.

"I watched a video of her the other night," said Lou. "I sat and cried. It makes me hate people."

"Me too. I don't want to eat salmon for a while," I said. I felt like if I wasn't careful I would burst into tears.

"Oh, don't worry about that. I have no desire to buy salmon anytime soon. To be honest, I'm more inclined to join Earth First! and start blowing up dams," said Mom.

"I'm in," said Lou.

"Me too," I said. "I can't imagine her pain."

"There!" Lou stood back and admired his work. "Do you all have any hair product?"

"Be right back," said Mom, disappearing into the house.

I wanted to talk about this, but I thought they were afraid to go too deep into this topic with me.

As soon as she was out of sight Lou planted a little kiss on my cheek. "You look totes adorbs dot com."

I blushed. Mom returned, handing Lou a pump bottle of hair cream. Lou squirted some into his palm, rubbed his hands together, and then smoothed it through my still-damp hair. His hands felt nice on my scalp. Mom handed me a hand mirror to inspect. I had to admit it looked pretty good. I felt almost cute.

"Not sure this is hottest new style in the Mommy-sphere, but I think I like it," I said.

"I love floppy mohawks," said Lou.

I wanted to talk more about the orca mom and her baby, about animals and grief, about losing Gray, and how I felt like I would never be able to keep Gracie safe in this terrifying world, but I kept quiet. I didn't want to be a downer, and besides I didn't feel like I could find the words anyway. The feelings I had floating through me were like a fine mist that I couldn't quite get a hold of.

I needed to make an appointment with Anna soon. I hope Tahlequah has an Anna in her pod who can help her.

"Banjo? Why are you crying?"

I hadn't realized I was. I shrugged. "Hormones," I said.

Chapter 12

I sat on the couch texting with Lou when Gracie woke up and began to fuss. I ignored her, hoping she'd conk back out with the motion of the swing. The exhaustion that filled every cell of my body made my nerves raw and electric. The humid air felt suffocating. My emotions seemed to bounce from pure defeat to burning rage.

I had barely slept in days. Gracie seemed to only sleep in fits and spurts and never at night. Nighttime was for screaming. Even the swing had stopped working. I was no longer tired though; I felt electric. I was restless.

"Want me to get her?" Mom yelled from the kitchen.

"No Mom, she's fine."

Oh my god, my mom is making me crazy, I texted to Lou.

Gracie upped her fussing.

Mom appeared and began unbuckling her from the swing, "I'll take off her diaper," she said. "It's so hot maybe she needs some air."

"Mom! I told you she's fine. Would you just listen to me for a change? Jesus." Anger surged through me.

Mom's face registered shock and then hurt. "I'm sorry, Banjo. I . . . I was just trying to help."

"Well, I don't need your help."

Mom handed Gracie to me and then returned to the kitchen without a word. Why did she always have to butt in? If I had wanted to hold her,

I would have picked her up myself. I lifted my shirt and slid her onto my dripping boob. Maybe she'd eat and pass out. Henry ran in from outside, slamming the door behind him and causing my already frayed nerves to startle. He dashed straight to Gracie, "Yo Gracie Dog, you're looking swag today," he said as he slid his finger into the palm of her hand.

"Knock it off Henry, I'm not in the mood. And don't say swag, it makes you sound like a jerk."

Henry frowned, "I was just joking around. Why are you so grumpy?"

"Wash your hands before you touch her. They're gross," I said through clenched teeth.

Just then Sam emerged from the kitchen.

"Hen, go help Grams in the kitchen."

"I want to play with Gracie Dog," he complained.

"Henry, I told you not to call her that." I was almost shouting.

Sam put her hand on Henry's shoulder, "Go help Grams."

Henry let out a loud huff of air as he stomped off to the kitchen.

"Hey Banj, you need to chill out. Henry didn't do anything wrong and you need to ease up on Mom. She's just trying to help."

"I don't need her help."

"Well clearly you do. All new moms need help. And even if you don't need her help why you gotta be a such a dick to her?"

I didn't answer.

"She's just trying to help you."

"It would have been nice if she'd been this concerned when I was a kid."

"She did the best she could. And that has nothing to do with right now."

"She did the best she could for you, she ignored me. You're only defending her because she's always given you every damn thing you ever wanted. And she did all that while ignoring me."

"Dude, I thought you two already worked through that. I thought all three of us had worked through that. Like are you going to resent her forever? Are you going to resent me forever? You know, she's been trying to make it up to you. And Jesus, check your privilege. Your childhood wasn't that bad." Her voice was heavy with irritation. "You aren't making any sense. Like why are you suddenly so mad? Where is this even coming from? I think you need some sleep, sis." Her voice softened. "Do you want me to watch Gracie while you go nap?"

I ignored her offer for help. Gracie was my kid and I could handle her myself.

"You're always defending Mom. You weren't even here when my childhood was being highjacked. I was here taking care of Henry and being ignored and you were off being manic and having the time of your life."

"I know it wasn't easy, but really? Can you really claim it was some sort of horror show? Mom knows it wasn't easy for you. And trust me, I feel plenty of guilt over what a mess I was and the chaos I caused, but there's nothing I can do to change that. All I can do is move forward from here. All Mom can do is move forward. Cut her some slack and check the attitude. You're acting like a spoiled asshole. And by the way, you don't do a damn thing around here. Ever since Gracie was born you don't even do your own laundry, much less take out the trash or wash a damn dish. So just knock it off."

She tried to smile and took on a more gentle tone trying to undo the mounting tension. "Dude, you're not making sense. You need to get some sleep. You look awful and you can't keep this up. It's dangerous."

"Can you really make up for screwing up someone's childhood? Cuz I really don't think you can." I clenched my teeth against the bitterness that sat heavy in my guts.

"Ditch the drama. My God, your childhood wasn't some

picture-perfect American Dream. On the other hand it wasn't some sad tale of neglect and abuse either. As a matter of fact, in the great scheme of childhoods, yours wasn't half bad. Like come on, you had everything you ever needed and a family that cared. Mom was poor as shit, but she still found a way to give art classes and homeschool you when you were being bullied. She worked extra hours to make sure you had swim lessons and you got to be in Girl Scouts and she took you on camping trips. Remember when you wanted that super fancy scooter? Did you know that Mom bounced a check just to get it for you? It ended up costing her almost sixty dollars more because of all the fees, but she knew it was important to you.

"No, your childhood wasn't perfect, but whose is? What the hell is your problem, Banjo? I'm seriously worried about you. You're going to snap. C'mon sis, let us help you. Please?"

I didn't know what my problem was. For the past couple of days all I could feel was a whole lot of anger. Anger at Mom, anger at Sam, anger at Gray, anger at the world. Apparently even anger at Henry. I felt nothing other than pure pissed-off, bitter, mean anger. I wondered for a moment if maybe this was postpartum depression or something, then I shoved that thought away. I had a right to be angry. I deserved to feel resentful. To be honest I liked being angry. It felt good to feel the fire of resentment in my guts. It felt good to see how my words could make Mom shrink into herself and to see how they made Henry's face melt into confusion and to see how they sparked Sam's fury. It felt good to be pissed off at Gray for ditching me.

Like how could Gray do this to me? I had been waiting so long for us to take our relationship from friends to something more and when we finally did I was so happy. I felt like our life together was really just beginning. And then they had to go and die by suicide on that same night? How could they do that?

When I arrived at Gray's apartment that night I found them crying. This wasn't all that unusual and I wasn't worried about it. Gray missed their mom deeply and even years after her death the wound was still sore for them. That night while I was comforting them we suddenly—somehow—ended up making out. And then we were having sex—the first time for both of us. Looking back to that night, it wasn't the sex or the making out that I remember so much as after when we lay in their bed just talking quietly. The way they played with my hair and traced their finger over my bare shoulder. I felt so safe that night. But it turns out that all along they had been planning to die. They sent me home that night with their apartment key and a promise to return in the morning.

My gut told me not to go. My gut told me something was really wrong. And yet I left. I will never forgive myself for leaving. Never. The next day when I returned they were gone. All that remained was a note and Rags.

They destroyed my life that night and today I hate them. I hate them so much. It scares me to feel this way, but I do.

The thing that was starting to bother me was that I'd finding myself feeling anger at Gracie but what could Gracie possibly do to cause me to feel anger towards her? She was just a baby who never asked to be born. What kind of mother was angry at her own baby just for existing? I didn't tell anyone this, but last night when she was up all night fussing, I imagined shaking her until she shut up. I didn't, of course; still, I found myself shoving my fists into my pillow to keep from putting my hands on Gracie's tiny body.

I glared at Sam, "Please just leave me alone."

I picked up my phone, ignoring Sam, and sent a text to Lou. *I need to get out of here. What are you up to? Want to go to the beach or something?*

A minute later Lou answered, *Sure, Dude. You okay?*

No, but whatever. Let's go do something. I'll leave Gracie with my mom.

Aww, you should bring her, Lou replied.

Sometimes I wondered if Lou was only into me because of Gracie. Anger rose. Look at me, I thought, now I'm even angry at Lou.

"Who are you texting?" Sam asked.

I ignored her.

"Banj, something's up with you," her voice was gentle. "Do you want to talk? I'm seriously getting worried. You know I got hit with all that postpartum shit when Hen was about Gracie's age and you know how that ended. You don't want to end up in the hospital again. Are you sure you're okay?"

"It's none of your business, Sam," I said as I unlatched Gracie from my boob and set her into the bouncy seat.

"I'm sorry, Banjo, it is my business. You're acting crazy."

"Well you should know about that, eh?" I shot back.

"Why are you acting like such a complete bitch?"

"Am I, Sam? Am I acting like a complete bitch? Or do you just not like the fact that I'm finally standing up for myself? Maybe you should think about that. You're worse than Dad. At least after he abandoned us he had the common sense to stay away. You ditched Henry with me and Mom while you had fun going crazy, and then you think you can just come back and be mom-of-the-year and sister-of-the-year and daughter-of-the-year and we'll all be so happy. So happy to have the wonderful and perfect Sam back in our lives."

Sam sprang forward and slapped me across the face. I fell back and touched my cheek. I had never been hit before. "How dare you," she hissed.

Gracie began to wail in her seat.

Just then Henry emerged from the kitchen. "Mama, stop!" Henry yelled as he ran to comfort me. I shoved him away. He stumbled trying to keep his balance.

Mom rushed back into the room, "Stop. Stop this right now." Her face was a mixture of anger and fear. The anger scared me, but the fear in her made me want to punch her. She was weak and I hated her for it. Henry ran to her and she pulled him into a hug. "Banjo. Sam. You two need to stop right this minute. Banjo, I'm not sure what is going on with you. I'm making you an emergency appointment with Anna." Her voice shook.

She turned to Sam. "Sam, can you take Henry in the other room." Henry let go of her and ran to Sam, burying his face in her chest. She hugged him for a moment and then directed him down the hall to their bedroom. Mom sat down next to me on the couch. She lifted the crying Gracie from the seat. I didn't care. Compassion replaced the fear and anger in her face. "Sweetheart, something is wrong with you. I think you might have postpartum depression. It's normal and it will go away, but it can turn dangerous. Very dangerous. And you cannot lash out at people like this. Anna can help you, okay?"

I didn't want help. I was sick of needing help. The jagged electricity that was surging through me made me feel powerful and I liked it.

"I'm leaving. There's milk in the freezer," I seethed. "Rags! Come!" For some reason I wanted the dog to come with me. Rags inched towards me unsure and nervous. I scruffed her head, grabbed the leash off the hook on the wall, hoisted my backpack off the floor, slung it over my shoulder, and I was out. It took everything I had not to slam the door like an angry 11-year-old. I didn't even kiss Gracie goodbye. I didn't even care that she was screaming.

A jackhammer of rage pounded through me. I paced back and forth on the front porch waiting for Lou. I examined the rotting steps and jiggly hand railings with paint chipping off in large flat slabs. I hated this dump. Mom always says, "Better to own a dump than rent a palace." Bullshit, I thought. It was becoming increasingly clear to me that Mom was a giant mess and because of that she had made me into a giant mess.

Rags whined with excitement at the thought of a walk. I placed my hands on both sides of her face and pulled her to me for a kiss. "You and me, Rags, let's run away," I whispered into her matted ear. "Just the two of us. What do ya say?"

The sounds of Gracie's crying and the muffled voices of my family filtered out to the porch. "Come on Rags, let's go wait by the street."

Just then Lou's Prius pulled into the weedy gravel driveway. He rolled down the passenger window and yelled out, "Waz up, Dude? Where we going? Rags! Ragsie, come see Uncle Lou." I let go of the leash and Rags ran to the car putting her feet up on the side and peering through the passenger window at Lou. Lou unbuckled and got out. Rags ran around the car to greet him.

"You sure you don't want to bring Gracie too?" Lou said as he ran his hands up and down Rags' back.

"No, I do not want to bring Gracie. Is that a problem?"

"Geez Banjo, relax. I was just asking. Calm down."

"Whatever," I hissed.

Lou looked at me for a long time. I tried to pretend I didn't notice. "You sure you're okay?" he asked squinting at me.

"Come on, Rags, load up," I said as I opened the back passenger door to Lou's car and waited for Rags to jump in.

"Mmmkay, don't answer me. So where are we going?" he asked, climbing into the driver's seat and buckling his seat belt.

"Anywhere but here."

"Hey, why don't we drive up to the mountains?" Lou suggested.

"Actually, let's go to the spot," I said.

He cocked his head, "You sure about that?"

"Yeah, I'm sure about that." I turned and looked out the passenger side window avoiding Lou's eyes.

He put the car in reverse and rolled down the back windows so Rags could stick her head out.

We drove past the *Your Job Is Your Credit* used car lots, the bikini espresso stands, the massage studios with the blacked out windows, the legal weed shops, the sketchy motels, and the scattered fast food restaurants until we reached the trailer park set back off the highway. Lou turned into the trailer park driveway and drove through until we hit the overgrown vacant lot that sat between the edge of the trailer park and the freeway below. He pulled up into a parking spot marked "visitor" and killed the engine. Rags began to whine.

"Ready?"

I didn't answer. I grabbed Rags' leash and let her lead the way to the hole in the chain link fence that Gray had cut way back before I even met them. Rags charged ahead with her nose to the ground and her tail wagging. She remembered this spot and it always tore me up a little when I brought her here. I think every time we came here she expected to see Gray. I guess a little part of me always sort of expected to see Gray too.

Lou followed Rags and I through the hole in the fence and to the spot by the thin oak tree. The altar that I had made for Gray was still there. I picked up the Virgin Mary candle that I had left here way back before Gracie was born. I turned it around in my hands. The glass was hot against my fingers and the wax was soft. The photocopy of Gracie's ultrasound picture had bleached almost white from the sun. It occurred to me that I should bring a current picture of Gracie to add the altar.

Being here calmed me in some weird way. This had been Gray's secret paradise. A place they once lived. When they arrived here with just a backpack and a handful of cash they had come to this trailer park hoping to find a cheap place to rent, but the cost of housing in

Washington was several times the cost of housing in Florida. They realized that day that there was no way they could afford a place with the small amount of cash they had. Instead they had taken their money to the local Fred Meyer and bought themself a tent and a sleeping bag and made a home under the oaks by the freeway. After they finally saved enough to rent an apartment, they still returned to this place when things got to be too much. It was beautiful here and special.

The first time they brought me here I was blown away by how peaceful it was. Even though you almost had to shout to be heard over the drone of the speeding traffic on the freeway below, the trees, grass, wild flowers, and city wildlife still made it feel like a secret world. Even the droning traffic could be soothing. It was easy to trick your mind into believing the swooshing of cars and trucks was the sound of a rushing river.

Gray had come here when they decided to die. Maybe that night when they walked out into traffic they imagined themselves walking into a river instead.

I picked a couple poppies and a stem of foxglove and laid them in front of the candle that I had left here months ago, before settling down with my back against the tree. Lou sat down next to me.

I pulled a blade of grass and twisted it in my fingers. "I'm thinking about seeing if that couple is still interested in adopting Gracie."

Before Gracie was born I had considered placing her for adoption and had found a nice gay couple who I thought might be a good fit.

"What the hell? You're joking, right?"

"No Lou, I'm not." I turned to look at him. "She would be better off in a normal family. My family's crazy and I suck as a mom. She deserves better. I could still see her now and then . . ."

Lou jumped up, "No! No Banjo, you are not giving away your kid. Are you insane? If you need a break, I'll take her. Seriously, I'll take her." Panic rose in his voice. "Hell, I'll take her forever. I'm eighteen, it's legal. I'll adopt her. Please don't give her up, I mean it. She already knows you, already loves you." Lou stood towering over me. "Do not give that baby away."

"You can't raise a baby. Janice and Doug would kick you out and cut you off so fast. What are you gonna do, raise her in that stupid car of yours?" I shot back.

"What is wrong with you? Have you talked to Anna about this? I think you need to go see Anna. Like you need an emergency appointment. You're acting crazy."

"It's not crazy to want to actually be a teenager. It's not crazy to be burned out at seventeen. It's not crazy to realize that Gracie would be better off without me."

"Gracie would not be better off without you. Don't talk like that. You're scaring me."

I shrugged.

"Dude, you put too much pressure on yourself. Let your mom and Sam and James and me help. And Dylan too. Dylan loves that kid. C'mon we can all raise her together. It will fuck her up if you give her away now. It will fuck you up and seriously what about Henry? It will fuck him up. He worships that kid."

"Don't you mean, what about you? You're the one that will be fucked up if I give her away? This isn't like what happened to you. You remember your mom, and you had to move to a whole different world than what you were used to. She won't remember me and there won't be any sort of cultural adjustment or learning a new language or anything. And I will still be able to see her if I want, like she'll know who I am. And I'll pick her family. I won't let her get stuck with parents like Janice and Doug."

"Don't do this."

"You can't stop me, Lou. Nobody can. I can do whatever I want. Maybe me and Rags will leave and start a brand new life. I still have Gray's money."

"You're so fucked up." Tears ran down his face. "You seriously need help." He turned and walked back up the hill.

"Where are you going?" I yelled. "LOU? LOU?"

He slid through the hole in the fence and disappeared.

"FUCK!" I screamed. "FUCK! FUCK! FUCK! FUUUUUCK!" I slammed my fist into the ground again and again until I couldn't stand the pain any longer. What was wrong with me? Was I falling apart again like I did before Gracie was born? Why was I being so mean to everyone? I scooped up a handful of dirt with my throbbing hand and threw it towards the freeway. Anxiety skittered through me like a thousand angry mice.

Rags crouched up to me and began to lick my bruised hand. I stared at the freeway and imagined myself making the same choice that Gray made. Gracie wouldn't remember me and maybe without me she would stand a chance. Rags began to whine. If I ran out in front of the next big truck to pass by, would she follow me? Of course she would. Harming Rags just wasn't an option. She'd already been through so much. If she had been with Gray that day they came here to end it all, would Gray have made a different choice?

God, I wished I had a razor blade to dig into my shoulder.

I lay down in the grass, curled up into a ball, and began to sob. Rags licked my face and lay down next to me to stand guard. Despite the horrific heat, I wrapped my arms around Rags and hugged her to me like an old ratty teddy bear.

Chapter 13

"Dude, wake up." Lou was on his knees shaking me. I groaned as I wiped the drool and bits of dried grass from my cheek as I sat up. My clothes were soaked in sweat. I could feel the sun baking my cheek and right arm. Great, I'm going to have one of those weird one-sided sunburns. I sat up and blinked the sleep from my eyes. My head throbbed and my mouth was sticky. The combination of crying and the baking sun left me dehydrated and groggy. This must be what it felt like to be hungover.

I squinted at Lou. "You came back."

"Yeah, I'm sorry. I shouldn't have left you. You just . . . you made me mad. The stuff you said . . ."

"I'm sorry." I closed my eyes as embarrassment washed over me.

"Um Banj?"

"Yeah?"

"Ah, your shirt."

I looked down to discover that my clothes were not, in fact, soaked with sweat, but were actually a milky mess. I looked back up at Lou. "I guess I missed feeding time."

"You smell a little curdled," he said and we both smiled.

"Come here." He pulled me to him. "I shouldn't have stormed off. I'm sorry."

I wrapped my arms around his neck and held on, smooshing my

soggy boobs against his chest. He ran his fingers through my hair. "I shouldn't have left you," he repeated.

"Yeah you should have. I was being awful. I don't know what's wrong with me. I'm sorry," I said. I pulled away so I could see his face.

"I left and then I got scared you were going to—

"Do what Gray did?" I finished his sentence for him.

"Yeah, I freaked out and turned the car around and ran back. You were already asleep. I wasn't even gone ten minutes and you were already sound asleep. So me and Rags just sat over there in the shade." He pointed to a small maple behind us. "And watched you sleep. I was worried your face would get sunburned, so I propped my backpack up to try to shade you. It wasn't super effective, but I thought even with a sunburn you should sleep. Besides it might be sort of cool to have a red and white striped girlfriend."

This was the first time he had used the word girlfriend to describe me. A lump rose in my throat. "You watched over me?"

He looked down at the ground, "Yeah, I guess. I sat over there and texted with Sam and your mom. I hope you're not mad," he added quickly.

"You talked to them?" I felt anger starting to seep back in. I tried to push it away. I needed to stop raging at everyone.

"Yeah, I was just so mad and sad and so so scared. Your mom and Sam think you have postpartum depression. They say it can be serious. They say you aren't sleeping at all and that you're not letting anyone help you. Dude, you can't do that. You have to let us help you, okay?"

My face crumpled.

"Whoa, why the tears?"

My words were stuck under the lump in my throat. "Thank you," was all I managed to say.

He let out a little laugh. "You're welcome."

He pushed the tears from my face with his thumbs.

"So while you were sleeping I came up with a plan."

"A plan?"

"Yep. A plan."

"What're you talking about?"

"A plan for how to make things better for you."

"Like what kind of plan?"

"Well maybe it's a dumb idea, I was thinking we could do some regular teenage things together. Like just because you're a mom now doesn't mean we can't go out and be dumb teenagers sometimes. Your mom and Sam think it's a good idea. They said it would be good for you." He pulled his backpack over, unzipped it, and pulled out three water bottles. "Here," he said handing one to me. "Judging by the front of your shirt you might need a little rehydration. I'm sorry they're pretty warm. They've been in my car."

I had forgotten all about my sopping wet shirt and with his words I instinctively reached to cover myself with my free hand.

"Is that okay with you? The plan I mean."

I nodded, not actually sure that the plan was okay with me, but I didn't want to hurt his feelings. I uncapped the bottle and drank the entire thing, barely taking a breath.

He pulled Rags's collapsible water dish from his pack, uncapped one of the bottles, and poured it into the bowl. "Here Rags," he said, swishing his finger in the bowl to show her the water. She drank nearly the whole bowl. Sometimes I'm blown away by how thoughtful Lou is.

"So hey, are you feeling a little better?" he asked.

"Yeah, I really am sorry about earlier. It's just that, I don't know, it's like I keep sliding into these waves of panic. Like I'm ruining my life and ruining Gracie's life. Not to mention everyone else's and then I get so mad. I don't even know why I keep getting so mad. Maybe Sam and Mom are right and it is postpartum crap. I don't want to give up Gracie. You know that, right?" My stomach knotted at the thought of not having my baby and of Lou thinking I didn't want her.

"I know. You put too much pressure on yourself."

I nodded.

"It's just really hard. I feel like everyone's judging me. I feel like I have to be perfect. I want to be a good mom to Gracie. I don't want to mess her up or let her down. And at the same time, I feel like there's no way to protect her from the world."

"Dude, you're going to mess up and you're going to let her down. Nobody's perfect. All you need to do is love her as hard as you can and don't worry about messing up. And why in the world would any of us judge you? That doesn't even make sense." He took another sip of his water and handed it to me. "Here, finish it. You need it."

I didn't argue. I was so thirsty. I downed the bottle in seconds.

Lou was right of course, I knew Mom and Sam, Dylan and Lou, my brother, Megan, Alice, Anna . . . none of them were judging me, but I knew pretty much everyone else in the world was and it was so hard to hold on to my confidence. I mean, my family was sort of crazy and my friends were all weirdo misfits. Maybe all the normal people were right and we are just a bunch of losers telling ourselves that we aren't.

I picked an orange poppy and twisted it in my fingers, letting my mind shift gears.

"Can I ask you something?" I asked, keeping my eyes on the flower in my hand.

"Of course."

"Earlier you said you thought it would be neat to have a red and white striped girlfriend. Does that mean that like you think of me as your girlfriend?" The heat of the sun was no match for the heat of my embarrassment. I shot a glance at him. His face was one enormous nervous smile.

"Well, yeah. Is that okay with you?"

I looked back down at the flower, trying to hide the enormous smile that was now swallowing my face.

"I take that as a yes?" he said.

I nodded as my tears dripped onto the dusty ground.

He crawled over to me and ducked his face underneath mine so he was looking up at me. "Dude, why are you crying?"

I shrugged my shoulders, trying to avoid his eyes. The poor poppy was now a mangled mess.

"Hey now," he said as he pulled me to him. "Shhh shhh. Don't cry. It's all going to be okay. I promise."

I began to sob. "Why are you so nice to me?" I asked.

He held me tight. "Because you're the best thing that ever happened to me," he said. "The very best thing that ever happened to me."

"Can we go home?" I asked.

We walked back to the car hand in hand. Neither of us spoke other than to keep Rags in check. On the drive home Lou played Tupac on low. The song "Dear Mama" came on and the tears returned.

He put his hand on my thigh. "Want me to turn this off?"

"No," I said turning it up.

We didn't speak again until we got back to my house. We pulled up and Lou killed the engine.

"Would you mind waiting outside for a few minutes?" I asked.

"Not at all."

Time to face the music, I thought. Rags and I made our way onto the porch and I pushed the front door open. Mom and Sam were sitting on the couch reading. Gracie was asleep on Sam's chest. Dylan's cat, Petunia, was curled up next to Mom.

"Hi," I said.

Sam smiled.

"Hi sweetie," said Mom.

"Where's Henry?" I asked.

"Out back," said Sam.

I went through the kitchen and called Hen in from the back. "Hen, will you come sit on the couch with Mom and Sam?"

"Why?"

Irritation bloomed. I shoved it down. "Please, buddy."

He ran into the living room and dove onto the couch between Mom and Sam. I followed him and sat down on the floor in front of the couch.

"I just want to say I'm sorry," I said. I could feel tears trying to surface. I was determined to keep them buried. "I've been awful. I don't know what's wrong with me." The tears rose higher. "I'm just so tired and so—I don't know—afraid of everything."

"What are you afraid of?" asked Henry.

"It's complicated, buddy. I guess I just worry too much about being a good mama to Gracie."

"And you miss Gray too?" he asked.

The tears were fighting to be released. "Yeah, I miss Gray too."

Henry jumped off the couch and wrapped his skinny arms around me. "Me too," he said. I stood, lifting him with me, and settled us on the couch between Mom and Sam. Sam laid her hand on my thigh while balancing Gracie with the other. Mom scooched over and draped her arm around my shoulders. Rags looked up from her spot on the floor, cocking her head from side to side before she jumped up to join the family.

"I really am sorry," I said.

"It's okay," said Mom. "You just need to ask for help. You can't do this alone, nobody can. You don't have to prove anything to anyone, sweetie. If you were thirty it might not be super easy to ask for help, but if you did you would know that nobody would judge you for it and they would actually help you. Just because you're young doesn't mean you have to somehow be perfect. If people judge you because of your age, well screw them."

"Screw them to hell," said Henry.

We all burst out laughing.

"Screw them to hell and back again," said Sam.

"Screw them to hell and back again sideways," said Mom.

"What do you mean, sideways?" asked Henry.

We all burst out laughing again.

"Nothing, your grams is just being silly," said Sam.

"Um Banjo?" said Henry. "You kind of smell bad."

"Yeah, I should probably go change my shirt, eh?"

I stood up to go find a clean shirt. "Oh damn, I forgot about Lou."

"He's still here?" asked Mom.

"Yeah, I asked him to wait outside while I talked to you. I swear my brain doesn't work anymore."

"You have mom brain. Don't worry, it will start working again in . . . well I'll let you know when mine does," said Mom. "Now go bring that child inside. You know he adores you?"

I turned away fast to hide my smile.

Chapter 14

om pulled up in front of Anna's house, which also served as her office. A sign that read *Anna Rios Counseling* hung next to her front door.

"Are you sure you don't want me to take Gracie?" Mom asked.

"Nah, I sort of want to show her off. Anna hasn't seen her for a while," I said as I unclipped her from her seat. I didn't feel like hauling the car seat in.

"Okay, I'll see you in an hour," she said as I grabbed the diaper bag and pushed the car door shut with my hip.

This was my first appointment with Anna since Gracie had been born. It felt good to be back. I pulled open the rickety wooden gate and made my way down the path that ran through the overgrown English garden to the oversized front porch. Her yard smelled amazing. Her cat, Giles, was fast asleep on the porch swing. I gave him a quick pat on the head before knocking on the heavy front door. Seconds later Anna pulled the door open.

"Oh Banjo, welcome," she said, stepping aside to let me in. I saw her glance at the elephant necklace around my neck. "Love, love, love your hair!" she gushed.

"Hey Anna," I said. "Thanks. Lou cut it."

Anna's border collie, Betsy, stood behind the gate in the kitchen, wiggling her entire body in excitement at the sight of me.

"Hi Bet-Bet," I called to her.

"Can I have the little bean?" asked Anna.

"I'll trade you," I said handing Gracie off to her and heading across the small living room to greet Betsy. Back when I first started seeing Anna, Betsy acted as a therapy dog at my appointments. I didn't realize it then, but I do now. Anna is sort of a brilliant counselor. Her office is in her living room, so it doesn't feel like you're in some formal setting working through your problems with a know-it-all professional. Instead you go into her house and hang with her cat Giles and her dog Betsy. The walls are covered in vintage posters and framed art. She conducts her therapy sessions right from her worn purple couch.

A Zen sand garden sits on the coffee table, as well as a bin of sharpies and notebooks, in case her clients want to fiddle with the sand or doodle and take notes. There's also a tea cup full of rubber bands on the coffee table for the people like me who struggle with self-injury. "If you feel the need to cut, just grab a rubber band and snap yourself. Of course, it's not nearly as satisfying as a razor blade or cigarette burn, but it's a good weaning tool and it can definitely help when we're discussing the tough stuff," she would say.

I opened the baby gate that separated the kitchen from the living room and Betsy sprang out, wriggling her skinny body in a frenzy as she pushed herself into me. I bent down and kissed her right on her snoot. "Hey girl, I've missed you."

"She's missed you too," said Anna, sitting down on the couch with Gracie. "Come sit. Have a cup of tea." Anna always had a little pot of mint tea, and a jar of raw honey, ready and waiting for her clients.

I settled in on the floor and pulled a rubber band from the tea cup. I didn't feel any urge to cut myself, but it gave me something to fiddle with. Betsy lay down next to me. For a while Anna and I were silent as she made faces at Gracie who smiled and waved her hands in delight.

"She sure is a treasure, Banjo. How are you doing?"

I let out a deep sigh. "I don't know. I feel like I'm all over the place. I know you know about my little freak out since apparently everyone in my life called you." My words came out with a little more irritation than I actually felt.

"They did call me. They were very worried about you. I told them all to let you know that they had called me, and it sounds like they did?"

"Yeah, they did. I'm not mad at anyone. I mean I get it. They were scared, especially after what happened before."

"How are you now?"

"I'm okay. Better, I guess."

"Any idea what led you to fall apart that day?"

"Well exhaustion for one. Gracie just doesn't sleep."

"So, you just think it's the lack of sleep? I remember that on the day of Gracie's welcome to the world party you had been crying, so maybe the exhaustion was more of a trigger than the root?"

It was definitely more than being tired and both Anna and I knew that. I appreciated her calling me out on that.

"Nah, I'm sure it's just exhaustion," I said. "I don't think it has anything to do with me having a baby at seventeen and the baby's other parent being dead by suicide and me falling in love with someone else before I've even fully processed it all. And it doesn't have anything to do with how it feels like the world is unraveling and I just brought a baby into this Trumpocalypse. It also has nothing to do with how some of the people treated me in the hospital because I'm a dreaded teen mom. It has nothing to do with endless news reports on a mama whale carrying her dead baby for weeks. I'm just tired. A few hours of sleep and I'll be just fine."

"You're probably right," she said. "Would you like to go nap in the back bedroom? No charge."

We both laughed.

"Did Lou tell you about his plan?" I asked.

"He did. And I need to tell you that I told him I couldn't discuss anything about you with him. While I see you and your family as my friends, when it comes to talking about your mental health or our sessions that is strictly between you and me."

"I know. I trust you." I twisted the rubber band tight around my finger. "Do you think his idea is a good one?" I asked without looking up.

"I think it's an excellent idea," she replied. "It's important to remember that you're more than just Gracie's mom. All mothers struggle with that. I imagine it's even harder for a teenage mom."

I twisted the rubber band tighter and watched the end of my finger begin to change color.

"Anna?"

"Yes."

"Me and Lou . . . We're like dating. I guess he's my boyfriend now. Like officially."

"Congratulations," she said, smiling. "Though I have to admit I thought you were all along."

"I guess we were. It's been complicated. Anna?"

"What is it, Banjo?"

I gave the rubber band another little twist and then released it. Blood exploded into my finger, causing it to tingle with pain. I swallowed over the brick in my throat. "Do you think that I'm a terrible person for being with Lou so soon after Gray? Do you think it's disrespectful to Gray or that this means I didn't love them or something? Do you think Gracie will hate me one day? I mean Gray died the day I got pregnant and then I ended up in the hospital several months later and met Lou. It hasn't even been a year since Gray died and already I'm with someone new and I'm thinking about letting him maybe be a parent to Gracie. Is that messed up?"

I twisted the rubber band around my finger again. I didn't look at Anna.

"Banjo, there is no right way to grieve. There is no timeline and there are no rules. You went through something extremely traumatic, and you have survived. You have not only survived, but you're finding your way back to happiness and that's huge, sweetheart. You deserve to be happy, and Gracie deserves to have you happy."

I nodded. "Do you think it's okay that I'm thinking about letting Lou be a parent to her?"

"I think it's absolutely okay as long as Lou has Gracie's best interest at heart, and from what I've seen and from what you've told me, I think that's the case. There are no guarantees in this life, as I'm sure you know, so we can only do the best we can, right? I think that when love presents itself to us, we would be wise to let it in. You have let Lou's love in, and I think that's not only very brave of you, but also very wise.

"Think of it this way, what would it accomplish if you took a break from Lou or kept him at arm's length from Gracie?"

"Nothing," I said, unwrapping the rubber band from my finger. "But what about Gracie? Like her other parent, and her other grandma, both died by suicide and that's this thing that's always going to haunt her in some way and what if I let her get attached to Lou and he leaves or what if when she grows up she thinks I'm a terrible person for getting with him so soon?" The words gushed from my mouth.

"Banjo, I think it's amazing that you are so thoughtful about Gracie's future and her emotional well-being. You're an excellent mother. You really are, but one thing I think you need to remember is that Gracie has her own story. She'll have her own challenges and her own traumas. It's not your job to write her story. It's your job to help her navigate her story.

"It's natural for parents to want to protect their children. It's natural to want to keep them from pain, unfortunately that's simply not possible and it's not healthy. What you want to do is help her find her own inner strength so she can understand and navigate her past—and her future. Does that make sense?"

"Motherhood is really hard," I said.

"Why do you think I don't have kids?" She laughed.

"You're an intelligent lady."

She adjusted Gracie in her arms. Gracie was silent, just looking all around Anna's colorful living room. "You did good with this one, Banjo."

"Yeah, I like her."

"You're going to mess up. You're going to cause her pain. You're going to let her down and you're going to repeat some of the mistakes that your own mom made. That's okay. When you give birth, you don't suddenly become some perfect being. Parents are people and people are flawed. Everyone is flawed. Everyone is insecure. Everyone is a mess. It's just how it is, so what you need to try to work on is forgiving yourself for the mistakes you will inevitably make. Your mom made a lot of mistakes, huh?"

I let out a little huff. "You could say that."

"And you still love her?"

"Yeah, of course. I wish she had tried harder sometimes."

"That's valid, and maybe she should have, but I bet you're starting to see how complicated it is to be a mom."

"Yeah, that's true," I admitted.

"And maybe some of the hard things you've gone through have helped you be the wise young woman that I see sitting here in front of me?"

I could see where she was going with this.

"What if your mom had been able to protect you from everything? What if you had lived a life with no challenges and no traumas? Do you think you would have been able to get through Gray's death the way you have? Don't get me wrong. I'm not saying that any of the things you've been through are positive or spouting any of that resiliency bs. But maybe you've developed some coping mechanisms or strengths because of your past?"

"I don't know."

"I'm not in any way saying your trauma was a good thing or asking you to look on the bright side of what you've been through. What you've been through sucks and you didn't deserve any of it. I'm just saying that we all have challenges and traumas—that's part of being a human—and if we're really lucky we might gain some skills as we navigate the pain. I think in your case you have. You have at least learned the things you don't want to do as a parent. You may fail, and that's okay, but you have an idea of the kind of parent you do want to be. No?"

"Maybe." I wasn't completely sure about any of this.

"My parents came here as undocumented immigrants," she said. "I was born here, but I grew up worrying every day about what would happen to them, and to me, if they got caught. When I hit my teen years they became citizens—it was easier to do back then—and once that happened I got angry. I was angry at them for all the times I worried that they would be deported, for all the times I had to lie to my friends, and for the way we struggled financially. As I grew older I began to see things from their perspective. And I began to see that the tough times did have some value. What I mean by that is that I learned very early that I was strong and capable. Would I do it again? No. I'm not saying that at all." She smiled.

"But I have a choice to look back and only see the pain, or I can look back and absolutely acknowledge the pain and unfairness of it all, and at the same time I can try to look at the things that have made me who I am today.

"My mom did her best to protect me and she was always there when I needed her, but she also made sure to let me fight the battles that I was strong enough to fight on my own. Probably because she was too caught up in her own problems, but she did try to be there when I really needed her.

"I'm not saying that I advocate parents creating trauma for their kids of course. I guess what I'm trying to say is that if you go through difficult times and if you have adults around to help you go through it, often times you just might come out with a set of tools that will help you later on.

"I think I've mentioned to you that I've survived a loved one taking their own life?"

I nodded.

"My first partner chose suicide. I was in my early twenties and at first I didn't think I would survive, but slowly I began to find that pocket of strength that I had deep down inside. The challenges of my childhood had left me with a strength that I was able to call upon when I thought I had no strength in me. For example, I learned that I can get through hard things and be okay. I learned that pain doesn't last forever. When I face difficulties in my life today I try to remind myself that I am a survivor. When things feel impossible I think back to what I have already overcome in my life and that gives me hope that I will overcome the challenges that I face now and will continue to face in my lifetime.

"I also spent a lot of time baking polvorones—Mexican wedding cookies." She laughed. "My mother also taught me that when times are tough you should make delicious foods. That's where I got this," she said, patting her belly. "Nothing like baking to ease anxiety.

"In all seriousness though, can you think of any skill you may have developed because of what you've been through? Can you think of anything you've learned?"

I shrugged.

"Okay, well for your homework this week I'd like you to come up with one thing that your trauma has taught you or one way it has made you stronger. I do not want you to discount your pain or the unfairness of it all, but instead of focusing on what you couldn't control, maybe focus on one thing that you did control or one positive change that happened inside of you. Just one and it can be tiny. If I were to give on example from my own life, I would mention those cookies I learned to make."

I smiled. Gracie began to squirm in Anna's arms.

"She's probably getting hungry," I said.

Anna handed her to me. We both watched her eat while I thought about the things that Anna said.

"So it's okay to love Lou?" I blurted out, almost surprising myself.

"It's more than okay to love Lou," she replied.

"There's something else, Anna. There is something that I think might make me a bad person." My eyes got hot and I felt tears begin to form. I craved the rubber band, but my hands were full of baby.

"Sometimes I wish . . . I wish that Lou was actually Gracie's other parent. Like, sometimes I wish that it could just be easier and that makes me feel so guilty. And it makes me feel guilty to know that I wouldn't even know Lou or Dylan, or even you and Alice, if Gray had lived. Is it okay to be happy about the good stuff about Gray choosing—" I couldn't finish the sentence. It was like my throat closed up to try to prevent me from going any farther with these thoughts. I looked down at Gracie. She dropped the nipple and grinned up at me.

"Forget it," I said. I didn't want to hear her answer. "I should go." I said, but I didn't stand up.

"Banjo, you cannot know what would have happened had Gray lived. You cannot know what twists and turns your life might have taken or who you would have met or not met. You only have this day, this moment, and you have to make the best of it. You have to find happiness where happiness exists for you. I would like you to try to work on not seeing your relationships with the people you love as a consequence of Gray's death. I know that's hard, and maybe not even entirely possible, but I want you to try.

"Being present in the moment is the hardest thing we can do as humans, and it's also the most valuable. It's true that you might not know any of us if Gray had lived, and it's also true that you might. Are you still journaling?"

"No, I tried to start again, but it didn't work out," I said, remembering the morning that I decided to list my goals and instead fell into the hole of grief as I watched Tahlequah carry her dead calf. I came here wanting to talk about Tahlequah, and now my emotions felt too tangled up to even let myself go there.

"Well, it might be a good idea to give it another try," said Anna.

I reached up and touched my necklace, hoping it would do its magic and help me with the grief that was sitting like a boulder in my guts.

"How's the cutting been going? Or the not cutting, I should say."

I shrugged. "Good. I mean I haven't really done it since she was born. I've wanted to, but I haven't."

"I'm glad to hear it," she said.

Chapter 15

Lou and I sat with Gracie on an old blanket in the backyard under the shade of the apple tree. The tree was heavy with fruit and already starting to fill the yard with the sweet apple smell of fall. Gracie was getting her daily tummy time, which she loved. At first she hated it anytime I put her on her tummy, but now that she got the hang of it I think it was one of her favorite parts of the day. It was amazing how fast she was changing. As soon as I laid her down she would push up with her arms and look all around. Twice now she had rolled over all on her own. It was exciting each time she learned a new thing, but it also made me a little sad. Time was going too fast.

"We should get a hold of Dylan and go to the beach for a while," I said.

"I sent him a text earlier and he never replied."

At that moment Lou's phone rang. "His ears must have been ringing," he said, holding up his phone so that I could see that it was Dylan calling. Lou switched it to speaker as he answered.

"Yo dude, we were just talking about—"

All we could hear was chaos: sirens, shouting, crying, and Dylan barely able to speak through his stuttering.

"C-c-come. P-p-please c-c-come," he sobbed.

"What happened? Come where? Are you okay?"

"Th-th-the hospital. They're t-t-taking m-m-me to the ho-ho-hospital." And then the phone went dead.

"Oh my God, what do you think happened? Do you think he's going crazy again?" I asked, gathering up Gracie.

Lou didn't answer. We ran into the house. I passed Gracie off to him and ran into my room to change into clean clothes that weren't covered in baby slobber. He gathered up Gracie's diaper bag and car seat, and together we ran to the car.

Lou sped into the emergency parking lot. I had barely even opened my door before he was in the backseat unclipping Gracie's car seat and handing it to me.

We rushed through the Emergency Room doors and I couldn't help but remember the last time I had come through these doors at this hospital. That time I had been completely checked out. My brother had carried me in, and I didn't get to go home for three days. I pushed that memory from my mind as I clutched Gracie's heavy car seat with both hands. We made our way to check in and asked for Dylan Moretti.

"Family?" the woman at the counter asked, giving Lou a bored look.

"Ah well no. We're his friends and he called us and asked us to come," replied Lou as he bounced from one leg to the other.

"Names please?" she asked curtly.

"I'm Lou Anderson and this is Banjo Logan," he replied.

"Have a seat and someone will be with you shortly."

We turned and found ourselves two side-by-side overstuffed chairs. The ER waiting room was packed full of people and I worried about what sorts of diseases or viruses Gracie was being exposed to. I draped a blanket over the handle of her car seat to insulate her from the swirling germs.

There were old fashioned, country-style end tables that sat randomly scattered between blocks of chairs trying to add a feeling of hominess and comfort to the room, but the glaring overhead lights and moaning, crying, and coughing people prevented them from offering even the slightest feeling of comfort.

Almost instantly Gracie began to fuss. She grabbed the blanket and pulled it onto her face and then began to scream. I unclipped her from the car seat and pulled her to my chest, stood, draped the blanket loosely over her head, and began to pace the large room filled with people in all types of distress and pain. She yanked the blanket off again.

We sat in the ER for almost three hours before Lou decided we needed to ask about Dylan again.

"Dylan Moretti?" the woman at the counter said, her ponytail pulled so tight that it looked like she had a facelift. A bad one.

"Yeah the lady that was here before said for us to wait over there," he pointed towards the waiting area, "and someone would take us back to see him. That was like three hours ago."

The woman squinted at him and then began tapping her long red fingernails on the keyboard in front of her. "How do you spell the last name?"

"Um, I'm not completely sure M O R E T T I, I think? His first name is Dylan and he was brought in here about three hours ago."

"Are you family?"

"We're his friends. He called us and asked us to come." Lou's impatience was causing his voice to take on that familiar manic tone he gets when he's upset or excited.

"Go have a seat. We'll need to get his permission to release any information to you. I don't see a form on file here, so we'll need to check up on that."

A low growl escaped from Lou's throat as he led Gracie and me back to our seats.

"Looks like the ER is about as well-run as the psych ward," he grumbled. "And seriously, if they aren't supposed to release any information without permission, didn't she just violate that by letting me know that he's actually here?" His leg was shaking furiously.

It occurred to me just then that Doctor Jack was probably right here in this very hospital at this very second. What if we ran into him in the elevator?

"I just realized that Doctor Jack might be here. Like I mean not just here in the hospital, but actually here in the ER doing a psych admission or something," I whispered to Lou.

"Oh God, I hadn't thought about that. I swear if I see that guy I'll punch him right in the face," Lou said.

Just then a rail-thin man with wispy blond hair stuck his head out of the double doors that separated the waiting area from the emergency examining rooms, "Lou Anderson and Banjo Logan?" he called in a slight southern accent.

We stood and Lou slung his backpack onto his back and then grabbed the diaper bag and car seat. I carried a now sleeping Gracie in my arms.

"Hey guys, my name's Lucas and I'll take you up to see your friend. Sorry about the wait. Everything takes forever in here. We had to find the form that stated it was okay to let people know he was here and then the form that said he was down with having visitors. He was sleeping and, between you and me, this place isn't always super organized, so it took a little bit longer than usual."

Lucas seemed very nice and maybe a little gay. He held the swinging door open for us and as I passed by him he leaned over to get a closer look at Gracie, "Oh my gosh, that is one cute baby. Name?" he asked.

I stopped so he could get a closer look, "Her name's Gracie."

"She's adorable. Good work, Mama. My husband and I have

two kids."

Well that answered my question on the whole gay thing.

He led us to a set of elevators. "You all want to head on up to the 5th floor, room 516. I'm Mr. Moretti's nurse, so I'll be seeing you all in a bit. Just have to go grab his x-rays and then I'll be up." He winked at us as he turned and walked back towards the ER. The fact that Dylan was on the fifth floor and needed x-rays meant he was here for something other than a psych admission.

We stepped inside the elevator and suddenly there was no air. I couldn't stop worry about running into Doctor Jack. When I had my breakdown after Gray died he had threatened to do what he could to have my baby taken from me.

"X-ray? I wonder what happened?" Lou asked and then must have noticed my panic. "Dude, you okay?" He set the car seat down so he could touch my shoulder.

I nodded. "What if Doctor Jack appears?"

"He won't. Don't worry."

Still, I was worried. I hated this place.

Almost every floor of this hospital held a memory for me, I thought. The first-floor emergency room was where they brought Gray that terrible night when we had made Gracie, the same night they had walked out onto the freeway hoping to free themselves and join their mom. They took their last breath at this very hospital. I couldn't stop picturing it in my mind. I kept seeing their broken body on a stretcher with doctors and nurses gathered around. They died alone under bright lights and surrounded by noise.

And a few months later I was back here being carried by my brother after I detached from reality and Mom panicked. And then to the third floor, where I had met Lou and Dylan. The horror of the psych ward had given me the first real friends of my life. And then two months later

I landed on the second floor where the three of us had met Baby Gracie for the first time. And now here we were on our way to the fifth floor to see Dylan, with no idea what had happened to him.

I swallowed the lump in my throat and shoved the tears back as the elevator passed through each floor without stopping. I was glad we sailed past the third floor without anyone needing to get on. The elevator dinged and the doors slid open, revealing an empty hallway. We followed the signs to room 516 where the door stood slightly ajar. A pale blue curtain at the far side of the room hung from the ceiling, providing a wall of privacy from hallway passersby. The bed nearest the door was empty.

We stopped at the door. "Do we just go in?" I whispered.

Lou shrugged as he pushed the door open wide enough for us to pass through. He crossed the room, peeked around the curtain, and then waved me to follow him into the room. He set the car seat and diaper bag down under the window, slid his arms out of his pack, and then slowly approached the bed where Dylan lay sleeping. A purple bruise was painted across his freckled cheek and his fluffy red hair formed a lumpy helmet around his head. His casted leg stuck out from under a thin white blanket

"Dyl? Dylan?" Lou said softly.

Dylan's eyes fluttered open and then slowly shut.

Just then Lucas appeared. "You found him. He's pretty knocked out right now. We have him on some pretty serious pain meds. You all can just make yourselves comfortable. I imagine he should be waking up soon. Lucas maneuvered himself around Lou and took the spot at the head of the bed, checking Dylan's vitals and adjusting his I.V. Dylan's eyes fluttered open a few times and he looked around without comprehension before falling back into a drugged sleep.

I went around the foot of the bed to the small love seat and settled in with Gracie. Lou came around the end of the bed and settled himself down on the floor, his back against the wall.

Lucas finished up with Dylan, "See y'all later," he said as he disappeared behind the curtain and out the door.

"What do you think happened to him?" Lou asked quietly.

I shrugged. Gracie squirmed awake. Before her eyes were even open, she was fussing and frantically rooting around the front of my t-shirt looking for a boob. I felt my boobs grow full and hard as a mild tingling announced the let-down of my milk. I pulled up my t-shirt and unclipped the front of the nursing bra as I brought her searching lips to my nipple. She latched on instantly and began to drink as if she hadn't eaten in a week. Her little hands clenched into fists against her face.

Lou stood and began to pace the small room, brushing against the pale blue curtain, causing it to flutter like an ocean wave. Every few minutes he obsessively pulled his phone from his pocket and checked his text messages as if he was expecting someone to contact him. Between phone checks he would stop every so often and press his palms against his eyes for a moment, and then resume his manic pacing and phone checking.

As he was checking his phone for the seven-millionth time Dylan stirred in the bed and let out a low moan. Lou shoved his phone back in his pocket and rushed to his side.

"Dude, you're awake."

Dylan looked around the room squinting, as if he was looking into the sun. "It's real," he said quietly. "I thought it was a dream, but it's real." Tears slid from his eyes.

I stood up slowly, trying to keep Gracie latched on as I rose. I held her in the crook of my arm as I made my way to the side of the bed next to Lou.

"Hey Dyl," I said.

He blinked up at me. "B-B-Banjo? How'd you guys get here?"

"We came as soon as you called us." I noticed that Dylan was barely stuttering, which was weird. I wonder if it was the pain meds.

"I c-c-called you?"

"Yeah," I said. "You scared the hell out of us. You called and asked us to come. You said they were taking you to the hospital."

He closed his eyes and took a long slow breath, as if trying to locate this lost memory.

"We were so afraid you were on your way back to the psych ward," said Lou. "What the hell happened to you? Did someone do this to you? Were you in an accident?"

Dylan turned away from us and looked out the window. "I-I-I went to see my little b-brother . . ."

His words trailed off and an awkward silence fell over us.

Lou reached over and smoothed Dylan's white-boy afro. "You went to your parents' house?"

Dylan nodded. "I didn't think they'd b-b-be home, or I guess I didn't think m-m-my dad would be home . . . and he wasn't when I-I-I got there." He swallowed hard and the tears started up again. "Jacob called me. One of his little friends got a phone and he let J-J-Jacob use it. He's been afraid to call me from the home phone in case my dad checked the outgoing c-c-calls." He swallowed again. He looked at me as he wiped away his tears, "J-J-Jacob is the same age as H-H-henry."

"Yeah, I remember you telling me that," I said.

"I thought J-J-Jacob hated me. I thought they brainwashed him into hating me, but when he c-c-called he was crying so hard. He thought I had abandoned him. They told him I left. They never told him that they k-k-kicked me out. He begged me to come and see him and so I d-d-did." Dylan spoke drug-slow as tears rolled down his cheeks.

Gracie had fallen back to sleep and her mouth slipped off my boob. She gave a few sucking motions in the air and then her mouth was still. "I'm going to lay her down," I whispered and turned back toward the worn love seat. I knelt down over her car seat, trying hard not to startle her awake. I set her in the seat and began to slowly remove my arm from beneath her. She squirmed and her eyes flashed awake for a spit second, her lips smacking at the air trying to find the boob. I held my breath as she fluttered back to sleep. One inch at a time I pulled my arm from beneath her, laid a thin receiving blanket over her and backed away. I returned to Dylan's bedside. Lou stood next to him, still smoothing his hair.

"Did your dad do this to you?" I asked.

He closed his eyes as he nodded, his face twisting with the memory.

Chapter 16

There was a tap on the door and a second later Lucas came in with two cops trailing behind him, a man and a woman. Lucas glanced at Dylan apologetically. "Hey, you're awake. These officers want to get a statement from you, are you up for it?"

Dylan's face flushed, "Yeah, I-I-I guess."

"Dylan Moretti? I'm Officer Swenson," said a short and very muscular white cop with a crew cut. He smiled and swept his hand towards the woman, "and this is Officer Jameson."

She nodded, "Good to meet you Mr. Moretti." She wore her dark blond hair in a bob. Her flushed cheeks and made her look as if she were perpetually embarrassed. She didn't smile.

Officer Swenson looked at us, "If you'll excuse us, we need to get a statement. It won't take long."

Lou and I glanced at each other and then at Dylan, "Will you be okay?" Lou asked.

Dylan nodded. Gracie and I followed Lou out into the hall.

"I don't like that he's in there alone," said Lou. "Cops scare me."

"Me too," I muttered.

We paced the hall for what felt like forever. Finally, we saw the cops come out and head towards the elevator. We rushed back into Dylan's room. He lay there with his eyes closed.

"Dude, are you okay?" asked Lou.

Dyl opened his eyes and nodded.

A red-haired woman dressed in a faded blue Winnie the Pooh t-shirt and high-waisted mom jeans peeked her head around the curtain. "Dylan?" she whispered.

A chubby boy around Henry's age with thick black hair and olive skin darted around the woman and burst into tears as he leaned over the bed. Dylan winced in pain as he awkwardly wrapped his arms around the little boy.

Lou stepped forward, positioning himself between Dylan and the woman.

"L-L-Lou it's okay. M-M-Mom, what are you doing here?"

Lou and I exchanged glances.

The woman rushed past Lou and stood behind the little boy. She seemed afraid to touch Dylan. "Oh my baby, my baby," she sobbed. "My baby. My baby. My baby. Oh my baby, I'm so sorry."

"W-W-Where's D-D-D-Dad?" Dylan asked. His stutter suddenly uncontrollable.

Dylan's little brother squirmed out from under the woman, "He's in jail. Mom said he's not coming home ever."

"M-M-Mom?"

The woman began to finger the tiny cross necklace that hung around her neck.

"I've kicked him out," her voice shook.

"A-A-Again?"

"Not again, for good. I want you to know this time it's for good. I've already contacted a lawyer and I'm going to apply for a restraining order against him. I'm not going to bail him out or even take his calls. I promise, honey. I promise . . ." her words were cut off by a sob.

The boy turned and wrapped his chubby arms around her. "It's okay, Mom."

Lou and I stood awkwardly at the foot of the bed. Gracie began to fuss. Lou welcomed the convenient distraction and quickly moved to take her from me. He paced around jiggling her and cooing in her ear.

Dylan's mom blinked at us as if noticing us for the first time. "Uh hello, I'm Dylan's mom, Sandy. And this is Jacob," she said, motioning down to the boy who was now clinging to her. He gave us a backwards wave, not bothering to turn around or let go of his mom.

Lou stepped forward, reaching his hand towards her while balancing Gracie on his shoulder with the other, "I'm Lou."

"Nice to meet you, Lou." The woman took his hand briefly.

"I'm Banjo," I said, giving a small wave.

"Your little sister?" Sandy said to me, as she glanced towards Gracie.

"M-M-Mom, that's Banjo's baby. Her n-n-name is Gracie." Dylan's stutter was beginning to subside again.

"Oh. Oh my. Oh, well she's very sweet." Her hand made its way back up to the cross around her neck again. "It's very nice to meet the three of you."

Lucas popped his head into the room, "Knock-knock. Looks like I'm just in time for the party." He greeted Sandy and Jacob. "Hello there, my name's Lucas and I'm this fine gentleman's evening nurse."

"I'm Dylan's mother, Sandy," she said.

"Hello there, young man," Lucas said to the back of Jacob's head. Jacob gave another backwards wave.

"Time for some vitals," Lucas chirped. "How's the pain? Doing okay?"

Dylan nodded.

"Before I give you the once over, I just have to have another look at that sweet angel baby." He moved behind Lou so he could look into Gracie's face. "Makes me want another, this one does." He looked at me, "May I hold her?"

I smiled, "Of course." I realized this was the first time anyone other than Alice, Anna, or my family had asked to hold Gracie.

Lucas fussed over Gracie and then got to work taking Dylan's vitals.

"Your vitals are great. Blood pressure is a little high. That's to be expected given the pain you've been in and the stress. Your CT scan came back okay. Looks like they'll be releasing you in the next couple of hours. You'll be on crutches for a couple of weeks and then you should be fine with a walking cast. I'll be back a little later with your paperwork," he said, giving Dylan a wink before disappearing out the door.

"Will you come home with me, honey?" said Sandy.

Dylan stared at her for a long time. "No Ma, I-I-I can't."

"Please? Please?" whined Jacob, turning around to face Dylan.

"I'm s-s-sorry buddy, I can't."

Sandy and Jacob both began to cry.

Lou stepped forward and faced Sandy. "We'll take care of him. Don't worry."

Sandy looked at Dylan, but he turned away. She turned back to Lou. "Thank you," she said and then she kissed Dylan on the cheek and left with Jacob. We could hear Jacob's sobs growing faint as they made their way to the elevator.

"Do you want to stay at my place tonight?" I asked.

"N-n-no, I sh-sh-should go back to my place, but c-c-could we go to your house for a wh-wh-while? I want to see my cat."

We got back to my place and Lou and Sam wrestled our old ratty recliner into my bedroom. The footrest kept popping out and they would stumble forward. "Goddamn," mumbled Sam.

"Do you need my help, Mama?" asked Henry.

"No," snapped Sam. Sweat was dripping from her forehead.

"You don't have to yell at me."

"Henry, stop complaining, alright? I'm in no mood." Sam's voice was solid irritation.

Dylan leaned on his crutches over near my bed. "I'm s-sorry."

"No, don't be," said Sam. "It's just so damn hot out and this piece of crap recliner won't cooperate. Not your fault."

Sam and Lou finally got the thing through the door and then shoved it over by my dresser. It took up most of my room.

"Your throne has arrived, sir," said Lou, as he gestured to the hairy chair. Rags jumped up and settled in. "Not you, Rags. Git," he said, as tried to shove Rags out of the chair.

"Sh-she's okay. We can sh-share the throne. Thanks guys." Dylan said, as he maneuvered himself into the chair next to Rags. Lou and I each took one side of his casted leg and gently lifted it as he pulled the handle to raise the foot rest.

"Hold on," said Sam, grabbing a pillow from my bed and placing it on the foot rest. "You need to keep that leg elevated when you're resting."

Lou gently lifted his leg and then lowered it onto the pillow.

"Alright," said Sam, "my work here is done. You children have fun. I'm going to go get a beer and find myself some shade." She turned to Henry, "C'mon Hens, let these guys have some time to themselves."

"I want to hang out with them," complained Henry.

"You can come hang out later, little dude. I promise. Just give us a little time and then maybe I'll take you out for some ice cream or something," said Lou, grabbing him in a mock headlock and ruffling his hair before swinging him up over his shoulder. Henry giggled as Lou set him down in the hall. Henry jumped up and pretended to karate kick Lou. Lou fell backwards against the wall as Henry ran off.

Lou slid down the wall and then crawled into my room. "Can we get you anything Dyl?"

"Nah I-I'm fine."

Lou came and sat next to me on the bed. Gracie sat happily in her swing grasping her favorite toy, a tiny lavender blanket with a bunny head. She studied it and then awkwardly moved it towards her mouth to slobber on it, her legs kicking in delight the whole time.

"Is your dad still in jail?" I asked.

"Yeah, they haven't set bail yet. I really hope she doesn't bail him out."

"Thank God, he's locked up for now," I said.

"Sh-she wants me to m-m-move back."

"Are you?" Lou asked.

"No. Not yet. F-f-first of all, I don't think it's s-safe. I mean if he gets out of jail and comes b-b-back to the house and finds me there I'm afraid he might k-k-k-kill me. But also, I actually sort of like the place I'm at. I-I-I mean, the rules sort of suck sometimes, b-b-but everyone there is gay—all the kids and all the people running it—so I don't know, I guess it feels more like home than m-m-my home."

We sat in silence for a while.

"Has your dad always been abusive?" Lou asked.

"A-actually, he's not my real dad. He's my st-st-stepdad. And yeah, he's always been like this, especially to m-m-me."

"Wait, he's not your real dad? What do you mean?" Lou pulled a small bag of chips from his backpack and began shoving handfuls into his mouth. I realized we hadn't eaten in hours. My stomach growled.

"He married my m-m-mom and adopted me when I was six.

"Why didn't you ever tell us this?" Lou asked.

"I guess be-be-because I have pretty much grown up just thinking of him as m-m-my dad. My real dad died of a heroin o-o-overdose when I was five. I barely remember him. I've been thinking about him a lot lately though . . ."

"Shut the front door. Your real dad was a heroin addict? I thought your family was hella into God?" asked Lou.

"My stepdad is h-h-hella into G-G-God and after Mom got with him she got that w-w-way too, before that she was some sort of h-h-hippie or something. I was named a-a-after Dylan Thomas."

"Who?" I asked.

"Some dead p-p-poet guy. My dad was a poet."

Lou closed his eyes and put his hand on his heart. "Do not go gentle into that good night, Old age should burn and rave at close of day; Rage, rage against the dying of the light," he said in a dramatic voice. "Dylan Thomas was not just some dead poet guy," he said, showing off his thirty-thousand-dollar-a-year private education.

I ignored him. "Wow Dylan, that's crazy," I said, fiddling with the breast pump. I was thankful that Lou and Dylan treated the milk-sucking-machine as just a normal part of my day.

"So your real dad was a heroin addict poet," Lou said, shaking his head.

"Yeah, he and Mom traveled around in an old v-v-van. I don't remember s-s-sleeping in a real bed in a real house until after Dad died. They did o-o-odd jobs and sometimes Dad got jobs teaching poetry at community c-c-colleges and stuff. Mom used to write too and p-p-paint some. They were like old school bo-bo-bohemian artists or something. Then dad d-d-died and Mom met my stepdad and became born again."

"Wow, that's intense," I said, as I adjusted the cup on my left boob.

"So your little brother is actually your half brother? That explains why the two of you look almost nothing alike," said Lou.

"Yeah, m-my stepdad is Italian. My real d-dad was German and Irish. Jacob doesn't know that I have a different dad. I wish he h-h-hadn't seen this happen." He glanced down at his casted leg.

I finished up pumping and capped the bottle. Gracie began to fuss so I pulled her from her swing and handed her to Lou. "Dyl, I need to go put this in the fridge," I said, holding up the bottle. I'll be right back. I'll grab us some snacks while I'm up."

Lou sat Gracie down on his lap so she was facing him, her back settled against his knees. "Gracie, Gracie, Gracie loves her Lou," he sang as he took her hands in his and gently clapped them together. She gave him a lopsided smile.

I went into the kitchen, opened the fridge, and swapped the little bottle of breast milk for some grapes. I snagged a box of crackers from the pantry and a package of Trader Joe's mini chocolate chip cookies. I returned to the bedroom to find Gracie in Dylan's lap.

He looked up. "B-B-Banjo, would it be okay if she called me U-U-Uncle Dylan?"

"What else would she call you?" I said, as I set the plate down on the bed and went to my closet to fish out my hidden stash of Cokes.

"Let me take her so you can eat," I said, taking Gracie from him and laying her down on her tummy on a blanket on the floor. She immediately lifter herself up and looked around at the toys scattered about. I doled out the snacks and the cans of Cokes and settled back in next to Lou. "What did I miss?"

"Nothing, we waited for you. Figured you'd want to hear the story. So Dyl, what exactly happened?" Lou popped the top on his Coke and took a long pull.

"Well after J-Jacob c-c-called me I decided to go see him. I figured my mom and dad—s-s-stepdad—would still be at work and they were when I g-g-got there. J-J-Jacob stays home alone after school, so I thought I w-w-would just h-hang out with him for a little while and be g-g-gone before anyone knew I was there. I didn't go in the h-house—I was too a-a-a-afraid—so we sat out on the porch. It was so n-nice."

Dylan's eyes filled with tears. "I miss that little guy so much. But then the n-n-next thing I-I-I knew my d-d-dad was there. He accused m-m-me of . . . of . . . of d-d-doing things to J-J-Jacob." He shook his head, trying to clear the stutter.

"D-D-Dad and I got into a screaming match. He called me a f-f-faggot child m-m-molester and took a swing at me. He caught me right in the eye. J-J-Jacob tried to protect me, but Dad shoved him out of the w-w-way and threw me down the p-p-porch stairs. Mom pulled up just as everything was exploding and called the c-c-cops. I snapped my l-l-leg when I landed."

Just then Petunia Rhubarb jumped up onto Dylan's lap and bumped her face against his chin.

Chapter 17

Dyl was excused from chores at the halfway house and he had to take vacation time from his job because of his leg, so he was coming by a lot more. It was nice having him around. We were lounging in my room screwing around watching dumb YouTube videos when Lou made an announcement out of the blue.

"Okay I have officially decided that it's time for Operation F.D.A.B, or Operation F-dab for short."

"F-dab?" Dylan and I asked at the same time.

"Find Dylan A Boyfriend."

"That s-s-sounds like a terrible idea," groaned Dylan.

"I hate to say this, but I agree with Dylan on this one," I said.

"Pshaw. It's actually one of the best ideas I've had to date. Dyl needs a boyfriend and if we combine our talents we will totally be able to find him the perfect hot boy toy . . . I mean boyfriend," Lou grinned.

Dylan groaned again.

"How exactly are we going to find him a boyfriend?" I asked.

"How does anyone find anybody? Online. Tinder, Bumble, OkCupid. Grindr, Hinge, Hornet. Um, there's also Jack'd and one called something like Scruff. Let's see, what else? GDaddy, Surge, Gayer. I think most of those might be a little too much for a Baby Gay."

"I'm n-n-not a baby gay," Dylan complained.

Lou ignored him. "Definitely not Plenty of Fish or Match. I think those are for old straight people. Or maybe just old people."

"Yeah, I know my mom went on there before," I said.

"Serious?"

"Yeah. She said it was a bunch of creepsters wanting to hook up, and that was just the lesbians. She was on OkCupid, but she probably took her profile down now that she's seeing Alice."

"Oh my god, we should totally look and see if it's still up!"

"Um, no thank you. I prefer not to think too much about my mom's online dating life. I mean what if she's into BDSM or threesomes or something?"

Lou burst out laughing.

"It's not funny! It's gross," I complained.

"G-g-guys, I really don't know if I-I-I want to try online dating."

"Wait just a second, how do you know so much about online dating?" I asked Lou.

The answer was painted all over his face.

"Are you on those sites?" My stomach collapsed.

"NO. I swear I'm not. But I was. Right before I turned seventeen I got on there and made profiles on a couple of places."

I interrupted him, "You have to be eighteen to be on those sites." I tried to keep the accusation out of my voice.

"I lied about my age and nobody checks your I.D. or anything. I took it down after we all got released from the hospital. I promise."

"It's okay. I mean you don't owe me anything." I felt like I was going to cry.

"Banjo! I'm telling you the truth. I swear! I'm not on any sites now. I was before we all met. Please tell me you believe me. And I do owe you something. I owe you my loyalty. You're my person. I would never hurt you. Please believe me."

"I do," I said as the tears began to fall.

"Why are you crying?"

I shrugged. Stupid hormones.

Dylan hoisted himself out of the chair that was still crammed in my room and onto the floor, and scooched over to me, being careful not to bang his casted leg on anything. He pulled me into a hug which only made me cry harder. Lou made his way over, kneeled down, and wrapped his arms around both Dylan and me. Suddenly all three of us were crying.

"Why are w-w-we c-c-c-crying?" asked Dyl.

"I don't know," Lou and I said in unison and then all three of us busted out laughing.

"I need to blow my nose," I said, reaching for the tissue box near my bed.

"Samesies," said Lou.

"Samesies s-s-samesies," echoed Dylan.

"Man, if Doctor Jack saw us now it would be right back to the ward with us," I said.

"Doctor Jack can go fuck himself," said Lou as he blew his nose. "Now back to the topic at hand, finding Dylan a cuddle pal."

"Th-thanks Lou, b-b-but I think I'm okay."

"C'mon, it'll be fun. And what do you have to lose? Like why not at least look? Let's just see what happens."

"Maybe he's right, Dyl. I mean what do you have to lose? And if you find yourself a boyfriend then we could all double date," I said.

He let out a deep sigh, "We c-c-can look, but I seriously d-d-don't want to online d-d-date. I've never even been on a real-life date."

"Sweet!" Lou jumped up, pulled his MacBook out of his backpack. He flopped back down on the floor as he opened the computer. "Okay, I say we start slow. Let's try OkCupid first. Like this will just be for practice before we put you up on the real sites. I promise this is just a practice. You have to have at least one picture with me and Banjo in it. Oh, and you should have one of you holding Gracie. That will make you look sweet."

"Um, I don't know how I feel about having Gracie's picture on a dating site," I said.

"We could have one that doesn't really show her face."

"D-d-don't I get a say in a-a-any of this?"

We both ignored him. "You should totally have a picture of him snuggling Petunia Rhubarb as well," I offered.

"Great idea. Let's get a picture with Dylan on the couch holding Gracie, with the cat and the dog curled up next to him AND showing his cast. Can you even imagine the response? Dylan prepare for a full collection of boy toys." Lou slammed his hand down on the floor in triumph.

"Okay, so what should his username be?" he continued.

"Hmmm I don't know. Maybe something to do with his red hair? Or is that too cliche?" I asked.

"That might work. Or maybe something to do with music? Something like Indie Music Nerd? I hate picking usernames."

"Hmmm . . . what about something like Indie Petunia? Like name him after his cat or something."

"H-h-hello! I'm right h-h-here," Dylan said, waving his hands in the air.

"What was your user name?" I asked Lou as we both ignored Dylan.

"I don't remember."

"Yes, you do! What was it?"

"No comment," said Lou. "Let's stay focused on the task at hand." He wouldn't look at me.

"C'mon, tell us."

Lou pretended to ignore me.

"Seriously, what was your username?" I said, feeling a mix of anger and panic rising up in me.

He let out a loud sigh, "Okay, okay if it will make you happy, I'll tell you, but it makes me feel so stupid."

"What was it?" I wasn't about to cut him any slack.

"Prunella Playa."

I nearly choked on my own spit as the laugh exploded out of my mouth.

"See? This is why I didn't want to tell you!" He pouted.

"I'm sorry. But that's pretty damn funny. And I had totally forgotten how you used to call yourself Prunella. That's how you first introduced yourself to me that day we met in the ward."

"Yeah." His face glowed in embarrassment. "It made Janice crazy when I would tell people that my name was Prunella rather than Prudence. Though I bet now she'd do anything for me to have that name back. She'd much rather have a daughter named Prunella than a trans son named anything."

"Poor Janice," I said letting Lou off the hook. "Okay, back on topic. What the hell should Dylan's user name be? I sort of think I should pick it because, no offence Lou, you sort of suck at it."

Lou whapped me with a pillow. "Whatever, I can totally pick him a good name."

"Y-y-you guys, I'm right h-h-here!" Dylan said again.

"Okay, so what do you want your user name to be?" asked Lou.

He shrugged.

"I rest my case. Banjo and I will handle this. You just sit back and relax. Or be a good boy and go make us some food. We need nourishment. This is hard work."

"There's some of that pie that Sam made yesterday in the fridge. It's so good, just don't let Henry follow you back here."

Dylan hoisted himself up from the floor, leaned onto his crutches, and let out a deep sigh. "H-h-how am I supposed to c-c-carry food back while on cr-cr-crutches?"

"My mom will carry it for you. Or get Henry, but tell him I said he can't hang out right now," I said.

Dylan hobbled out the door on his crutches.

"I know what his username should be!"

"Care to share?" I asked.

"Dragon Boy."

"Oh my God, that's perfect."

"I. Know." Lou smiled triumphantly.

Dragon Boy was the nickname Lou and I gave Dylan when we all met in the psych ward last year. One day in group we had to do this stupid get to know you exercise where we all had to introduce ourselves and then name one thing about us that was unique. Dylan had announced that he collected dragons, which was about the stupidest thing he could have done. Announcing your weirdness in a teen mental ward is like wearing high-water pants and a bow tie to the first day of middle school. Lou and I never made fun or laughed at him like some of the others, but we did nickname him Dragon Boy.

"Okay, let's see if this username is taken," he said, typing in the username. "Damn, it's taken."

"How about Red Dragon?"

"Dude, he's gay. Red Dragon sounds like a penis reference." Lou lowered his voice and waggled his eyebrows, "Hey baby, wanna meet the Red Dragon?"

"Okay yeah, you're right. Maybe we should just avoid dragon altogether." I glanced over at Petunia Rhubarb curled up on my pillow. "Maybe we really should base his name on Petunia Rhubarb. Oh! How about Rhubarb Crisp?"

"Ha! That's perfect for Dyl." Lou said, typing in the new username. "Score! It's available."

There was a knock at the door. "May I come in?" It was Mom.

"Yeah, come in," I said.

She came in carrying a mixing bowl filled with pie and ice cream. Dylan came behind her, maneuvering himself on the crutches. Mom sat herself down on the edge of the bed.

"What are you kids up to?" she asked.

"We are finding Dylan a boyfriend," said Lou.

"Well that shouldn't be hard," replied Mom. "Would you like me to take the bean for a while?" she asked.

"Sure, if you want to," I answered.

Mom scooped Gracie up off of the blanket on the floor and held her up in front of her. "Come here you sweet little pea," she said, smacking her lips against Gracie's cheek. Gracie reached out unsteadily and grabbed Mom's lower lip.

Mom turned to Dylan. "If there's anything you need you just ask me. Do you understand?" she said with Gracie still grasping her lip. Gracie thought this was hilarious and her whole body burst in wiggles.

Dylan nodded.

"And you stay here as long as you'd like, okay?"

He nodded again, tears building in his eyes. Mom excused herself to go back to the kitchen.

"Your mom is the best," said Dylan after she had left.

I nodded. It made me uncomfortable when Lou and Dylan gushed about Mom.

Lou passed out the forks and we all gathered around the bowl of pie and ice cream. We all dug in. Lou took a huge forkful of ice cream.

"You should try this pie," I said to Lou. "Sam made it from the raspberries in the garden."

"No thanks, I just want ice cream."

"You eat more ice cream than any person I've ever met in my life," I said. It was true. Lou ate a lot of ice cream.

"Maybe I'm pregnant," he said.

"Whatever."

"I scream. You scream. We all scream for ice cream," he said.

"What?"

"It's a th-th-thing people s-s-say," said Dylan.

"Never heard it before. I was homeschooled remember? I don't know all the hip sayings."

"If I ever join a roller derby team my derby name will be I Scream, only I'll spell I e-y-e. Get it? Eye Scream?"

"Wh-wh-what's a derby name?" asked Dylan.

"In roller derby you make up names for yourself—sort of like when you're online dating—and you use that name for all roller derby events. Usually the names are a play on words. Like Lou's Eye Scream name," I said.

"Wh-wh-what is roller derby anyways?"

"It's sort of like beating the shit out of each other while on roller skates. And you wear crazy outfits to your games," Lou said with his mouth full of Breyers vanilla.

"They're not called games, they're called bouts and it's more than weird outfits and knocking people down," I corrected. "Actually nobody beats up anybody. It's way less violent than football."

"How do you know so much about derby?"

"My mom dated a derby girl back in the day."

"Well Miss My Mom has the Gaysees so I Know All About Roller Derby, we should totally join a team," said Lou.

"I am not playing roller derby. I don't even know how to skate."

"M-m-me either," said Dylan.

"I had no idea you two were the Official No Fun Zone. Well, can we at least make up derby names for ourselves? Oh and by the way, Dylan, we chose your dating name. It's Rhubarb Crisp," said Lou.

"No. No way," said Dylan

"We'll talk about that later," said Lou, "right now we're picking derby names."

"Dylan, what was the name of that guy you were named after?" I asked.

"Dylan Thomas. You know? The famous poet," said Lou. "Ya homeschooler."

I rolled my eyes at him. "Dylan your name should totally be Villain Thomas only you should spell Villain V-y-l-a-n. Get it?'

"Genius," said Lou. "So," he continued, "what should Banjo's derby name be?"

"Dueling B-Banjo?" offered Dylan.

"Oh good one, Dyl. Or maybe HomoSchooler?"

"Guys, I already know what my derby name is," I said.

"Do tell," said Lou, shoveling more ice cream into his mouth.

"Teen Mama. Nothing is more terrifying to most people than a teen mom."

"Ha. Brilliant! The Three Must Be Queerdos Derby Team featuring Eye Scream, Vylan Thomas, and Teeeeeeeeen Mama," Lou said in his best derby announcer voice.

"W-we should g-get shirts made," said Dylan.

"We totally should." Lou immediately pulled out his phone and began googling custom-made shirts.

"We can make them ourselves. We have all the stuff here. It's easy. We can either design them on the computer and do iron-on transfers or we can cut our own stencils and paint them," I said.

"Painting them ourselves sounds like fun," said Lou.

"Let's take the kids and walk to the craft store for t-shirts. I'll have Mom find the paint and stuff while we're gone."

"Ah guys, I'm on crutches, remember?" said Dylan.

"Oh yeah, good point. Maybe you should wait here and take a little nap," I said. "We could drive, but I really want to get Gracie out for some fresh air. Is that okay?" I asked.

"Yeah totally. I could use a nap anyway," Dylan replied.

I went to the dresser and pulled out a tiny t-shirt for Gracie. It was just one of those plain white baby undershirts. It was too hot out for anything fancy. I tossed it to Lou. "Will you go get Gracie and put this on her while I find something halfway decent for me to wear?"

"You're feeling better, huh?" asked Lou.

"What do you mean?" I asked, knowing exactly what he meant.

"Like emotionally. You're feeling better emotionally."

"What tipped you off? The fact that I'm going to put on a clean shirt to go out?"

I was feeling better, but I didn't want to talk about it. It still felt too raw. "Do you think this shirt will look okay with these shorts?" I asked, holding up a sleeveless tank that most people call a wife beater, but mom calls a wife-hugger.

"If you don't mind looking gay as hell," said Lou. "I mean that shirt with those basketball shorts make you look a little queer, just saying."

"Don't mind if I do." I turned my back to Lou and Dylan and pulled off my baby puke encrusted t-shirt and slipped on the tank.

Dylan had abandoned the plate of pie and lay on my bed curled up around Petunia Rhubarb with Rags at his feet. Petunia was aging fast and Dylan spent every second that he could with her.

"Lou while you're out there can you go find Henry and see if he wants to go with us and if he does make sure he pees before we go."

"No problem." he said.

"You sure you're okay here alone?" I asked Dylan.

"Absolutely. The pain m-m-meds are making me tired. I'll just nap with the cat."

His stuttering was so much better. I'm not sure that being put in the psych hospital did Lou or me any good at all. I'm pretty sure—that for me at least—it just added a big pile of trauma to my already complicated life, but I think in some weird way it was good for Dylan. Not the actual time in the hospital and definitely not anything Doctor Jack or that ineffectual therapist did or said, but because it got him connected to the halfway house.

Lou turned to leave to get Gracie, then at the last minute he turned around and kissed me right in front of Dylan. My face went scarlet, but it felt good.

"Y-y-you two are cute," said Dylan.

"True that," said Lou and then he disappeared out the door.

From the kitchen I heard Henry yell, "Yay." And then a second later the slam of the bathroom door.

Mom appeared in the doorway, "You're taking Henry out to the craft store?"

"Yeah. Can you find the fabric paint and stencils and stuff? We're going to make t-shirts."

Mom smiled a *I'm so glad you're doing better* smile. "Of course. Do you mind if I join you kids later? I have a great idea for a shirt."

"Only if you join our roller derby team," said Lou, coming up behind her with Gracie in his arms.

"Your roller derby team?" asked Mom.

"Our pretend roller derby team," I said. "We aren't going to skate. We just want to pick derby names and make jerseys. So far it's me, Lou, and Dylan. And we plan to recruit Henry and Gracie."

"Well in that case I definitely want in," said Mom. "My name will be Grrrrrams."

"Of course, it will," I said.

Henry came running down the hall from the bathroom.

"Did you wash your hands?" Mom and I asked in unison.

"Yeah. Lou said we're going to make t-shirts for our roller derby team. Are we going to go skating tonight?" he asked.

"No, this is just a pretend roller derby team," I said.

"Can we please go skating? Please? Please? Super please?"

"Maybe someday, but not today. Do you want to come along or not?" I asked.

"Yes," he said.

"Then plug your pie hole and let's go," I said.

Lou put his arm around Henry. "I promise that you and I will go skating soon. We'll leave those fuddy duddies at home."

Henry hugged Lou.

Lou kissed the top of Henry's stinky head. "Now start thinking of a good derby name for yourself and let's go."

"How about Diet Coke?" asked Hen.

"Diet Coke?" asked Lou.

"Yeah, diet coke is so bad and Grams says it will kill you."

Lou busted up laughing. "Henry, you are the best."

Henry rolled his eyes and grinned. He loved impressing Lou.

We left Dylan on the bed to nap and headed out onto the porch and down the steps. I took Gracie from Lou and strapped her into the stroller. At the sight of this Rags began running in circles yipping, expecting a walk.

"You stay this time, girl. It's too hot to leave you tied up outside a store," I said, leading her back onto the porch.

"Come, Rags," Mom called from the living room. Poor Rags put her tail between her legs and went back into the house.

The four of us headed down the driveway, gravel crunching under out feet and the stroller wheels.

I was happy.

Chapter 18

y phone dinged. I picked it up to see a text from Lou. *Be ready in an hour.*

Why? I'm not sure I'm up to going out, I replied.

Turn off Unexpected. I'll see you in one hour. He added a GIF of a rainbow-farting unicorn. I smiled despite myself as I reached for the remote and turned off *Teen Mom*. Mom, Sam, and I had long ago finished *Unexpected* and I was on to new things. I started to type a reply to protest, but knew Lou well enough to know it was pointless. So I just typed, *okay.*

Gracie was still asleep so I thought a shower might be a good idea. If Lou was on his way over I should at least wash the crusty spit up out of my hair. I mean the leaky boobs, hot flashes, and random crying fits are already pretty damn sexy, I wouldn't want to overwhelm him by adding in some crusty baby puke with a side of dried baby poo.

I worried that Gracie might wake up while I was in the shower, but honestly I was way past due in the cleanliness department. It felt like it might be totally *Teen Mom* of me to ask Henry to watch her while I showered. Mom and Sam weren't home, so it seemed like the only choice.

I opened the back door. Henry and Rags were racing around the yard oblivious to the heat. "Hen, can you come here?"

"Why?"

"Because I need you to watch Gracie."

He abandoned Rags and raced up to the back door. "Really? You're going to let me babysit?"

"Well, sort of. I need to shower. Can you just keep an eye on her? Just come get me if she wakes up."

"Yay! I get to babysit."

"I just need you to watch her while she sleeps."

Henry followed me back into the house and settled in on the couch. The bassinet was set up in the corner of the tiny living room.

"Go wash your hands. And use soap."

Her ran to the bathroom and returned minutes later.

"Let me see."

He held out his hands for my inspection. He passed.

"Okay don't forget, just come get me if she wakes up."

Henry put his hand to his forehead in a salute, flopped down on the couch, and then leaned over the edge of the couch to stare at Gracie in her bassinet.

"Dude, you don't actually have to watch her like that. Just stay in the room in case she wakes up Remember that she rolls over now, so don't leave her unattended."

He waved me away without removing his face from the bassinet.

I went into the bathroom and undressed. I didn't get in the shower right away. I sat on the edge of the tub and tried to decide if leaving Hen in charge of Gracie was irresponsible. Maybe I should just wait on the shower until Mom or Sam got home. I mean, what if she stopped breathing and Henry didn't notice? Babies die of SIDS every day. What if he picked her up and dropped her? What if there was an earthquake and I couldn't get out of the bathroom before the house collapsed on her? They keep saying the Big One is coming and it could be any time. It could be today. Right now.

I grabbed Mom's ratty bathrobe of the hook on the door and pulled it on. It wouldn't hurt to check on her.

"Henry! What are you doing?"

Henry sat on the couch with Gracie in his arms. He was making faces at her while humming the Sponge Bob Square Pants theme song. She grinned up at him. Her arms were flapping wildly in excitement. He looked up, "I'm holding her. She woke up. She really likes the Sponge Bob song. You should definitely sing it to her."

I left him alone for one minute and this is what he does? I felt the anger building,

"That's dangerous. I told you to watch her and to come and get me if she woke up. I didn't say you could pick her up." I tried to keep my voice even.

"I've held her a million times before."

"Yeah, you've held her with an adult around to make sure you didn't drop her."

"You're not an adult. You're a teenager. And I'm almost ten. I can hold a baby. Why are you being so mean?" His face reddened and he looked like he might cry. "I would never drop her."

He was right. He would never drop her, and I used to take care of him all the time when I was his age and he was Gracie's age.

"You're right. I'm sorry. I just worry about her so much."

He stared down at Gracie. "I would never drop her," he said as tears slid down his face.

I sat down next to him and leaned in to look at my baby. She looked at me and smiled. Henry scooched over so his body was pressed against mine. "Is it okay if I keep holding her?" He sniffled.

"Yeah you can keep holding her, but on one condition. You can't drop snot in her face. Let me get you some toilet paper." I went into the bathroom, pulled off a wad of toilet paper and returned to Henry. I held it to his nose. He blew hard into the tissue and then I crumpled it up and wiped off the last few tears from his cheeks.

"Remember when you were little and I used to help you blow your nose?"

He smiled. "Yeah and I didn't get it, so I would blow into your hand with my mouth."

"Yep, until the day you did get it and blew snot all over the place."

"Can I be the one to teach Gracie Dog—I mean Gracie—to blow her nose?"

"You're such a weirdo. Do you realize that?"

"Yep. So can I?"

"Yes. you can teach her how to blow her nose. Okay, I'm getting in the shower. Just don't walk around the house with her. Stay on the couch. Do not set her down anywhere other than her bassinet. Don't put her on her belly on the couch. Only on her back. Remember that she can roll over so actually now that I'm thinking about it, don't lay her on the couch at all. Don't feed her."

He nodded his head, "Aye aye, Captain. As you wish."

I closed the door to the bathroom and took some deep breaths. I could hear Henry go from humming Sponge Bob to loudly singing. "Who lives in a pineapple under the sea? Gracie Bob Square Pants!" I smiled. She will be okay, I reassured myself. Henry would never let anything happen to her. Man, this motherhood thing is stressful. I think I'm starting to understand why Mom is such a mess. I can't imagine having to worry about three kids and a grandkid . . . two grandkids.

I turned the water on and let it run until it was steaming and then I hit the shower button and climbed in. It was far too hot out for a hot shower, but somehow I craved it. The hot spray stung my skin and instantly turned me as red as a cooked lobster. The pain felt good. I stood there as long as I could stand it and then turned up the cold until I wasn't cooking myself alive.

I dumped what seemed like half a bottle of shampoo onto the top of my head and lathered up until suds ran down my back. I grabbed the lump of farmers' market soap and scoured every inch of my body. I rinsed and then smeared my head with Sam's expensive coconut conditioner. The smell of the soap and conditioner took me right back to the day I found out I was pregnant. I had used Sam's conditioner on that day too. And then I had sawed off all of my hair with Mom's dull rusted hair scissors and filled my backpack with a collection of pills in case ending my life became my only choice. On that day I had snuck out of the house with Rags and headed to my brother's to think.

I hid out in his spare bedroom all day and then after dark I climbed out the bedroom window of my brother's trailer with Rags. We wandered around in the night before ending up at the beach. Finally, around midnight Rags and I headed home. That night I faced the secret fear I had been carrying around since right after Gray died. I had stopped having my period and I was nauseous all the time. For a while I told myself it was just the stress of everything, but eventually I had to face the truth. My boobs had started to hurt and there was really no explaining that away. I bought a pregnancy test and carried it around in my backpack for days before I finally got up the courage that night to take it.

I sat on the edge of the bathtub and peed on the magic stick that in just a few short minutes told me my whole life was about to change again. I was pregnant. My brain pretty much went numb at that point. I became a zombie.

Thinking back to that night I'm not sure how I didn't just go crazy right then and there. I mean I was sixteen years old and my only friend—the person I loved most in the world outside of my family—had just walked onto the freeway and taken their own life and then several weeks later I discover that I'm pregnant by them? Looking back, I can see just how traumatic it all was, but when I was in the middle of it I couldn't see anything at all.

I suppose that even now I'm not seeing things clearly. Maybe I'll make another appointment with Anna.

I rinsed the conditioner out of my hair and let the cool water run over me. I stared at Sam's razor. I had the urge to crack it against the side of the tub to break the plastic housing and release the blade inside. I imagined digging it into my arm and letting the physical pain ease the emotional pain of thinking about Gray. I had kept my urge to cut under control since Gracie was born, but at that moment gouging my arm with the sharp metal blade sounded amazing. I didn't do it though, and I was proud of myself for that.

I turned off the water, grabbed the scratchy old towel, and dried off. I rubbed Mom's mint body lotion into my skin and savored the cool tingle before pulling on my green basketball shorts, stained nursing bra, and my orange octopus t-shirt. It was time to push the memories to the back of my brain and come back to my present reality. I had a baby who needed me.

I wandered back to the living room feeling strangely relaxed.

Henry sat on the couch holding Gracie on his lap so she was sitting up facing him. He was quietly singing her the Six Little Ducks song.

"And the one little duck with the feather on her back, she led the others with a quack quack quack," he sang.

I stood in the hall watching him and my heart swelled with love. I loved that little kid so much. Ever since Gracie was born Henry looked so grown up to me. It was hard to imagine that one day Gracie would be his age. Nine years seemed like an eternity, and at the same time it seemed like Henry was born just yesterday. I was under no illusion that time wouldn't pass in a blink of an eye and that before I knew it Gracie would be as big as Henry.

I needed to work hard to not let time slip away from me.

And then I realized that worrying too much about letting time slip away from me might make me so anxious that I would become over-whelmed again and let time slip away. Motherhood is like some sort of tightrope covered in butter over a pit of alligators and you have to walk it wearing clown shoes and a blindfold while carrying your baby who just keeps getting bigger and bigger with each step. No wonder my mom is such a mess and my sister went crazy.

I stepped into the living room.

"Hey Peach Pit, how was she?" When Gracie heard my voice she turned to look for me. When she saw me her face lit up. She was so beautiful. I was afraid she would demand a feeding, but by some miracle she didn't seem to be hungry and was quite content in the care of her doting uncle.

"She did great. I sang her some songs and told her about the time Rags pooped in the house and you stepped in it," he said.

"Thanks for that."

"I can keep babysitting if you want," he offered.

"You know what? I'll take you up on that. I'm going to go make some coffee. Just don't walk around with her, okay? And if she starts to fuss call me."

"Roger that," he said, nodding.

I went into the sweltering kitchen to make coffee. Hot coffee on a hot day was probably not a great idea, but I'd hardly had any since I found out I was pregnant and I was seriously craving it. Better hot coffee on a hot day than a razor blade to the arm, I reasoned.

I measured six scoops of coffee into the French press and put the kettle on the stove. While I waited for the water to boil I pulled out my phone. *Please tell me where we're going*, I texted.

A minute later my phone pinged, *Okay. Okay. I'm just taking you out for hotdogs and some beach time. I texted Sam and she said she'd be home soon and can watch Gracie if you want.*

Would you mind if we brought Henry along?

Your wish is my command, he replied. *Though not sure this is keeping to the plan to be regular teenagers.*

Maybe being a regular teenager is overrated? I replied.

I stuck my head into the living room. "Hey kid, put her in the swing and get ready to go. Lou and I are taking you out."

"Hurray!" he cheered. He gently set Gracie down in her swing, buckled the straps, turned it on, and raced off to his room.

Chapter 19

drank two cups of steaming coffee and then fetched Gracie from the swing so I could go get ready. My body buzzed with exhaustion making me feel oddly manic. Even though I was letting Mom and Sam help out more, I was still so damn tired all the time. The coffee wasn't helping. I carried Gracie into my room and laid her on the bed. She looked around the room wide-eyed. It was amazing how alert she was. I leaned over her. "I'm going out with Lou and you're going to hang with Aunt Sam, okay?" I said in a sing-song voice. It's weird how it's somehow impossible to talk to a baby in a normal voice.

She looked at me for a long time and then she looked away. It's like babies can only handle so much eye contact. She turned towards me again and her face erupted in that smile. I grabbed her little plastic ring of keys and held it over her. She got very serious as she stared at them reaching both hands towards the bright keys. When she finally grasped them with her right hand she pulled them to her mouth and began to chew. I leaned over and kissed her tiny, slobbery face, "Mama loves you so much. So much. So much." I whispered. "How about some lunch before Mama has to leave?"

I lay down next to her and lifted up my shirt. She latched right on and gazed at me as she drank her lunch, keeping the keys grasped tightly in her fist. I felt the oxytocin surge through my body. They say oxytocin is the love hormone and I believe it. For many people breastfeeding releases oxytocin in buckets and so every time I feed her I feel like I'm bathing in love for her. I caressed her head and started to cry. Again.

I thought about Gray's mom breastfeeding Gray. I can't even imagine how I would feel if I couldn't prevent someone from hurting Gracie the way Gray's dad hurt Gray. I imagined the shame that Gray's mom must have felt and I wished I could hug her.

I startled awake. I must have dozed off. Gracie was asleep next to me with her milky lips still on my nipple and those keys still in her hand. I slowly detached myself from her and reached for my phone. I was only asleep about ten minutes. Good. I still had some time before Lou arrived.

Groggy as I was, I forced myself to get up. I gently lifted Gracie, carried her to the living room, and placed her in her swing. I went into the bathroom and studied my face in the mirror. Bruise colored circles sat heavy under my bloodshot eyes. I splashed cold water on my face and then did something I've never done before: I opened up Sam's makeup bag and pulled out a tube of waterproof mascara. I carefully painted it onto my nearly invisible blond eye lashes. I have to admit that I sort of liked the way it looked. I considered applying some base and powder to my face, maybe a little blush as well, but then changed my mind. I'll just stick with the mascara for now.

My hair was a mess. I took a finger-full of hair cream and rubbed it into the mess. I ran my fingers through my choppy floppy fauxhawk until it stuck up just enough, but still flopped over in just the right way. I studied myself again. I'm cute, I thought to myself. I returned to my room and searched through the clean laundry for my brown flannel. It goes perfect with the orange octopus shirt that I was wearing. It was way hot out still, but just in case we stayed out late I figured I should take a jacket of some sort. I slid my feet into my threadbare black Chuck Taylors.

Back in the living room I found Sam and Henry sitting on a blanket on the floor playing with Gracie. That nap sure didn't last long. Sam looked up, "Dang Banj, you look cute today."

I squirmed in embarrassment. "Thanks for watching Gracie," I said in an attempt to change the subject.

"I'm excited to be the third wheel," said Henry.

"Where in the world did you hear that?" Sam asked.

"Hear what?" asked Henry.

"Third wheel. Do you even know what that means?" Sam asked, glancing at me. We both tried not to smile.

"I'm not a baby, Mama. I know what a third wheel is." He rolled his eyes at her and I had to look away to avoid laughing.

"Well, Mr. Third Wheel, you are not going out with Banjo and Lou."

"Mama, you should totally change your name to The Lady Who Never Lets Her Kid Have Any Fun."

"Okay Mr. Third Wheel."

"Actually, I invited him along," I said.

"You sure?" asked Sam. "I mean, don't you want some alone time?"

I shrugged, slightly regretting inviting Henry. Sam was right, alone time would be nice, but it was too late. Henry was so excited.

"There's some fresh milk in a bottle in the fridge and plenty more in the freezer if you need it. She just ate though so she should be good for a while. I changed her about an hour ago."

My phone buzzed. *I'm here. Bring Rags if you want.*

"He's here. Are you sure you're okay to watch her? I don't have to go." I felt panicky at the idea of leaving her.

"Go."

"Henry, be sure to grab a towel if you plan to go in the water," I reminded him. He raced down the hall and returned with a bath towel.

"Wait a minute," said Sam. She went into the kitchen and returned with sun screen which she proceeded to smear all over Henry. She handed it to me and I stuffed it in my backpack.

I got down on my knees and bent to kiss Gracie. God, I loved her so hard. I hoisted my pack onto my back and grabbed Rags's leash off the hook on the wall. The moment I touched the leash Rags erupted in yips. She loved her walks.

"Come on, Hen." I opened the front door. Rags and Henry charged for the car. Henry opened the back, passenger door for Rags and she jumped in, eager for her dog adventure. He followed after her. I slid into the front passenger seat and leaned over to kiss Lou. The cool air of the air-conditioned car wrapped around my body and caused goose bumps to explode across my arms, or maybe it was the kiss.

"You look beautiful," he said.

"I bet you say that to all the girls."

"Nah, only the hot moms."

I punched his shoulder as he backed the car out of the driveway. I realized that I really loved this guy. I reached over and put my hand on his thigh. It felt nice. He turned out of the driveway and onto the road.

"You guys are cute," Henry said from the back seat.

Lou and I glanced at each other. That kid.

"Can we roll the windows down?" I asked.

"It's ten thousand degrees out there."

"I know, just for a few minutes. Please? I want to feel the wind on my face."

He hit the buttons on his door handle and all four windows slid down. Rags hung her body out the window.

"Good idea Rags," I said as I stuck my head out my window. "Turn up the music!" I yelled over the wind.

He cranked up the music.

"What is this?" I yelled.

"Soy Yo' by Bomba Estéreo," he yelled back.

"I love it," I yelled into the wind.

"Me too," yelled Henry, sticking his head out the window.

I let the music carry me right into the best mood ever.

Chapter 20

We parked at the ferry dock and climbed out of the car. Henry held Rags's leash.

"Okay, let's go get those hotdogs and then we can sit on the beach and have a picnic," Lou said as he reached into his back pocket. "Shit, I forgot my wallet."

"That's okay. We can eat later," I offered.

"No, I'm starving. My house isn't very far from here. We can walk, if you don't mind."

"I don't mind, but what about your parents? Won't they freak out about me and Henry and the dog?"

"I doubt they're home. If they're not working late then they're probably out for drinks. Let's go. The sooner we get there the less likely we are to run into them."

I hated this idea. Meeting Lou's parents was about the last thing in the world I wanted to do and this felt way too risky. "Okay." I shrugged.

Lou led us up a hill past a collection of cute little specialty shops to a small bluff that overlooked the water. The houses were all beautiful historic mansions. I knew Lou's family had money, I just hadn't expected this. He led us to a steel-blue house with white trim. Every window had a flower box exploding with flowers. The pillared front porch held an old-fashioned swing and huge ceramic pots filled with more flowers. His house was the kind of house you see on magazine covers. I felt my stomach knot up. Ancient apple and plum trees filled the side yard between the house and the old-fashioned detached garage.

"Let's put Rags in here just in case Janice and Doug come home," said Lou, opening a side door into the garage. "They'd flip out if we had a dog in the house."

Henry hesitated.

"It's okay. We'll only be a few minutes. Rags will be fine," I said, reassuring him.

We closed Rags in the garage and then climbed the wide wooden porch steps.

"Wow, you live in a mansion. Are you rich?" Henry voiced what I was thinking.

"No little dude, I'm not rich. But my parents are," Lou said, slipping his key into the lock.

He opened the door onto a stone entryway. The smell of honeysuckle and lavender wrapped around us. I thought of my own house that smelled of herbs and essential oils, like the organic food co-op, with a base layer smell of musty mold and dampness. A smell not unlike dirty socks that belonged to an old hippie.

"Prudence? Is that you?" A woman's voice said.

"Shit, they're home early," Lou muttered.

"Yeah, I forgot my wallet," he yelled.

"Whose Prudence?" whispered Henry.

"Shhhh, I'll explain later," I said.

My heart sank as Lou led us to a kitchen gleaming with granite and stainless steel. The far wall of the kitchen was made entirely of glass. The view was breathtaking. The house overlooked the ferry dock and gray-green Salish Sea. The late afternoon sky was a watercolor painting of orange, pink, and high thin white clouds and it cast the kitchen in a warm golden light.

Two very tan and very blond white people stood leaning against an oak and granite kitchen island.

Two glasses filled with icy brown liquid sat sweating next to a nearly empty bottle of Pappy Van Winkle whiskey. The woman, Janice I assumed, took a long drink from her glass and then refilled her glass with the last of the bottle.

"Mom, Dad, this is my friend Banjo. And um, this is her nephew, Henry," Lou said, placing his hand on Henry's head. "Banjo, Henry, this is my mom and dad, Janice and Doug."

The man stepped from behind the island and extended his smooth hand to me, "Good to meet you, Banjo." His white shirt was untucked from his dress pants and a paisley tie hung loose and undone from his neck. His cheeks were red from the alcohol and his words were a little soft around the edges—not quite slurring, but almost. He looked like a fashion model for a California beachwear company or something

I knew Lou's parents were white, but seeing them in person was sort of shocking. They both had sun-bleached blond hair and perfectly even paid-for tans. They almost looked like siblings. It was nearly impossible to imagine them as Lou's parents. I remembered the day I first met Lou at the psych ward and he had told me that his parents were white. He had said, "They're whiter than you. All white and tan with a free side of skin cancer all for the low low payment of just $30 a month." He was right.

"Hi," I said. For some reason I felt terrified.

Doug reached his hand out to Henry. "It's nice to meet you," said Henry, taking his hand.

The woman stared at me. She was dressed in a woman's version of her husband's outfit, pressed slacks, a silk button-down shirt, and one of those thin lady ties. Her blond hair hung loose past her shoulders. "Hello," she said, smiling a bit stiffly.

She turned to Lou. "Banjo? The girl you met at the hospital?" Her tone was sharp and her words were slurring. She moved in that weird slow-motion way that drunk people move.

"Yes, Mom."

She smiled at me again, this time making more of an effort to look like she was actually glad to meet me. She then reached out to shake Henry's hand.

"Hi," he said. "Nice to meet you."

She smiled at him but didn't speak.

"I just need to grab my wallet and then we're going to the beach," Lou said, as if to let her know we wouldn't be staying.

"Prudence, your father and I would like you to have dinner at home one of these nights."

"Mom, my name is Lou."

Janice stared at Lou for a long minute and then turned and walked out of the room without a word.

Doug stood frozen for a split second, looking from Lou to me and back to Lou. He closed his eyes as he let out a loud sigh and then went after Janice, "Janice, sweetie, come back. Let's talk about this." He turned back to us, "And um, good to meet you Banjo, and you too Henry."

Lou rolled his eyes. "Always the same thing," he said. "I'm sorry, guys. Dad's a passive drunk. Mom's a mean drunk. And drunk is their favorite thing to be. They aren't so bad when they're not drinking, sadly they're always drinking. Guess how much that bottle cost?"

I shrugged.

"Right around fifteen hundred dollars. And they drank it in one sitting. Now do you see why I take what I can get from them? They suck. Come on, let's get my wallet and get out of here." His voice was shaky.

Henry and I followed Lou through the enormous house to a thick wood door with an antique crystal doorknob near one of the two living rooms. "I'd offer you a tour of the house, but I really don't think that's the best idea. My room's down here," Lou said, pulling open the door to reveal a gorgeous oak staircase leading down to a room that seemed bigger than my entire house.

"Dude, you could fit ten of my houses into your house."

"Wow, this is so cool," said Henry. He seemed mostly oblivious to the tension in the house.

"Yeah," Lou said quietly.

We reached the bottom of the stairs and I looked around in amazement. Lou had a full-sized couch, a king-sized bed, a huge T.V. mounted on the wall, two MacBooks sitting side by side on an antique desk, a small refrigerator, and a microwave all in his bedroom. The room was painted a muted green and trimmed in ornate white wainscoting. A large Ethiopian flag hung above his bed. The polished oak floors shone. A door off to the side opened into a bathroom that was bigger than my bedroom. His room was much more apartment than bedroom. A really nice apartment.

I thought about my shabby little bedroom with its matted carpet and dingy walls and felt a rush of shame. If I had known Lou lived like this I never would have let him into my cruddy room, or my cruddy house for that matter.

Henry interrupted my thoughts.

"What's this?" he asked picking a doll up off of Lou's bed.

Lou looked up from the pile of clothes he was rifling through. "That," he said with a hint of sadness, "is Doll Doll. I've had her my whole life, or at least as long as I can remember."

"She's beautiful," I said.

"I think my real mom made her for me. I remember having her at the orphanage. Janice spent years trying to get rid of her. She would bribe me with those horrific American Girl dolls, but I always refused. Janice hates Doll Doll. I'm actually shocked she didn't toss it as soon as she got me back to the states. I guess she wasn't quite so awful back then. I think in the beginning she actually tried to love me, but maybe she loved her whiskey more. Maybe if she had never brought the whisky home she would have been able to love me. I dunno. Maybe I'm giving her too much credit."

Henry ran his fingers over the beaded up, filthy doll. It was a brown felt doll with stiff curly black hair made from rope. It wore a simple faded cornflower blue cotton dress with tiny yellow flowers. Its eyes and mouth were stitched on with black thread. The doll was threadbare and tattered from age and wear.

"I'm glad you still have her," said Henry.

Lou smiled. "I'm sorry little dude, I shouldn't be talking about this in front of you."

"It's okay, Lou. I'm not a little kid any more. Mama and Grams and Banjo talk in front of me all the time. How old were you when you were adopted?" he asked.

"Six."

"You don't have any memories? I mean other than that foggy one of the day they took you to the orphanage?" I asked.

"I have some flashes of memories, or at least I think they're memories. Sometimes it's hard to know for sure. And I do have some very clear images, not many, but a few. Why?"

"I dunno, it just seems like six is an age where you would be able to remember your mom," I said.

Lou was quiet for a long time and I realized I'd upset him.

"Do you think I'm making up that memory of being taken? Do you think my mom is really dead like Janice and Doug said?"

"No! I just mean I have memories from before I was six."

"Dude, think about it. I was taken from her when I was five and I was put into the orphanage. I lived in the orphanage for almost a year. They never spoke of my family once I was there. All they did was concentrate on teaching us English. Do you know they taught us how to sing songs in English and then they'd film us singing? And not in a group. They'd make us stand all alone and sing and then they'd put the video up on our adoption profile page."

"Adoption profile page?" I asked

"It's pretty much like a dating profile. The adoption agencies put up pictures and videos of us so that prospective parents can pick and choose their future children."

"Wait, like people literally pick out a kid?"

"Yeah. Oh and they offer discounts for disabled kids."

"What the hell?" I couldn't believe it. It made my stomach hurt. I thought about Gracie on one of those pages and I wanted to puke.

"I don't remember anyone at the orphanage ever talking about my first family or even acknowledging that I had one. All they talked about was how fantastic our lives would be once we got to America or Europe. And of course, once I got here Janice and Doug never asked me about my old life. When I asked Janice when I would be able to see my mom again she would say, "You get to see her every single day. I'm right here.""

"Later when I would ask to go home she would get angry and yell at me. Doug would take me aside and tell me that I was upsetting Mommy and that I was home. It was like the biggest mind-fuck for a little kid. I remember the orphanage fairly clearly or at least the last months I was there, everything before that is just flashes.

"The only reason I still have Doll Doll is that I fought like hell to keep her. Any time anyone tried to take her I would become a rabid animal and bite, kick, scream, punch. I slept with her crammed down my pants so they couldn't sneak in and take her while I slept."

I glanced over at Henry. He held Doll Doll cradled in his arms as if she were an infant.

"So anyway, all of that is to say that they worked hard to make us forget our first families and it mostly worked. I mean, like I said, I do have some snippets here and there but not enough to be able to say I remember my time in Ethiopia before the orphanage.

I thought about my memories of Gray and how foggy they already are. I have photos and their stuff and Rags to help me remember and of course I'm much older than Lou was, but still sometimes my memories are so fragile and wispy. I could see how Lou can't remember.

The room fell into silence and then Henry said, "We should make Gracie a Doll Doll."

"Little dude, that is the best idea I've heard all day," said Lou.

Henry beamed.

Lou resumed his wallet search. "Where did I put that damn wallet? I'm so frustrated!"

"Is that it?" asked Henry, pointing to Lou's wallet sitting right out in the open by his computer.

"That is in fact my wallet. C'mon, let's go eat," Lou said, grabbing the wallet and leading us up the stairs.

Chapter 21

Lou, Henry, and I sat on the grass overlooking the beach, eating hot dogs and chips, and drinking Cokes. Rags sat at attention waiting for bites of the hotdog that Lou had bought just for her. Henry was doling them out.

"Are you going to go do online school this fall?" Lou asked, before taking a bite of his hot dog.

"Yeah, I think so. I think maybe I should get an actual diploma from an actual high school. I mean since it's online school it shouldn't be all that much harder with Gracie around." I hoped that was true. "Or maybe I'll just keep unschooling."

"How long have you been homeschooling?"

"Since 4th grade. That's when I started getting bullied and the school wouldn't do anything about it."

Mom had been furious at the school and said if she hadn't been so poor she would have hired an attorney. "Hypocritical fascists that love to talk about diversity but throw a gay parent or gender nonconforming kid at them and they crap themselves," she had said. "I mean what the hell, do they think the other kids are going to catch the gaysies?" So she had pulled me out. She and Sam had never even bothered to send Henry to school.

"You're lucky you graduated," I said. "I hated real school. I'm pretty sure I'll hate online school too. I mean, I love learning and all that, but I hate formal school."

NINA PACKEBUSH

"Yeah, I totally get it. I'm so glad to be out," Lou said with his mouth full. Little flecks of mustard settled at the corners of his lips.

"I can't believe you went to Wayside. That place must cost more than my mom makes in a year, maybe two years," I said. Wayside was the most expensive private prep school in the state.

"Yeah, it was pretty rad being the only black kid in my grade and one of the only like six black kids in the school. You should go online and look at the website. I'm all over it. They made sure I was in every promotional photo taken the entire six years I was there. I am the face of diversity." He fluttered his hand up as if it were a butterfly while turning his face to the sky.

"Before Wayside I went to a Seattle public school. It was one of those ones that was really a private school in disguise. Janice and Doug drove me all the way to Seattle every day for school. They both worked at different Seattle law firms. Doug was a divorce attorney and Janice a corporate litigator. They work in Edmonds now. They have their own law firm, but back then they worked in Seattle and they loved talking about how they had me in a big city public school just like a regular kid. The school was one of those Seattle elementary schools that was in a fancy neighborhood and not anywhere near the bus line, so they were able to filter out most of the brown, black, and poor folk.

"Anyway, at the public school I went to we did community service as part of the curriculum and we did shit like go to homeless shelters and serve food or put together hygiene packages for poor black and brown kids at the falling down schools. The only time I saw large groups of kids that looked like me was when we were on some dumb community service project. All the white parents got to brag about that shit and trust me, I got invited to every birthday party of every kid in my grade.

"At the time I loved it. I thought I was the most popular kid in the school." He rolled his eyes.

He took another bite of his hotdog.

"Guess how many black teachers they had at that school?"

"Zero?" I said.

"Yup. Not one. Not even a brown teacher. But they did have a brown janitor, so you know, diversity."

Lou was talking so fast that the words tumbled out of his mouth. I liked it when his hyper ways surfaced. He took another bite of his hot dog and continued on, mouth full and crumbs flying.

"All the progressive parents loved to brag about how their kids went to public school because that made them part of the 99% or something. Like you know that kind, they love to go to the Women's March or protests on Saturdays to take selfies to post on their Facebooks, but then spend their Sunday mornings going over their stock portfolios. The kind that loved to talk about being colorblind and buy their kids black dolls and shit like that. I was surrounded by this growing up. Every single one of Janice and Doug's friends were this type. I didn't fully get it then, of course. I just knew that somehow I didn't fit. Now I see it and looking back I can see just how messed up it was and I understand why I always felt uncomfortable around the other families." Bitterness dripped from Lou's mouth.

"Are you going to college?" I asked.

"According to Janice and Doug I am. I could get into pretty much any college I want to, but I never applied to a single one. I brought home all the applications and filled them out and then accidentally dumped them in trash rather than the mailbox. Oops, my bad. They freaked out when no acceptance letters arrived. I told them I'm taking a gap year and since that's all the rage these days they settled down."

"Why aren't you going?"

Lou looked out at the beach. The tide was coming in and the sun was sinking low in the sky. "I'm going to find my real mom and if I find her,

I'm going to go back to Ethiopia to meet her. Maybe I could even bring her here." He paused as if picturing it. "If I'm in school, I won't have time to look for her. Neela gave me information on a bunch of Searchers and I'm going to take all my savings and hire one. So many kids were basically stolen from Ethiopia that now there's this whole industry where people make their living reuniting families. Ethiopia doesn't even allow transnational adoption any longer because the adoption agencies were basically just child trafficking operations. I watched a few documentaries about it.

"There's one called *Unwanted Children—The Shameful Side of International Adoption*. It's really good. I cried all the way through it. What's really crazy is that they feature a kid from here, or actually from Everett. There is also this report I read called, "They Steal Babies, Don't They?" I've learned so much. I wish more people would pay attention to this stuff."

"Maybe we could watch that documentary together some time?" I asked.

He smiled. "That would mean a lot to me, Banjo. Did I ever tell you that when Janice and Doug adopted me they thought I was four, but I was really six?"

"I remember you telling me that." This was the most Lou had ever talked about this stuff with me. He seemed to need to get this off his chest.

"Yeah, it was what a lot of adoption agencies did. They lied to Americans about our ages because most people wanted younger kids. They tricked our parents into giving us up and then told the Americans that we were younger than we were. It was crazy. When I got here they celebrated my fourth birthday, but I was actually turning six. I tried to tell them that, but they wouldn't listen, plus my English was still pretty shaky. Then finally, when I turned nine, stories started to surface about how corrupt the Ethiopian adoptions were and they couldn't deny it any longer. So one day I was seven and the next I was nine."

Lou reached over and ran his hands down Rags' back.

"Janice and Doug were pissed and it was a giant mess with school.

"So yeah, about college. I found some of my adoption papers hidden in Janice's office at the house. I don't have my original birth certificate though and my birth parents' names are blacked out on the paperwork that Janice and Doug have. I'm pretty sure they're the ones that did that. Did you know that when you get adopted you get a brand-new birth certificate with your adoptive parents' names on it?"

"Really?"

"Yeah." He sighed and then went on. "I copied all the documents that I could find and have them stashed. I have four thousand dollars saved up and I'm totally going to hire a Searcher to find my mom. The website I found says it only costs like nine hundred dollars or something, but I've been stealing money from the folks forever, so I have a nice stash. A twenty here from Janice's purse, a ten there from Doug's wallet, lie about the cost of something and keep the extra. It adds up fast.

"The only thing that's sort of freaking me out is that I worry my real mom won't understand all this," he swept his hand across his body. "My mom knows she had a daughter. What will she think about the fact that now I'm a son? Honestly the only reason I haven't gone forward on getting top surgery is the fear of what my real mom might do. I did some checking and my insurance totally covers top surgery. Now that I'm eighteen I can get it done without the consent of Janice and Doug." He shoved a handful of chips in his mouth, "But not yet. I need to find my real mom first and then I'll figure that part out."

Henry looked up from his food. "Lou? Did you used to be a girl?"

Lou glanced at me and then at Henry. "Yeah little dude. When I was born everyone thought I was a girl, but I was really a boy. It's sort of complicated—"

Henry interrupted, "Oh so you're trans. That's why your mom called you Pru."

"Well, I guess it's not that complicated after all," Lou said, looking at me grinning.

"Don't you remember when we first met Lou, he went by Pru?" I said.

"Oh yeah, I totally forgot about that," said Henry. "I think I might be a they. I'm not sure yet."

Lou laughed. "Henry, you are the best kid I've ever met."

"I know," he said. "Can me and Rags go in the water?"

"Sure, but no deeper than your knees. Do you hear me?"

"Yes, sir," said Henry as he saluted me. Then he and Rags tore off towards the water.

I turned to Lou. "Hey, guess what I'm doing tomorrow?" I didn't wait for him to answer. "I'm going to go apply for EBT and TANF."

"What's EBT and TANF?" he asked.

"EBT is food stamps. That's what it's called now. You get like a debit card thing, but it's only good for food. And TANF stands for Temporary Assistance for Needy Families. It's a program that gives poor parents a little bit of cash to live on. Of course, it's not enough to even possibly live on—like maybe four hundred dollars a month—but it would definitely help.

"They give you a little bit of cash for like a year or something to sort of help out until you can go to work. I'm going to go apply. I figured if I can just get it until I graduate that'd be cool. My mom said I didn't have to because according to my her they're all fascist dicks, but Mom thinks almost everyone is a fascist dick."

"Do you want me to go with you?"

"Nah. I sort of want to do it on my own."

"That makes sense. Hey, can I ask you a question?"

"Depends on the question."

"Can I kiss you?"

I glanced towards the water and saw that Henry had his back to us and I leaned in.

Chapter 22

went on the Department of Social and Health services website to start filling out the application. It was hella confusing. They wanted to know everyone who lived in the house, how much each person made, and how much of the bills I was responsible for and even how much Gracie was responsible for. It didn't make any sense to me. I couldn't imagine trying to fill this stuff out if English was your second language, or if you didn't speak English at all, or if you didn't have good reading skills or whatever.

After about an hour of pure frustration and nearly smashing the computer to bits, I decided just to go to the office and apply in person. I pulled out an empty file folder from the file cabinet next to the desk in the living room and started gathering up the things they said I needed—social security card, my birth certificate, Gracie's birth certificate, a hospital bill with my name and address on it, and a copy of my homeschool declaration of intent. I stuffed the folder into the side pocket of the diaper bag, doubled checked that I had enough diapers and wipes as well as a change of clothes for Gracie in case she had a blow-out, grabbed my water bottle, and stuck everything in the cargo basket of the stroller.

I went into my room and found a clean short-sleeve button-down shirt and then changed my mind. It's too hard to nurse in a button down. Well, actually it's not really harder, but it draws more attention. People notice when you start unbuttoning your shirt in public. I found a clean t-shirt instead. I changed out of my cut-off sweat pants and put on a pair of my nicer messenger-style shorts. I tried to tame my hair, regretting the floppy Mohawk with all my might. I mean I loved it, but I knew the official people would most likely not love it. Oh well, too late now.

I lifted Gracie from her swing where she had been happily chilling, changed her diaper, put her in a clean flowered onesie, and then tried to convince her to eat a little before we headed out for a day of adulting.

"C'mon Gracie, let's top off your tank, okay?" She nursed for a few minutes, more out of habit than hunger, Hopefully it would be enough to keep her quiet for a while.

I strapped her into her stroller, handed her the bunny blanket toy she loved, and we headed out into the bright September day. The Department of Social and Health Services office was only about half a mile from my house. I remember going there with Sam when I was little. I don't remember it being a particularly fun place to spend a summer day, but oh well. I guess this is what adulthood is all about: spending beautiful days in dreary buildings doing dreary things.

Gracie and I had to cross several intersections between my house and the DSHS office, so by the time we arrived I was dripping sweat. The glass doors slid open and I was temporarily blinded as I waited for my eyes to adjust from the bright sunlight to the dimmer florescent lights. Once inside I regretted not bringing a hoodie. The air conditioning was on high. I pulled a blanket from the diaper bag and draped it over Gracie's bare legs.

The room was filled with chairs and the chairs were filled with people, almost all women. There were little kids everywhere. I hoped none of them were sick. There was a number dispenser up near the front, so I took my number and then found an empty seat to wait. My number was eighty-six and they were only on number fifty-four. I wondered how long this would take. I seriously thought about going home, but I knew that I needed to stay and do this. Not only was it the grown-up thing to do, but I felt like it might also help keep my depression under control.

Two hours later, after feeding Gracie twice, changing her diaper once, and standing and jiggling her forever, they called my number.

A screen over one of the windows lit up with the number eighty-six as the woman behind the desk called it.

I shifted Gracie into my right arm and tried to direct the stroller through the rows of people with my left. The woman called my number again. Her voice was both bored and irritated.

"Number eighty-six. Last call. Number eighty-six."

"I'm here," I called. Anxiety began to flutter in my chest.

I reached the window and sat down in the metal chair, settling Gracie on my lap facing the woman. I thought that maybe if she saw how completely adorable Gracie was, she would be more likely to give me the things I needed. The woman didn't even glance at my baby.

She looked to be about thirty. She had a giant iced Starbucks drink sitting near her computer screen. I bet the drink cost more than what most people here spend on food for one day. The little name plaque at her window read Diane.

"What can I help you with today?" Diane asked.

"Um, I'm here to apply for food stamps and, um, TANF. I need some help with the forms. I started to fill them out, but I got confused." I pulled the half-filled out forms from the diaper bag and slid them towards her. She barely glanced at them.

"This is your baby?"

"Yes."

"I'll need to see your birth certificate, your baby's birth certificate, your social security card, and proof of address. How old are you?"

"I'm seventeen."

"Okay then, if you want TANF I'll need proof that you live with a parent or guardian. If you don't, we will need to approve your living situation."

"I live with my mom."

"Okay, have you graduated?"

"No."

"Are you enrolled in high school or a GED program?"

"Well, not right now, but I plan to be in a month or so. I've been homeschooling since 4th grade. I brought my declaration of intent."

She ignored this.

"How old is the child?"

"Um, twelve weeks, almost thirteen."

"You need to be in school by the time she's twelve weeks."

"Well, I'm homeschooling and I was thinking about doing online school."

"You'll need to be in some sort of schooling to receive benefits. And you do understand that if you're approved for TANF the money will go to your parent or guardian or other approved adult and they will be the ones dispersing it to you, correct?"

"I told you I homeschool and have since fourth grade. But why will my money go to my mom? I'm the mom of my baby."

"You're a minor. Your child will qualify for TANF, and if you meet the criteria you will as well, but because you're a minor you must have an adult payee."

"What if I had abusive parents or like lived on my own?"

"If your parents are abusive we can open up a child protective case."

"No, no my mom isn't abusive." I felt like I might vomit. "I'm just asking what if she were and she kept my TANF money? Like what about teen moms who have abusive parents who would take the money and keep it? Or like what if a teen mom had a parent addicted to drugs or something?"

"You would need to let us know that and we would investigate. Or you would need to move into another qualifying home."

"What's a qualifying home?" I had no idea why I was continuing to push this since it didn't apply to me, but I just couldn't let go of how messed up this was.

"Well any safe home with an adult who is not your boyfriend, unless your boyfriend falls within the approved age range. If you don't have any place that fits that criteria we can place you into foster care."

"That doesn't make any sense," I felt anger rising in me. Like what if my mom treated me terrible and just kept my money for herself? Or what if I was on my own? If I was on my own and needed TANF I would have to go into foster care? " I tried to calm myself. Freaking out on this robot lady would not get me food stamps.

"Can I please see your birth certificate as well as the child's?"

My baby has a name, I thought.

I pulled the birth certificates from the file folder and slid them towards her. She inspected mine and then looked at Gracie's.

"You'll need to list the father if you want to receive benefits."

My stomach clenched. "Gracie's other parent is dead."

"Do you have proof of the father's passing? A death certificate?"

"Gracie's other parent wasn't a father. Gracie's other parent used the they pronoun and identified as genderqueer, or non-binary."

"Excuse me?"

"I said her other parent wasn't a father, they were just . . . they were just her parent, but not a dad. They were non-binary."

"Yes, I heard you. I'm asking what you are talking about. You're saying that her father wasn't a male. I'm not quite sure I understand. There had to be sperm involved and, no offense, you seem a little young to have just walked into a sperm bank and—"

I cut her off. "I didn't. Her other parent was her biological parent but didn't identify as male." My face grew hot. "They weren't male. They were non-binary and used the they pronoun. Their name was Gray Lanstrom."

"Okay, let's try this. Do you have a death certificate?"

"No, I don't."

"Any sort of paternity evidence?"

"No."

"Are you certain that this person was the father?"

I took a deep breath. In. Out. I knew I needed to let go of this father argument, but letting go of it felt disrespectful to Gray, and to Gracie.

"Yes."

"Okay, well this is definitely going to complicate things. I'm going to have to refer this to the Prosecuting Attorney."

"What? Why? What did I do?"

"The prosecuting attorney will send you paperwork to help determine who the baby's father is. It's how things work when there is no father listed on the birth certificate and when the mother is unable or unwilling to name the father. Don't worry, you aren't being accused of a crime."

"I already know who her other parent is. I told you. And I'm not unable or unwilling to name them. I'm telling you they died."

"I don't make the rules. The paperwork will ask you who you had sex with in the past year, if there were any witnesses to the act, if there is anyone who can verify the identity of the father, and things like that. This information will be used to help track down anyone who may be the baby's father and then they will issue a summons for paternity tests. The prosecutor's office will do an investigation in an attempt to locate the father."

"I didn't have sex with anyone else."

"Well, you can put that on the form then."

"I'm telling you who the other parent is and that they died."

"And again, I don't make the rules. Now we can go ahead and issue you food stamps and begin processing your TANF application. You may be approved for TANF while they sort out paternity. Be sure to put down who you want as your payee."

"This is stupid. I'm the mom, why do I have to have someone else handle the money?"

"And again, I don't make the rules. Maybe you should have thought about all of this before you had that baby?"

Breathe in. Breathe out.

I carefully gathered up all of my documents, put them into my file folder, and stood. I calmly placed Gracie back into the stroller, buckled her in, and handed her the bunny. Violence coursed through my veins, but I kept my breathing even. Would it really be so terrible if I picked up this cheap metal chair and broke out a few windows? Maybe screamed right in her smug face? Would all the other people here rise up with me? We could have a little food stamp riot. A class war. Moms and dads and kids tearing the place to pieces while the horrified workers huddled in the corner clutching their overpriced coffees.

But instead of throwing the chair through the window and organizing the uprising of the poor I just said, "Nobody deserves to be treated like this. You may not make the rules, but you could at least be nice. Do you think anyone wants to be here? Do you think anyone wants to ask for help? Just because you're a miserable person with a miserable job doesn't mean you need to try to make everyone else feel bad."

"You need to leave right now."

"Oh don't worry. I'm leaving," I said as I turned the stroller around. "Have fun spending this beautiful day inside being mean to people. I think me and my baby are going to go spend the day at the beach. Have fun wasting your life," I added. Maybe that was immature, but what could she expect from someone who wasn't even old enough to handle their own money?

Mom was right, they were all fascist dicks.

So much for adulting.

Chapter 23

After the horrible experience at the DSHS office Mom suggested I give up on food stamps. Instead she suggested that it might be a good idea to apply for WIC benefits. WIC stands for Women, Infants, Children Nutrition Program. It's this program that gives parents coupons for free food and stuff. It also offers classes on breastfeeding and nutrition and things like that. Mom said they were much nicer than the people at DSHS and admitted that we could really use the free food. Both Sam and Mom had been on WIC back in the day.

I waited for a break in the traffic and was about to jay-walk across the street to the WIC office when a vision of a speeding car crashing into Gracie's stroller flashed in my mind. I decided to walk the extra two blocks to the light. That thought triggered a brief memory of Gray. I shoved it aside hard. I couldn't afford to let those thoughts surface when I was already so nervous.

The WIC office was a tiny storefront in a tiny strip mall on the main highway through the city. As a matter of fact, it was only about six blocks from Gray's spot on the freeway. The office looked pretty bleak from the outside.

I stood outside the hand-print smeared glass door, took a deep breath, silenced my phone, pushed the door open with my back and pulled the stroller in behind me. It was a small room with basic doctor office style chairs lined up along each wall underneath posters of the food pyramid and photos of moms breastfeeding and little kids eating healthy foods. In front of me were two plexiglass windows separating the WIC workers from the clients. There was one woman at the window filling out forms and two other women sitting in the chairs along the wall, waiting to be called. I wasn't sure if I should check in or just sit down.

A girl about my age with a toddler whispered, "If you have an appointment you can just sit down and they'll call you when it's your turn."

"Thanks," I said.

I took a chair and situated the stroller out of the way of anyone coming in or out.

The small table next to me was scattered with all sorts of pamphlets about different services I may qualify for. I looked through them and stuck a couple into my file folder.

"Amanda Logan," the man behind the glass called.

That was me.

I wanted to throw up. After my experience at the DSHS office I felt like I had committed some crime or was lying about something and this guy was going to find out and I would be in big trouble. I said a silent prayer to the universe and the Virgin Mary that these people would not grill me about the blank spot where the father's name should be. I just couldn't handle that again.

I sat down in the chair in front of the window. The man behind the glass smiled a real smile. He seemed to be about forty with thick black hair and a pair of wire-rimmed glasses that made him look both intelligent and like he belonged back in the 1970s. A thick mat of matching black chest hair puffed out of the top of his checkered button-down shirt. I had heard him speaking Spanish to the women before me and his accent told me that English was probably not his first language. His name plate read, Luis.

"Hello, what can I help you with today?" he asked.

"Um, I want to apply for the WIC Program."

"Awesome. Well, you're in the right place. Did you happen to bring the documents mentioned on our website?'

"Yeah, everything is right here," I said as I pulled out the file folder.

"Cool. We're good to go then. I'll have you fill out these forms and then I'll need your child's birth certificate and two pieces of I.D. from you as well as proof of income and address."

"I brought my birth certificate and my social security card. I'm seventeen and still live with my mom, but I brought my hospital bill because it has my address on it. I have my baby's birth certificate and immunization record. I don't have any proof of income because I don't have a job. I homeschool so I brought my declaration of intent to homeschool." My shaking voice exposed my nervousness.

"You nailed it. I love when people come prepared," he said. "Do you need help filling out the forms?"

"I don't think so. Thank you. Do you want me to go sit back down?"

"No, just fill them out here that way if you have any questions I'm right here." He smiled. "While you're doing that I'm going to run in back and make copies of your documents. And while I'm at it I'm going to grab another cup of coffee. I'm having a mid-day crash. Be right back." He winked and disappeared around a corner.

This guy was so nice. Why can't everyone be so nice? He didn't even seem to care that I was only seventeen with a kid. I mean, he's probably used to it, but that lady at the food stamp office was probably used to it too and she was so mean.

I finished filling out the paperwork just as he returned.

"All done?"

"I think so," I said.

He handed me back my papers and then looked over each page of the forms I had just filled out. "Oops, you forgot to sign here."

I scribbled my signature.

"Perfect. Okay come around to that door over there and I'll buzz you in."

I collected my paperwork and slid it all back into the file folder and then slid the file folder into the cargo basket of the stroller. The door buzzed. He pushed it open and held the door for me and Gracie. Then he led us to a room in the back and directed me to have a seat in one of the chairs.

"I'm going to need to weigh your baby and take a few vitals, just to make sure she's healthy. Nothing scary or invasive. If you can just undress her down to her diaper that would be great."

I gently lifted Gracie from the stroller. She blinked awake, yawned, and did that adorable baby stretch. He leaned over to have a look. "Hi there, Gracie. You sure are a cutie pie," he said to her, making her smile. "I love them when they're this age," he said to me. "Good work, Amanda."

"Um, you can call me Banjo. Amanda is just my legal name."

"Sweet. Okay, so if you can just take off her diaper for a second and lay her on the scale, we'll get her weight."

He weighed and measured her and then listened to her heart. Making notes as he went.

"Okay, that's all over with. You can go ahead and get her dressed." He opened up a cupboard filled with plastic bags and handed one to me. "You earned yourself a goody bag."

Inside there was a sippy cup, a baby spoon, a small cookbook, a pen, notebook, a little rattle, a large fridge magnet of the food pyramid, some stickers, a pot holder, a paper growth chart to tack up on the wall, a pamphlet on domestic violence, information on free services I qualified for, and some other stuff. I shook the rattle for Gracie and she immediately reached for it.

"So Banjo, do you breast or formula feed? Or both?"

"Right now I just breastfeed," I said as I tried to slide the wiggling Gracie back into her onesie. I shouldn't have handed her the rattle before I got her dressed.

"Perfect. So for now since you're exclusively breastfeeding I won't give you any formula samples or vouchers. Instead you'll get a little extra to buy foods to keep you healthy and producing good milk. Later if you decide to use formula just let us know and we can change that. Give me one minute and I'll print out your vouchers and then you'll be on your way. We'll be switching to cards sometime next year, but for now we're still stuck with these pesky vouchers."

He returned with an envelope.

"Okay, your vouchers are in here. In that goodie bag you'll find the list of things you can and cannot buy with them. If you have any questions at all don't hesitate to call. We'll need to see you back here in a month for a mandatory nutrition class. Do you feel like you need any breastfeeding support? We have peer counselors on staff that can work with you if you're having any issues."

"I think I'm okay."

"Awesome opossum. Well, you're all done." He extended his hand and we shook.

And that was it.

I opened the office doors into the sunny day. In the short time I had been inside the WIC office I swear the temperature had risen ten degrees. I adjusted the sun shade on the stroller and considered my options. I could head home or maybe Gracie and I could go on our first mother-daughter outing. I had my new food vouchers, a twenty-dollar Starbucks card that I had gotten for Christmas and never got around to using, and a ten-dollar bill in my pocket. I felt rich.

"Where should we go, Gracie? Should we check out the Starbucks? Maybe buy ourselves a fancy coffee drink? We can pretend we work at DSHS. I think I deserve a fancy coffee drink after being such a grown-up, don't you think?"

She didn't object so we turned and headed the opposite direction from home. The Starbucks was about two blocks away.

Even though it was well past the morning rush the place was packed with people. I considered turning around but told myself that this was good for me. I wrestled the stroller through the door and the tables and approached the counter.

"Oh my gosh, what a sweetheart," the barista said, leaning over the counter to get a good look at Gracie. "I just love babies. I used to babysit too. Isn't it just the best?"

It took me a second to grasp what she was saying.

"Um I'm not babysitting. This is my daughter."

Her face twisted around from confusion to realization to something just this side of horror. She didn't even try to hide it.

"Oh wow, there was a girl in my high school who had a baby. She dropped out after her baby daddy left town. So what can I get for you?"

"Um a grande, vanilla, iced cold brew and a berry scone, please," I said handing her my gift card. I didn't know what to say and I didn't know what to do. I felt a twinge of sadness tickling the edges of my good mood.

"Name?"

"Banjo."

"Like the hillbilly instrument?"

"Yeah."

She scribbled my name on the cup.

As I turned to walk to the pick-up counter I saw the girl turn to her co-worker and say something as she nodded her head toward me. The co-worker turned and looked my way. They both laughed.

The tickling sadness melted into shame. Were they laughing at my name or at the fact that I was a mom?

Or both?

A minute later my name was called. I collected my drink and scone and found a table back by the bathrooms and away from the crowd. Before I could even take a sip of my drink Gracie began to scream for food. No warning at all. Great. I pulled her from the stroller as fast as I could, grabbed her blanket and threw it over my shoulder and then tried to attach her to my boob as discreetly as possible.

It wasn't possible.

She was frantic and when she was frantic like this it was near impossible to get her latched on without a struggle. My face burned. I tried to calm the creeping frustration and shame. "Damn it, Gracie," I whispered as I tried to reposition her while also trying to adjust the blanket to conceal us. The blanket kept sliding off my shoulder and onto her face which only made her scream harder. Screw it. I tossed the blanket back into the stroller.

I put her in the football hold and just as I maneuvered her to my boob again, she grabbed my shirt with her tiny fist. She drew her arm up in hungry fury and my naked dripping boob was exposed for all the world to see. Or at least for all of Starbucks to see. I looked up and was met with what seemed to be hundreds of shocked faces, although it was probably only about ten.

I turned my body so that I was facing the bathroom and tried again. This time it took and she began to gulp as if I hadn't fed her in weeks. Tears rolled down my cheeks.

"Excuse me," said a woman's voice.

I turned slightly to see two older women standing at my table.

"Are you okay?" said one of the women. She had to be in her

mid-seventies with the most amazing white hair, which made her blue eyes stand out like little electric beams. She wore a brilliant orange flowered muumuu. Her friend smiled kindly. She was wearing loose Bermuda shorts and a pink t-shirt that said Uppity Women Unite across her flat chest. She wore her long black hair in a thick braid that fell down her back. Her brown eyes were kind.

"Yeah, I'm okay. Thanks."

"Mind if we sit with you?" Muumuu lady asked in a raspy gravel voice.

Before I could answer Muumuu and Bermuda sat down at my table, plopping their giant whipped cream and sugar drinks down in front of them.

"Allow us to introduce ourselves. I'm Ethyl and this here is Rayleen," said muumuu lady.

"Nice to meet you," said Rayleen. "Call me Ray." She had the slight lilting accent of the local Indigenous tribal members.

"Hi," I said, not really sure how to react.

Muumuu Ethyl smiled. "We were behind you in line and saw the whole damn thing. That bimbo barista giving you the stink eye, making fun of your name, and then if that wasn't bad enough that adorable little nincompoop has to go and give you a hard time. Boy or girl? Or maybe you're not doing the gender thing?"

"Um girl. Her name's Gracie."

"Oh good choice," said Bermuda.

"We hope you don't mind that we invited ourselves over. It just looked like you could use a little back up. Lordy when your little titty popped out I thought the entire store was going to drop dead. I bet not one of them has a kid, well other than their fur babies, or whatever it is people call their dogs these days. I don't even know why we come in this joint," said Muumuu Ethyl.

Bermuda Ray snorted.

"So what are you, about eighteen?" asked Ethyl.

"Seventeen."

"Me and Ray here were both eighteen when we had our first kids. It was the summer of love and believe you me that was no joke. We were hippies before capitalism got ahold of it and made it into a fashion statement. Fuck the war. Fuck the police. Fuck the man. That was us.

"You know what they did back in those days? You either had to marry the baby daddy or you got shipped off to a pregnancy home and they forced you to give your baby up for adoption. They lied to us, tricked us, and then stole our babies. It happened to my sister. She got pregnant in high school and my folks shipped her off to a home. She came back nine months later with no baby and a year after that she had herself a nice little heroin addiction."

"My mom told me a little bit about that," I said as I moved Gracie to my other boob.

"And back then they were still stealing Indigenous babies and children, so Ray here was in even more danger than I was. When we found ourselves pregnant in the summer of sixty-seven we weren't about to become one of those lost girls. We packed up my 1958 Datsun Bluebird and hit the road. Like Thelma and Louise before Thelma and Louise, and pregnant, and without the violence, and no cliffs... so I guess nothing like Thelma and Louise now that I think about it.

"Anyhoo, we headed down the coast to California—Mendocino County to be exact—rented a tiny piece of property and a trailer, planted a nice garden and a big ol crop of weed and raised up our babies. We made ourselves a pretty nice living back in the day.

"Ray and I woulda run away even if we hadn't got knocked up. Ray here come from a mama who grew up in one of them Indian Boarding Schools and never was able to find her way after that. And I come from one of those families that's picture perfect on the outside and the definition of dysfunction on the inside. Getting ourselves pregnant just gave us the excuse we needed to get outta Dodge, as they say."

Ray smiled and nodded.

"Wow, that's crazy," I said. I pulled a cloth diaper from the stroller and tossed it over my shoulder as I lifted Gracie to burp her.

"May I?" asked Ray as she reached for Gracie.

"Yeah, sure." I handed Gracie and the burp rag to her. I noticed that her hands shook and for a moment I worried she might drop Gracie, but despite the shaking she lifted Gracie onto her shoulder like a pro and within two minutes she had Gracie burping up a storm.

"You're good at that," I said.

"Oh honey, I've done this more times than I can count. I have six kids and who knows how many grandkids and great grandkids."

"Wow, six kids?"

"Yep, six kids by four different men. Love the one you're with, they used to say, and so I did. Back then if a man took off his pants within a hundred yards of me I'd be knocked up in seconds."

I felt my face redden.

"Rayleen! You're making her uncomfortable."

"No, no, it's okay," I said.

"Well, it's the truth and there ain't no shame in it. You never heard of women's liberation? What's more liberating than enjoying some good sex, am I right?" asked Ray.

I giggled despite myself.

"Well, can't argue with that," said Ethyl. "Then one day we wised up and realized you don't need men for good sex, if you know what I mean." She winked at me as she reached across and took Ray's free hand.

"Amen to that," said Ray.

"Okay, we should get going. We've imposed enough. We just couldn't sit by and watch that ninny behind that counter treat you like that." Ethyl stood.

"Thank you," I said. "I'm so glad you did. Do you guys come here a lot?"

"Oh no, we normally go to Rainbow Grounds. Have you been?" asked Ethyl.

"No, I've never heard of it," I said, wondering how that could be possible.

"Oh it's actually fairly new and up in the north end of the Rucker neighborhood. It's a tiny place, but much better atmosphere than this dump. We generally go to open mic night. Ray here is a poet, and we're almost always there for their Saturday morning scones," said Ethyl.

"Oh I live pretty close to there. Maybe I'll see you?"

"Next open mic is Thursday at six o'clock and Rayleen will be reading for sure."

"Maybe my friends and I will come by," I said, though I knew there was no maybe about it. I was going. Maybe I could even invite Mom and Alice, Sam and Henry too.

Ray laid Gracie back in her stroller.

"I hope you make it," she said. "Maybe I'll write a poem about you." She winked, took Ethyl's hand and they were gone.

I glanced up to see the snotty barista staring at me. I scratched my nose with my middle finger, smiled, left cup and napkin on the table—I was tempted to accidentally spill the remains of my drink—and walked out into the beautiful day feeling pretty damn good.

Chapter 24

"Ugh. When is this heat going to end?" I said as I stood at the sink washing the dishes in cold water. Who cared about sanitation in this sweltering heat? "I have like heat rash under my boobs."

"Dude, this is the new normal, as they say. Welcome to the post climate change dystopian future," Lou said, wiping sweat from his forehead with his ratty green bandana before hoisting himself up onto the counter top.

"I can't deal," I said, tiny surge of panic rising in my chest. Why had I brought a child into this world? What kind of future would she even have on our boiling planet where college doesn't guarantee anything other than a lifetime of debt, and you have to be a millionaire to even buy a shack, and people like Lou are shot by police just for existing, and brown children escaping violence are locked in cages and stolen from their parents, and mama whales carry their dead babies for weeks?

"Don't worry Banj, I'm sure we'll get eight feet of snow this winter."

"Snow would be better than the endless rain we had in spring," I said, swatting at one of the flies that circled like a swarm in our kitchen. It had rained endlessly the entire spring, and not just rain, but monsoon rain. And then the rain had abruptly turned to scorching heat which had led to an explosion of mosquitoes and flies. Mom had to hire some guy to come and make screens for all the windows to keep us from being eaten alive by the mosquitoes. The flies though, they always found a way in.

I felt embarrassed by the cloud of flies. Lou didn't seem to care. It was still hard for me to wrap my brain around how our cruddy house could be better than his beautiful historic home with its shiny floors and granite counters and good smells and views of the water and the mountains. I guess Mom is right when she always says, *it's the people that make a home a home.* Lou's family was as cold as their stone entry way. They were rigid and shiny and unyielding. My family was an old wood floor covered in paint splatters and mud, worn smooth by memories. Love for Mom surged through me.

"Is your mom coming with us?" he asked as if reading my mind.

"Yeah, and apparently Alice is coming too," I said. We were planning to go see Ray's poetry reading later at the little coffee shop up the street. "My mom should be home in a couple hours. I think Alice will meet us there. What time is Dyl coming over?"

"Whenever he gets off work. I'm excited to meet those old lesbians. They sound rad," said Lou.

"They are rad."

"Are like all teen moms lesbians? Or are all lesbians teen moms? Because it sure seems that way hanging out around all of you guys."

"Sam's not," I said.

"Oh yeah, I forgot about that. I guess since she doesn't have a boyfriend I just assumed she was a big homo like the rest of you."

"Who knows, maybe she is," I said. "I mean it wouldn't surprise me."

"It is pretty weird that you and your mom and Alice and Ray and Ethyl are all homo teen moms."

"Yeah," I agreed. "My mom once told me that there was actually some official study that was done in New York that showed that queer teens are more likely to get pregnant than straight ones. It definitely seems to be true around this house."

"I feel sort of left out. Maybe I should get knocked up too." Lou grinned.

"You better not!" I threw wet dish rag at him. He caught it with one hand, nearly toppling off the counter, and then threw it back at me.

"Maybe you could knock me up," he said.

"I'll knock you out if you keep that up," I warned.

"You already knock me out." He waggled his eyebrows at me.

I rolled my eyes.

"Anyway Mr. Smooth, it's an open mic tonight. You should try reading some of your poetry."

"No damn way."

"Why not?"

"Because I hate public speaking, that's why not. Plus, I'm pretty sure my poetry sucks."

"Your poetry does not suck," I said. I had actually only read one of his poems, but it was really good. I mean, I was no expert, but Mom had made me read a ton of poetry over the years and so I thought I knew a good poem when I saw it.

"Who's your favorite poet?" I asked.

"I dunno. I guess I like Tennyson. Oh and also Langston Hughes."

"Do you only know dude poets?"

"Pretty much. That's all we were taught in school. Well, I take that back, we also read Emily Dickenson, but I wasn't so into her. And—damn what was that other chick? Oh yeah, Sylvia Plath. Mostly it was all dudes though. White dudes of course, well I mean other than Hughes."

"Oh man, I don't think I ever read a single poem by a guy. Mom filled my head with all the feminist lady poets when I was little and then later when I was older she and Sam took me to tons of queer slam poetry nights. Those were some of our best times together growing up. I don't think I know any man poets. Or I should say any straight cis man poets. Ever heard Andrea Gibson?"

"Never heard of her."

"Them."

"Never heard of them."

"I think you might love them," I said, drying my hands on the ratty hand towel and pulling YouTube up on my phone. I typed in Andrea Gibson and chose my very favorite poem, "Jellyfish." "Come watch," I said as I sat down at the table.

Lou jumped off the counter and came over to stand behind me at the table. He rested his hands on my shoulders and gently rubbed them as we watched.

"Holy shit," he said when it was over. "How have I never heard of her?"

"Them."

"Sorry, them. How have I never heard of them before? Why didn't we learn them in school?"

"I don't think most schools teach poets like that. Or even teach women or queer or people of color poets in general. Though what do I know, I haven't been to school in a million years."

"No, you're right. They mostly only teach old white dude poets. They throw in Langston Hughes so they can get the black and the gay over with all in one guy. I love his stuff, but damn, Andrea Gibson is a little bit easier to relate to, ya know?"

"Would you skip moon rocks to me?" I asked, referring to my favorite line in the poem.

Lou squeezed my shoulders as he leaned over and kissed my neck. "I'd skip moon rocks to you forever if I could."

Goose bumps exploded on my arms despite the wicked heat of the kitchen.

"Here listen to this one," I said to try to hide my sudden nervousness. "It's called Your Life. I think you might love it."

I felt Lou's hands tighten on my shoulders as the video began and Andrea spit out the first few words of the poem. Halfway through he lifted one hand off of me. I was pretty sure he was wiping away tears. I turned to look up at him. He tried to smile, but it came out twisted and the tears picked up speed. I reached up and put my hand on his hand and turned back to watch the video. When it was over he pulled his other hand away and pushed at the tears. I stood and pulled him into a hug.

"Shit," he whispered into my ear. "The start of the poem, what was it? It isn't that you don't like boys, It's that you only like the boys you want to be. That was me."

I rubbed the back of his head.

"I'm so glad I met you, Banjo. And your family. I've spent my whole life feeling like a freak."

"Welcome to the freak show," I said, accidentally quoting Ani DiFranco.

He pulled back a little and then leaned in for a kiss. We stood making out even though the heat from our bodies mixing with the heat from the day made me dizzy. We heard the front door open and quickly pulled away from each other.

"Oops. Sorry kids," said Mom. "Didn't meant to interrupt."

I wanted to sink into the floor.

"Why are you home so early?" I demanded, my voice sounding unintentionally accusatory.

"The air conditioning broke at work and they had to shut down. I'm going to go take a cool shower. Don't mind me."

"Well that was awkward," said Lou after Mom had disappeared into the bathroom.

"Seriously."

"I love your mom though. She's the best."

I shrugged.

"She is. I bet you never have to worry about being who you are or being rejected by her," he said.

"Well, I don't know. I mean if I were like a Republican she'd probably disown me. Or if I were like a stock broker or a CEO who worked for Exxon she might disown me."

"That doesn't count. Those are good reasons to disown a kid." He smiled.

"Yeah. I know what you mean though. She gets on my nerves a lot and sometimes I think the ways she's crazy has maybe helped make me and Sam crazy too, but I never feel like I can't just be who I am."

"You're lucky. Janice and Doug basically decided who I was supposed to be when they picked me out on the adoption web page and when I didn't turn out to be the appreciative rescue orphan they had their hearts set on they made sure to let me know every day what a disappointment I was." He oozed bitterness.

"How much does it cost to adopt a kid from another country?" I asked.

"Varies, but from what I've been able to tell the average is about thirty thousand dollars. Not sure what Janice and Doug paid for me. It was probably close to that or maybe a little less since it was well over ten years ago."

"Are you kidding me? Thirty thousand dollars? That's insane."

"Yeah and what's really insane is that a lot of the kids up for adoption aren't even real orphans. A lot of them come from poor families who are told that the kids will go to America or Europe and get educated and then they'll come back. The parents are tricked. They don't understand they're giving up their kids. Some kids are actually kidnapped. Some kids are given up because one parent died and the other parent feels like the only hope the kid will have is to be sent to a rich country.

"The worst part is that if all these people who care so much about orphans donated even like a third of that money to the family of the kid they wanted to adopt that kid would be able to stay with their real family and their whole life would change. Like dude, the average yearly income for a person in Ethiopia is something like three thousand a year. I can't remember exactly, but it's really low."

"That's crazy," I said.

"I'm sorry I keep going off about this stuff. I'm just learning so much lately and it helps to talk about it," he said. "I hope I'm not being too annoying."

"I like hearing about it. This is your reality and I want to know everything about you," I said.

He kissed me and went on. "If all these people really cared they'd donate ten thousand, save a family, and then adopt out of foster care here. But people don't want to adopt kids from here because it's harder to get a little kid or a baby, and also there's always the risk that the birth parents might get the kids back before the adoption is final. Adopting from another country means once you get that kid here you have no worries of having to give them back or possibly running into their birth parents at the grocery store or anything like that. Plus, when people adopt from other countries they can run with the whole orphan narrative and look like saviors. It's a joke." Lou's mood seemed to be crashing with this conversation.

"I had no idea."

"Most people don't," he said. "Hell, I didn't have any idea until I started doing research recently."

"Damn, it's so messed up."

"It's beyond messed up. Some people even adopt like six or eight or ten kids this way." Lou let out a long sigh.

"It's not uncommon for adoptive parents to decide they don't want the kid or kids after all and to rehome them. Do you know that up until recently it was legal to rehome kids on craigslist just like when you rehome a pet? I'm not even joking," he said. "They talked about it in that documentary."

"I think I told you about that couple that wanted to adopt Henry? The ones who were going to get the baby from Guatemala, but then decided it would be easier to get Henry?

"You did tell me. If that couple had adopted Hen I would totally go liberate him just like I liberated Petunia Rhubarb," Lou smiled, trying to lighten the mood.

"Ha, I could just see you sneaking into that rich white neighborhood and liberating little Henry," I said.

"I'd do it," he said with enough conviction in his voice for me to know he wasn't joking.

"I know you would," I said, smiling. I loved him so hard.

I suddenly felt so tired.

"I'm exhausted," I said, yawning.

"Why don't you go take a nap? I'll watch T.V. and watch over Gracie in case she wakes up."

I opened my mouth to object, but then closed it. I was so tired.

"You don't mind?" I asked.

"Of course not. Go rest so we can have fun tonight."

"Alright. Wake me up if Gracie needs me or if she gets fussy or hungry or anything. There's also a fresh bottle in the fridge."

"Dude, I can handle it. Just go take a nap, k?"

I smiled. "Okay. Come on Rags, let's go nap."

I kissed Lou and headed to bed with Rags on my heels and my brain swimming with images of kids in orphanages.

Chapter 25

I woke up from my nap to the sound of voices in the living room. I forced myself out of the mid-day nap grogginess that coated me, slid into clean clothes, and joined the pre-poetry party that was happening without me.

"Hey, sleepy head," said Mom as I stumbled into the room. "We were just getting ready to come wake you. Have a slice and we'll head out."

Henry, Dylan, Mom, Lou, and Alice were all hanging out eating delivery pizza. Gracie was asleep in her bouncy seat.

"Guess what? Dylan's mom is coming with," Lou said with his mouth full of pizza.

I turned to Dylan.

"Sh-sh-she called and I told her where we were going and she asked to c-c-come along. Is that o-o-okay?" he asked.

"Yeah, of course. But your mom? Will she be able to handle it?"

"My d-d-dad was a poet, remember?"

"Yeah, but she's super religious now and, I mean, it's a queer/trans poetry night and we are all a bunch of homos and queerdos. Is she up for that?"

He shrugged. "She's b-b-bringing Jacob."

"I'm going to be Jacob's friend," said Henry.

"We definitely need our own reality TV show," I said as I bit into my pizza.

Even though it was less than quarter of a mile from our house it took us over half an hour to walk to the coffee shop, because of Dylan's leg. He was in a walking cast now and used a cane. He was still pretty slow getting around. Mom had offered to drive him, but he insisted on walking. We arrived to find his mom and Jacob standing outside. Sandy had ditched her high-waisted mom jeans and Winnie the Pooh shirt for a tank top and a pair of denim overall shorts. She wore those weird flat Hawaiian sandals that my mom refers to as Jesus cruisers. I noticed that the cross she had worn around her neck that day in the hospital was gone. Her frizzy hair was pulled back in a loose ponytail. When Jacob saw us, he ran to Dylan and wrapped his arms around him.

"E-Easy there, kiddo. W-w-watch my leg." Dylan waved Henry to come forward. "Henry this is Jacob. Jacob, Henry."

The two waved at each other. Henry reached into the pocket of his cut-off shorts and pulled out a deck of Pokemon cards. "Wanna play?" he asked.

"Sure," said Jacob.

"Can we sit out here?" Henry asked Mom.

"It's okay with me, but you better ask Jacob's mom."

"Fine by me," said Sandy. "And by the way, I'm Sandy." She reached her hand out to Mom and then took turns shaking everyone's hands as they introduced themselves.

"S-s-sorry. I sh-sh-should have introduced you all," said Dylan.

We left the kids at an outside table with promises of Italian sodas and with strict instructions not to go anywhere. Mom and Alice went to the counter and ordered our drinks while the rest of us found three small tables to push together.

"I hope they show up," I said, feeling nervous that maybe Ray and Ethyl wouldn't show, but no sooner had the words left my mouth than the door swung open and the two of them flounced in.

"Well look what the cat drug in," Ray said, rushing towards me. She pulled me into a bear hug and then stood back to take in the rest of my entourage. Lou offered his hand, introducing himself, followed by Dylan and Sandy. Mom and Alice came up carrying a tray loaded with drinks and pastries, taking turns introducing themselves. The entire process was repeated with Ethyl's introductions.

Mom invited the two of them to sit with us, offering to buy them drinks. She and Alice returned to the counter with Ethyl and Ray's orders. When they got back to the table Ethyl fished in her pocket and produced a small silver flask. She winked at us as she poured a splash of brown liquid, obviously whiskey, into her and Ray's coffees. She offered a hit to Mom and Alice and they happily took her up on it.

My life was insane.

Ray excused herself to go add her name to the list of performers for tonight's open mic. I tried to talk Lou into doing one of his poems, but he was adamant in his refusal. Mom took Italian sodas out to the kids. Ethyl asked to hold Gracie.

The show began. A puffy-faced bear of a white guy with a long Santa beard was first, reciting his poem about climate change and polar bears. Next up was a pimply-faced Latinx teenager shouting out their spoken word poem about racist police. A nervous woman in her early thirties read her poem about being disowned by her family for being gay, and then finally it was Ray's turn.

She marched up to the stage, adjusted the mic, and then began.

"This poem was inspired by a fierce little queer mama that my partner and I happened to run into on a hot summer day in a corporate coffee chain that shall not be named."

She cleared her throat and began to shout into the mic.

"Patriarchal reversal

Takes what is real

And makes it fake news

Patriarchy says

The banjo is a hillbilly instrument

Poor white trash, they say

When in fact it originated in Africa

Rich history, beautiful tones, culture appropriated

Patriarchy says

Teenage mothers destroy themselves, their children, the world

It forgets that Jesus was born to a teenage mother

We survive, we thrive, we stay alive

We don't compromise, believe your lies, apologize

Patriarchy says

Homo, queer, trans, lesbian, gay

Abominations, deserve castration, practice indoctrination

Fake news and lies

We will not die, let you see us cry, lose sight of the sky

Put matriarchy into all-wheel drive

And patriarchy cannot survive

Smash the state, destroy the hate

It's not too late."

She thrust her fist into the air and flounced off.

The room burst into applause. I jumped up and wrapped my arms around her as she returned to the table. "Oh my god, that was so good."

"You are my muse." She winked, sat down, and drained her whiskey-spiked iced-coffee drink.

The MC came out on the stage "Okay, we have a few minutes left. Would anyone else like to jump up?"

Sandy raised her hand. "Could I?' she asked shyly.

Dylan shot me a terrified look.

"Come on up," cheered the MC.

Sandy climbed up on the small stage, adjusted the microphone, and cleared her throat.

"Um, I don't have a poem or anything at all actually. I didn't come here tonight planning to be up here, but wow you all were just so inspiring. You see I'm a straight Christian lady."

Dylan groaned and put his face into his hands.

"Well, let me correct myself. I'm a straight lady. Not so sure about the whole Christian thing right now. I'll have to get back to you on that." She laughed. The audience laughed with her.

"I just want to tell you all that I've made some big mistakes in my life and I let a man take me away from myself. I let him take away my power and in doing that he almost took away my son. You see my son is gay and I'm okay with that. Being here tonight, well I just feel so full of gratitude. I feel like going right out of here and smashing that patriarchy all to heck."

She raised her fist in the air. "Power to the people." Everyone cheered.

Alice reached over and gave Dylan's shoulder a little squeeze.

Sandy returned to our table and we all told her how brave she was to get up there. Ethyl stared at her for a minute and then shoved the flask towards her. "I think I like you. Care for a swig?"

Sandy hesitated and then grabbed the flask and knocked it back. She coughed a few times and then flashed us a wide smile.

"Yep, I like ya," said Ethyl. She turned to Ray, "We need to invite this lady over."

Ray nodded. "We do indeed." She turned and winked at Dylan. "And this young man as well."

Dylan looked like he might sink into the floor.

We gathered outside around the table the kids sat at. Dylan and his mom wandered away from us to talk.

A few minutes later he hobbled back to us, limping along on his walking cast. He hugged Jacob and told him to go on with their mom. Jacob waved to all of us, then hesitated. After a moment's thought he ran over to Henry and the two of them hugged goodbye. Dylan scruffed his head as he ran by him to join their mom.

"Sh-sh-she asked me again to move back home. And she g-g-gave me this." He reached in his pocket and pulled out a tiny silver dragon with a swirly rainbow stone in its belly.

"That's really sweet. She's trying to fix things," I said.

"I-I-I know," he said.

"Are you going to move back home?" asked Lou.

"No, I'm not ready and I-I-I don't trust her," he said.

"She seems like she's trying," said Mom.

"Sh-sh-she is, but she let me down for a lo-lo-long time."

Mom nodded. Alice put her arm around Dylan.

I thought about Gray's mom and what it must have been like for her. I thought about how Gray's dad made her feel like she was worthless and would never survive without him. I thought about how he held Gray hostage in so many ways. I wondered if Gray's mom had lived if it would have ended up like Dylan's situation. Would Gray have grown to distrust her? Would Gray have chosen to walk away from their mom to save themselves? Gray had said that having their mom die when they were only eleven froze their relationship in time. They never got to know their mom through a teenage or adult perspective and that complicated everything.

There are so many ways we trap ourselves. There are so many choices we make in life that lead to other choices that lead to other choices that sometimes lead us to terrible choices made out of desperation or lead us to no choices at all.

Ethyl had passed Gracie back to me as we left the café and now I adjusted her on my shoulder and nestled my face into her neck. She smelled like baby sweat and slightly sour milk, which is one of the best smells in the world. I breathed her deep into my lungs and vowed right there on the sidewalk that if anyone ever tried to hurt her I would give my life to protect her. I felt an arm slide around my waist. I turned to see Alice.

She smiled. "Motherhood is a real mindfuck, am I right?"

"That's a nice way to put it," I said.

Lou came up behind us, pushing Gracie's stroller with one hand and balancing Henry on his back with the other. I guess it was a good thing Henry was a twig of a kid.

"Miss Gracie's ride has arrived," he said, stopping the stroller next to me.

"I think I want to carry her," I said.

He nodded, and then he and Henry walked ahead, leading the way home.

Mom and Dylan took up the rear. They were deep in conversation. Little snippets floated up to my ears. They were talking about Sandy and maintaining healthy boundaries.

Alice still had her arm around me. I didn't really think of Alice as my obstetrician any longer but rather as an almost step-mom. In the past three months she had spent so much time at the house just doing normal house things. She fixed our leaking sink, she replaced the broken faucet out front, she repaired the garden fence for Mom, and sometimes she came by and made us dinner or took Henry out for the day. She had become part of our lives. The Alice that delivered Gracie, maybe even saved her life, seemed far away. This Alice that was walking down the street holding onto me, the Alice whom I had seen in her underwear one early morning when she was making her way to the bathroom, felt like she had always been a part of my life.

If she stuck around—which I was pretty sure she was going to—she would be Gracie's other grandma. Sometimes I felt overwhelmed at how lucky Gracie was. I hoped that wherever Gray was they can see us now. I hope they know that Gracie is growing up with so much love.

"That was a lot of fun," she said, snapping me out of my thoughts.

"It was. I love Ethyl and Ray."

"They're a hoot. I was telling your mother that we should have them over for dinner some night soon," she said.

"Damn, I forgot to get their numbers."

"Your mom and I did."

I leaned my head on her shoulder. "Thanks Alice."

"No big deal. It was actually your mom who remembered to ask them."

"No. I mean, yeah thanks for getting the number, but I mean thank you for just you know? Being so nice to all of us."

She gave my hip a little squeeze. "No need to thank me, kid. It's an honor to be a part of this clan."

She really is my other mom, I thought.

Chapter 26

The weekend after the poetry night Lou took me and Dylan on another adventure. We pulled up in front of the LBGTQ youth center and my stomach turned inside out.

"I'm not sure I'm up for this."

"Dude, let's just give it a try okay? I mean you've never been to a dance before. How do you know if you'll hate it unless you try it? If you hate it, we'll leave. Pinky swear." Lou lifted his pinky finger into the air

"I-I'd like to check it out actually. I-I've never been to a dance," Dylan said as he leaned on his cane and locked pinkies with Lou. I let out a loud huff and took my turn at the pinky swear.

"Look at this, the homeschooler and the Christian shut-in at their very first dance. Warms my heart," said Lou as he opened the door and climbed out of the car. Dylan and I followed. Lou hit the lock button on his key fob as we stood there staring at the drab brick building. All around us were groups of teenagers smoking cigarettes or leaning on cars or lining up under the huge rainbow made out of balloons that framed the doors.

We took our place at the end of the line. The kids in front of us were passing around a water bottle that I'm pretty certain was not filled with water. The smell of weed hung heavy in the air. The line was a sea of brilliant colored hair: blue, purple, red, orange, black, green, bleach blond, rainbow, you name a color and there was a kid sporting it on top of their head. There were kids in tight sequin prom dresses paired with combat boots and kids in fancy purple tuxedos paired with Converse. There were kids in tutus and kids in tiaras. There were kids wearing rainbow capes and kids with unicorn tails and horns. There were kids in traditional prom dresses and suits. There were a few kids wearing regular street clothes, like us, but even these kids had on elaborate sparkle make-up. I had never seen so much glitter in my life, but then I had never seen so many queer kids in my life.

I wondered if any of these kids had babies.

I wished we had glittered up.

Finally, we reached the door to the building. Just inside we were greeted by two Sisters of Perpetual Indulgence. The Sisters are a group of mostly gay men—though there are a few women—who dress up like drag queen nuns with painted white faces and wimple nun hats. The Sisters do volunteer work on social justice causes, mostly in the queer community. They started in San Francisco, but now we had them in Seattle too, and there was rarely a queer event without at least a few Sisters working.

Lou pulled out three tickets and handed them over to a Sister with a brilliant red wimple and matching red sparkle mini dress. The second Sister flamboyantly took our hands and stamped them with a tiny unicorn stamp before directing us to follow the rainbow duct tape arrows on the floor that would lead us to the main hall.

Lou led the way into the dark room thumping with the beat of dance music. Splashes of light bounced off the disco ball that hung from the center of the ceiling. Boys in fairy costumes, girls in combat boots, and non-binary kids in glitter capes moved their bodies in time to the music. A kid in a unicorn hat and rainbow hoodie was dancing with another kid wearing a formal tuxedo. Off in the corner stood a group of girls and guys and non-binary folks all in formal prom dresses.

I glanced over at Dylan. He had a definite deer in the headlights look in his eyes and his cheeks glowed red. I met eyes with Lou and we both had to look away to keep from laughing. I don't think Dylan had ever even met another queer person in his life until he met Lou and I. This was way outside his comfort zone. At least there was one other person here more out of place than I was.

Lou grabbed me by the hand and led us into the sea of kids. Dylan limped along behind with his walking cast.

"C'mon my queerdos, let's dance!" Lou shouted as he began to move his body wildly to the music.

"Um, I don't dance," I shouted back.

"Me either," yelled Dylan. "And you may have f-f-forgotten that I have a broken leg."

"What? I can't hear you? You're breaking up," Lou yelled back at us.

Dylan and I stood there. Me with my hands jammed into my pockets. Dylan leaning on the cane. I was grateful that Dylan was as awkward as I was.

Lou wiggled his way up to us and yanked my hands out of my pockets while grinning like a maniac. He then took me by the arm pulled me so the two of us were facing Dylan and he began to dance up to Dylan and then back again. "Move your shoulders," he yelled, "and loosen up those knee caps."

"M-m-my leg is broken," Dylan yelled.

"Then move your one good knee cap," Lou yelled back.

Dylan and I grudgingly began to sway our bodies to the beat of the music.

"That's it. Now move those feet. Stop being such self-conscious sticks in the mud. I mean Jesus, look around you. This place is filled to the brim with misfits and weirdos. Chill out and relax. This is supposed to be fun. Look at that guy," Lou shouted as he pointed to a glitter-covered boy lost in some sort of made-up interpretive dance. The boy spun around the room, oblivious to his surroundings. "Stop being such old men. My grandpa is more fun than you two and he's dead."

Dylan and I did as we were told and began to mimic Lou's body movements.

"Yaaassss! You old dudes are doing it. Grandpa Banjo and Grandma Dylan are crashing the gay partay."

Lou started play boxing us. "I call this the box trot. C'mon try it."

Dylan and I laughed as we began to play box with Lou. Soon we were surrounded by kids box trotting. An adorable Latinx boy in a pink tuxedo boxed his way up to Dylan and began sprinkling glitter on his head. Dylan turned the color of a fire truck, but he didn't stop box trotting, as a matter of fact after throwing a quick wide-eyed glance towards us, he hobble-danced off into the crowd with Glitter Boy.

"You aren't going to box trot off into the sunset with some gender-bending girl-boy and leave me, are you?" Lou yelled into my ear.

I playfully punched him on the arm and was about to connect with my other fist, when he grabbed my wrist and pulled me in for a kiss.

"It's a knockout!" he shouted.

We danced like this for two more songs and then made our way through the crowd to the refreshment area. Lou bought us a couple of lemon La Croix, two homemade chocolate chip cookies, and a bag of chips. We went and found a couple of chairs near the door and sat down to eat.

"Thanks," I said.

"How could we turn down homemade cookies and hipster water?"

"No," I said, "I mean thanks for all of this. Thanks for dragging me out and making me box trot."

"Don't mention it, Gramps."

"I mean it," I said.

"I know. I'm glad you agreed to come."

"I may have to go soon though. I can feel my boobs getting bigger. I really don't want to spring a leak here." Mom had offered me nursing pads soon after Gracie was born. I had rejected them after trying them one time. It was like having maxipads in your bra, but now I sort of regretted not using them. I was having fun and I didn't want to leave.

"Ha. Can you imagine the looks on these kids' faces if you started spraying milk everywhere? They'd probably think it was some sort of performance art or something."

"Would you be mad if we left soon?"

"Of course not. Let's go find Dylan."

We gathered up our snacks and went back into the throng of kids to find Dylan. We found him sitting across the room with the boy he had box trotted off with. He didn't notice us approaching. "Hey, we gotta be heading out pretty soon. Maybe just one or two more songs and then we have to go," said Lou.

"A-a-already?"

"Yeah sorry," I said, "but um, I'm about to spring a leak."

Dylan's face went scarlet.

"The bathroom is back behind the snack bar," said the boy.

"Uh thanks, but that's not the kind of leak I'm talking about."

He glanced at Dylan, confused. "I could drive you home. I mean, if you want to stay longer," said the boy.

Lou reached out his hand, "I'm Lou and this here is Banjo." The boy stood and took Lou's hand.

"Oh s-s-sorry." Dylan's embarrassment grew. "These are m-my friends. Banjo, Lou, this is Isaac."

"Nice to meet you both," he said, reaching for my hand. He turned back to Dylan, "Really man, I can give you a ride. It's no problem."

"W-would you g-g-guys mind?"

"Have fun, Dyl. Don't do anything I wouldn't do." Lou winked at him before pulling him into a bear hug.

Next it was my turn to hug him goodbye. "Isaac's adorable," I said into Dylan's ear, trying to quietly shout so he could hear me over the music, but not loud enough for Isaac to hear.

"I know," he yell-whispered back.

"I heard that," said Isaac smiling. "Nice to meet you all," he said as he and Dylan sat back down.

"You too," Lou and I said in unison.

We left them to gaze into each other's eyes. I guess there was no need to follow up on creating his dating profile.

"How about one more song before we go?" asked Lou as he took my hand and led me through the crowd.

Just then Bruno's Mars *Just the Way You Are* came on. Lou spun around and grinned at me. "It's a sign," he shouted. Lou loves Bruno Mars. He confessed that dirty little secret to me back on that first day when we met in the ward. Lou—Pru back then—came up to me as I was curled up on the couch that first terrible day and literally poked me in the back demanding I talk to him. And then he confessed his love of Bruno Mars and Celine Dion. We became instant friends.

He pulled me out onto the dance floor and began singing along while doing some sort of free-form dance. He clutched his chest and slid up to me. "Cuz you're amazing…" he sang and then he twirled around, landing on one knee in front of me. He took my hands in his, "your eyes your eyes," he shouted as he jumped up and danced around me. A crowd started to gather around us singing along until there were at least twenty kids watching, swaying, clapping out the beat, and serenading me as Lou's backup singers. Part of me wanted to sink into the floor and disappear, and yet I couldn't stop smiling. Nothing like this had ever happened to me before.

I felt love for Lou surging through me.

He grabbed my hand and pulled me to his chest. We finished off the song with him holding me pressed against his body as the crowd continued their clapping and singing. I rested my chin on his shoulder and closed my eyes. When the song was over the kids burst into applause and cheers and then scattered back out across the dance floor.

I pulled back from Lou and looked into his eyes. My smile felt like it might swallow my face. "That was amazing. You're amazing." I giggled. I didn't mean to giggle, but it somehow just fell out of my mouth. Lou returned my face-swallowing smile with one of his own.

"Aww shucks," he said, looking down and dramatically kicking at the floor.

He looked up and our eyes met, and our smiles evaporated. I felt so uncomfortable just staring into those deep brown eyes, but I couldn't look away. Finally, he leaned in and kissed me. It was a kiss that felt like it came with something more. When the kiss ended we just stood there staring at each other. My words dried up and my heart was pounding in my chest. And then I felt the heat in my nipples, but it wasn't the kind of heat you expect in your nipples after a really good kiss. The kind of heat that was surging through my breasts was the kind of heat that only meant one thing: it was past time for Gracie to eat. A Niagara Falls of milk began to flow from my breasts. Wet spread across my shirt.

Lou stepped back and stared at my chest. "I could make some completely inappropriate comment about the effect my kisses have on you."

"Don't," I said, unwrapping the flannel from my waist and pulling it on to hide the stains.

"I take it this is our cue to leave?" He laughed as he took my hand and we headed for the door.

We walked out into the cool night air. Fall was starting to finally take hold.

"We had our own private wet t-shirt contest," he said.

"I'm sorry."

"What are you sorry for? This was the absolute perfect ending to the best kiss of my life. I mean, I can tell you I will never forget this night. Your leaky breasts sort of fascinate me."

I started to say something and then caught myself just in the nick of time.

He noticed. "What were you going to say?"

"Nothing."

"You were going to say something. I saw the look in your eyes and you started to say something. What were you going to say?"

I couldn't look at him, so I just kept walking.

He stopped. "Hey, what were you going to say?"

I stared down at my feet. He took my chin and lifted my face, so I had no choice but to look at him. It was obvious that he knew damn well what I almost said, and he wanted to hear me say it.

Heat crawled up my face as milk ran from my boobs. "I'm in love with you."

I don't know why this was so hard for me to say. Maybe because I felt so serious about it. It felt so real and every day I seemed to feel it stronger than the previous day. It's scary to love someone this way. And even scarier when you have a kid that has a tiny heart that could be broken if you mess it all up.

He swallowed hard and then burst into tears. "I'm so in love with you too," he said. And then he leaned in and kissed me again which of course changed the slow river of milk into a level five rapid.

Chapter 27

ou and I sat on my bedroom floor drinking iced coffee and eating chocolate cookies. He was in one of his hyper moods. I could tell he was trying to keep his cool, but his bouncing leg and wide dancing eyes gave him away. I was reminded of that first day we met in the hospital.

"So I think I found a searcher," Lou said. "Last night Neela helped me go through the list of people that she said are legit. I started emailing them this morning. One guy already got back to me and he was the top person on her list."

"Really? That's so exciting."

"Yeah. He sounds okay and he doesn't charge as much as some of the others. Neela knows people who have used him, and she says he's awesome."

"Wow, so it's really happening? Are you nervous?"

"I'm puke-my-guts-out-and-collapse-into-a-quivering-heap nervous. I need about 30 Xanax and like a back rub and maybe a shot or eight of whiskey. Dude, I'm so scared. I mean, like I could find out who and where my real mom is in just a couple of weeks. And I'll be able to find my sister and maybe other relatives. I almost can't wrap my head around it."

I crawled the few feet over to him. "I'm fresh out of Xanax and whiskey, but I can rub your back." I maneuvered myself behind him and began working my fingers on his shoulders.

He let his head fall forward. "Man, that feels so good."

I dug into his shoulder muscles. "You have so many knots. You're all twisted up."

"All twisted up over you," he turned around to grin at me.

I play-smacked him on the side of the head, "Whatever. You better knock it off if you want a back rub."

"Okay, okay," he ducked his head back down.

I worked my fingers up and down his back, paying special attention to his shoulder blades and neck. "You should take off your shirt."

"Whoa, you're smooth."

"Do you want another smack?"

"Um, yes please."

"Oh my God."

He pulled his t-shirt over his head. He still had his binder on, but without the shirt it was much easier to really dig into his twisted-up muscles. It was hard not to stare at those muscles.

"So, will you come with me?" he asked.

"With you? To Ethiopia, you mean?"

"Yeah. If I pay for it, will you come with me?"

"Lou, I can't come with you. I can't leave Gracie."

"Bring her."

"No, that's not safe. She's too little and she'd probably need a bunch of shots and that could be dangerous. I don't want her to be pumped full of all sorts of unnecessary vaccines that might make her sick. And besides dragging a baby along will just make things harder. Plus, it's not super safe for queers there. I'm pretty sure this new haircut will tip them off."

"Yeah, I guess you're right."

"What about Dylan? You should totally take Dylan" My stomach curled up thinking about Lou and Dylan halfway across the world together and me all alone here.

"I wonder if he's allowed to go on vacation? Like do you think they'd kick him out of the halfway house if he took off for two or three weeks?" he asked.

My fingers froze on Lou's back, "You'll be gone that long?"

Lou turned around to look at me, "Yeah dude, I mean it's a long way to go and I'll be seeing my family."

"Yeah, of course. I mean I know. It's just . . ." I looked down, feeling my face flush with embarrassment and the threat of tears, "I guess I'll just miss you. That's a long time."

Lou put his fingers on my chin and lifted my face. I tried to keep my eyes down on the floor, but I couldn't help it and looked into his eyes. A tiny smile played at the edges of his eyes.

"You'll miss me?"

Hello tears.

"Oh hey, don't cry." He pushed the tears off of my cheek with his thumb. "I'll miss you too, Banj." The tears came fast now, faster than his thumb could keep up with. He pulled me into a hug. I wrapped my arms around his bare shoulders and heat surged through my body. I felt his lips on my neck, a tiny kiss that I wasn't even sure was a kiss. I held my breath.

"I love you," he whispered into my neck.

"I love you too," I said.

The smile that played along the edges of his eyes spread across his face. He slid his finger under my chin again and gently pulled me towards him as he leaned in and kissed me on the mouth. Heat shot through my body and suddenly I wanted nothing more than to be right here right now kissing Lou. His hands slid from my chin to the flat part of my chest just above my breasts. His hand rested there for a minute before it slid down and cupped my right breast. The heat grew. He squeezed my breast as his thumb massaged my nipple. I felt ready to explode with desire and then it happened; I felt my breast release the flood gates. I tried to pull away, but it was too late; a fire hose of hot milk shot directly into Lou's hand.

I wanted to die.

I wanted to vanish.

I wanted to sink right into the floor.

Lou pulled his hand away not quite understanding what was happening.

"Oh god! Kill me now," I said as I covered myself with my arms.

"Whoa! That is so freaky."

Shame washed over me. "I'm sorry."

"No, don't be sorry. That's like . . . amazing. Seriously, wow. Like obviously I've seen the results of your leaking many times, but to actually feel it happen? That's so cool. It sprays out. I had no idea."

I wanted to disappear. "How is that cool?"

"Like I don't even know, that's just . . . wow. I mean, obviously I know those things leak like a firehose when you're late feeding Gracie, but experiencing it first hand, as they say, well it's so cool. You make food." He sounded enthralled.

Just then, as if she could sense her dinner was ready, Gracie woke up and began to fuss and my other boob let loose. A dark stain spread across the other side of my shirt.

"Ah shit." I couldn't believe this was happening.

Lou rushed over and picked up Gracie and handed her to me "Plug the dyke, Baby G, plug the dyke."

"You think you're so damn funny," I smiled as I lifted my shirt and slid Gracie onto my left boob. I had to admit it was pretty funny. I mean it was mortifying and horrifying and probably not something that has happened to a whole lot of seventeen-year-olds who are trying to make out with someonc, but it's hard to deny that it was also hilarious. I bet

Lou never forgets this make-out session.

"You know what I love about all of this?" he asked.

"I'm sort of afraid to ask."

"What I love is that here I was talking about going to Ethiopia to find my family, and like how many eighteen-year-olds do you know who need to go to Ethiopia to find their families? And then I finally, finally, finally get up the guts to like do more than just kiss you and your boobs go all cray cray and shoot laser beams of milk all over the place. This is so not normal. You do realize that, right?"

"Yeah, I may have noticed."

"You know what else?"

"There's more?" I asked as I broke Gracie's latch and popped her onto the right boob to try to stop the slow leak that was still going on.

"Yes, there's more."

"Spill." Realizing too late my poor choice of words.

"You're going to miss me." He grinned.

My face flushed.

"Ha! And you're totally blushing."

I leaned down and whispered in Gracie's ear, "Do not listen to Uncle Lou."

"Uncle?"

Ugh, I felt my face light up even more.

"We need to think of a name for me. I don't think I want to be Uncle Lou. I mean, is that okay?" Suddenly the tables turned and he was the one fumbling and blushing.

"I was just joking about the uncle thing. We should totally pick a name for you. I mean, as long as you plan to stick around." I kept my eyes on Gracie as if it took all of my concentration to keep her stuck to the boob.

I glanced up to see hurt painted across his face. "I'm sorry. I don't know why I said that," I said.

"It's okay," he said in a way that made me know that it wasn't okay. "Maybe I should look up names in Amharic, that way maybe Gracie could learn to speak two languages. We could learn together."

"That would be so rad if she spoke Amharic. What would you want her to call you? Like what label do you want instead of uncle?"

His face flushed and he looked away. "I don't know. This is dumb. She should just call me by my name."

"No seriously, let's pick something and then if you want to translate it into Amharic we can."

"I guess I need time to think about it. It's no big." He smiled. I knew he didn't need time to think about it. I had a feeling he knew what he wanted to be called but was afraid to say. And I knew it was a big deal.

"Papa?" I offered.

His smile dissolved. "Don't joke around like that. That's not funny. Seriously, okay?" I saw the tears build up and fight to break free.

"Lou, I'm not joking. You'd make a cute Papa."

He stared at me.

"I'm not trying to be funny."

"You'd let her call me Papa?" he asked.

"Sure. I mean, unless that's not okay with you. I mean . . . I guess I shouldn't assume that's what you want . . . I uh, ugh, I'm sorry. What do you want her to call you?" I stumbled over my words. Suddenly it felt like the air was made of awkward and every breath I took just intensified it.

"How about Bapa?" he asked.

"Bapa." I smiled.

Chapter 28

woke up drenched in sweat, sandwiched between Rags and Gracie. The air hung heavy with early fall humidity and being squished between two bodies, one of them seriously hairy, was a particularly bad idea. Brilliant sunlight shone through my thin curtains. What I wouldn't do for a few days of rain. This heat and humidity was just getting to be too much but thank god I wasn't pregnant during this horrible heat. And thankfully the nights were finally beginning to cool down. There was an end in sight.

I rolled over and looked at my phone. It read 10:24 am. How had I managed to sleep so long? Actually, I knew the answer to that. Gracie had been up almost the entire night. I think we finally fell asleep around five. The sun was up and the birds were singing when we finally drifted off.

I rolled over to stare at my baby for a while. I loved watching her sleep. She was flat on her back with her arms and legs thrown out in all directions. Her little face contorted as she tried to wake up. She crinkled up her nose, smacked her little lips, and occasionally opened her blue eyes just the tiniest bit, before she finally opened them all the way and blinked up at me.

"Hello Sweaty McGee, did you sleep well?"

Her face erupted into a smile which caused my heart to erupt in love.

I turned back to my nightstand and grabbed my phone. I unlocked it and was met with a stack of notifications. Four missed calls and two voice messages from Lou, plus a text. Lou never leaves me voice messages. Something was wrong.

I started with the text.

Where are you? He found her! He found my mom! Please call me. I'm freaking out! Call me!!!!!!!

I sat up and shivered despite the thick heat.

Lou found his mom. I should be happy. Why did I suddenly feel terrified? And how did it happen so fast? I thought it would take months, not days.

I stared at my phone. I felt paralyzed. I couldn't bring myself to listen to the messages. I was not prepared for him to find her so quickly.

I closed my eyes and tried to concentrate on my breathing. In. Out. In. Out.

Gracie began to quietly fuss, letting me know that she needed her second breakfast. Okay, I decided, I'd feed her and then call Lou. I lifted Gracie to my chest and just then there was a knock at my door.

"Come in."

Lou burst through the door.

Rags jumped off the bed and rushed to jump all over him with her tail swinging. Lou kneeled, "Hey Ragsy, hey girl," he said as he ran his hands up and down her greasy back. He looked up at me. "Why didn't you answer?" he asked, holding back tears.

"I'm sorry. I just woke up. I literally just saw your text. Are you okay?"

"I don't know. I don't know. I. Don't. Know. The searcher found my mom," he said, standing and with that dismissing Rags who flopped onto the floor and began to suck on her gross feet.

"Banjo, he found my mom. She's alive. And I know my name. My name is Grace. Can you even believe it? Grace. That means something. It means something that me and Gracie have almost the same name and also like me and Gray . . ." His hands were shaking as much as his voice.

"Are you serious?" It seemed impossible that Lou's name could be the same as Gracie's and yet it also made sense in the way that all the crazy shit in my life made sense.

"Isn't it wild? Like my name is Grace and you named your baby Gracie and then there was Gray and . . . Jesus Banjo, they found her. They actually found her. They found my mom. And I practically have the same name as Gracie," he repeated. " I don't know what to do. I have a baby sister. My dad is dead or, maybe not dead, but he's disappeared." His words tumbled out of his mouth so fast and scattered that it was hard to keep up.

"I need to find my passport and apply for a visa. I need to be ready to go there," he said, more to himself than to me. "I have to tell Janice and Doug. I have to be ready."

"What's your mom's name?" I asked. I didn't want to hear about the details of him leaving.

"Niyyat."

He burst into tears. I laid Gracie down on the bed and went to him. Gracie was not happy to have her breakfast suddenly taken away, but I ignored her fussing. I pulled him to me, rubbing my hands up and down his back, hoping to calm the trembling.

"So now what?" I asked into his neck. "What happens next?"

He pulled back and began to pace, taking deep deliberate breaths. I picked up the increasingly frantic Gracie and resumed feeding her. Lou stopped and leaned against my door.

"The searcher is going to try to arrange for me to skype with my mom. She lives in a tiny village, so they have to arrange for her to travel to a place with a computer and internet. He said it shouldn't be too hard. She still lives in the house where I was born. The searcher asked her to bring my sister so I can meet her . . . or remeet her I guess would be more accurate." He closed his eyes and took a deep breath. "Will you be there when I meet them?"

"Yeah, of course," I said, though I couldn't even imagine what it would be like to be there. We sat in silence for a while, listening to Gracie slurp away. When she was finished Lou reached for her.

"Can I hold her?" he asked.

"Yeah, you don't have to ask. You know that."

He looked at me as if we didn't speak the same language. He was flying so hard and fast that he was only half here. He lifted Gracie so they were face to face and kissed her on the forehead. "I'm so glad you have her," he said, smiling through the tears that were flowing again.

I knew what he meant was, *I'm so glad that you didn't give her up for adoption*, but his words didn't upset me. I was glad too and I knew he had been right all along. I had once thought that the only way Gracie could have a chance in life was to give her up. Lou was completely against that and let me know every chance he could. It used to piss me off when he would start in, but now I know that I had been wrong and he had been right.

I tried to imagine my life without Gracie. I tried to imagine what I would be doing right now if I had given her up to that gay couple I had chosen. Thinking about life without her caused a wave of shame to wash over me, so I changed the channel in my brain. Instead I tried to imagine Lou as Grace. I could see it fitting. I mean, fitting back when Lou was Pru. Why in the world would Janice and Doug change his name from Grace to Prudence? Grace was such a good name.

"Do you think your mom is going to understand that you're a guy now? I mean, are you going to tell her?"

"I've been thinking about that a lot. I don't think so. Not now. Maybe not ever. It's illegal to be gay in Ethiopia, probably illegal to be trans too. Like you can go to jail for being gay."

"Are you serious?"

He nodded.

"I'm scared for you to go there. What if they find out you're queer? What if you get arrested? Or worse . . ." I felt sick to my stomach.

"I know. I've thought about that. I was thinking that maybe I could figure out a way to take Dylan with me. Like pretend he's my boyfriend or something. I don't know. Don't worry though, I'll be safe. I haven't even talked to her yet, so don't worry. Okay?"

I tried to breathe. What if Lou went to Ethiopia and got killed, or raped, or arrested? I couldn't lose Lou. I couldn't lose one more person. I just couldn't. Maybe it was selfish of me, but the idea of losing Lou after already losing Gray was just too much. I would be a nervous wreck the entire time he was gone and I probably wouldn't even be able to text him or call him. I would have no idea if he was safe or dead or in jail.

I could feel my lungs shrinking. I felt dizzy.

And then another thought hit me: what if his mom rejected him after all of this? What if she had actually wanted to give Lou up? What would that do to him? If she rejected him, I might lose Lou in a completely different way.

He placed his hand on my thigh while balancing Gracie in the crook of his other arm. "Look," he said, "try not to worry, okay? I mean, who knows what will happen when we skype. I just want to take this one step at a time. I can't think too far ahead right now. I mean I do keep future tripping, but I know that anything can happen."

He shouldn't be comforting me right now. I should be the one comforting him. I didn't say anything.

He lay back on the bed and lifted Gracie over his head and began to baby talk to her. "I don't even know, Grace Grace. Maybe my mom won't even like me. Maybe this is all a big dumb mistake. Tell your mama to chill the hell out. One step at a time," he said. Gracie's face erupted into a huge smile as a large blop of spit up fell out of her mouth and right onto Lou's face.

"Thanks a lot, Gracie," he said as he sat up.

I couldn't help laughing as I wiped the breastmilk puke off of his face with a t-shirt that I pulled from the pile of clean clothes at the foot of my bed.

"Damn. I found my mom," he said to me, while keeping his eyes on Gracie.

"You did," I said as I tossed the spit up t-shirt to the corner of my room. I sat down next to him so our thighs were touching, even though it was far too hot to be touching anyone. "I'm happy for you."

"But?"

"But nothing. I am," I said, trying to keep my voice even.

"Dude, you suck at lying."

"I'm not lying," I said defensively.

"Okay, maybe you aren't lying. Wrong choice of words, but something is bothering you." He turned his gaze from Gracie to me. I felt like he could see right through me.

"I am happy for you. I really, really am. It's just that . . . it's just, well I don't know."

"You do know. Tell me. Please?" he kept his soft brown eyes on me.

"I'm just worried is all. What if something bad happens to you there? I would have no way of even knowing. And we probably can't text or anything." God, I sounded like a whiny baby. Here he had finally found his mom after all these years and I couldn't even let him have his moment.

"I'll be okay. I promise. And we can text. I already looked into it and I can change my phone plan. We won't be able to text much, but I can at least check in once a day." He smiled at me. "Is there anything else bothering you?"

I swear sometimes I felt like he could read my mind.

I shook my head, keeping my eyes on the floor.

"Banjo, look at me. Please tell me what's bothering you," he sounded almost calm.

"I'm just afraid that . . . that you might decide to stay there or maybe you'll change and decide that, I don't know, that you don't like me or that—"

He cut me off. "Dude, I swear to God I won't stop liking you. I actually think this might be good for us."

"Good for us?"

"Yeah, I mean this whole mom thing is always on my mind. I'm always thinking about it. I'm always wondering where she is, if she misses me, why she gave me up, or even if she's still alive. I'm wondering when my real birthday is. I'm wondering if I look like her. Do we have things in common? There's just always been this huge piece of me missing. Up until I met you and Dyl, I never felt like I belonged anywhere. Finding the two of you pretty much saved me. You guys are like my first real friends, but even after finding you guys I still feel this particular sort of loneliness that I can't really explain. Hell, just knowing my birth name feels like a damn miracle.

"So, my point is that maybe finally having these answers will fill up some of that hole in me and I'll have more to give you. I'll be more me than I am now and . . . I don't know. Am I making any sense here?"

"Yeah, that makes sense. Just please be careful, okay?"

He leaned in and kissed me softly at first and then more intently. Warmth rushed through me, especially to one particular place. It felt good.

He kissed his way to my ear. "You're my family. You and Gracie. And your mom and Henry, even Sam. And Dylan too, of course. And Alice. I'm not going to forget you or stop loving you. I need to know my mom and I need to find my first family, but that doesn't mean you won't be my family," he whispered. Then he gently bit my earlobe sending the most wonderful electricity shooting through me.

I turned my face to catch his lips again. Gracie squirmed in his arms and I pulled away. We both looked down at her.

"I think she's jealous," he said.

"Nah, she's not jealous. It's just awkward. No kid likes to see their parents make out," I said.

Lou smiled. "Parents?" he asked.

I felt the embarrassment crawl across my cheeks. "Well, I mean yeah. I mean..."

"Shhhh," he whispered and kissed me one more time.

Chapter 29

ou sat at the kitchen table with his MacBook open in front of him. Dylan and I sat on chairs on either side of him. Mom, Sam, and Alice stood behind us, leaning over our shoulders to see the screen. Henry sat on Dylan's lap. Gracie snoozed in her car seat at our feet. Rags was next to her.

Lou took a deep breath. "Okay, it's going to be any minute. Are you all ready?" he asked. The skype call was supposed to come in at noon, ten o'clock at night in Ethiopia. It was already twenty past noon.

"Are you ready, sweetheart?" asked Mom.

Lou turned to look at her, rolled his eyes, and shrugged his shoulders. "Hell if I know," he said. "It's almost twelve-thirty. Do you think something went wrong? Maybe she changed her mind." He tried to keep his voice calm, but we could all hear the rising panic in his voice.

"She'll call. Don't worry about it, sweetie. I imagine getting connected to the internet there is a little different than here," Mom said as she placed her hand on Lou's shoulder.

Lou pressed his palms into his eyes and stayed that way, taking slow even breaths. Mom rubbed her hand up and down his back. I put my hand on his knee.

"She's going to call," I said. "She is."

Lou didn't move. He just sat slumped in his chair, his elbows on the table and his face pressed into his hands.

Suddenly the room erupted in the *boop boop boop. Boop boop boop bedoop* that was the skype ring tone.

"Oh my shit," moaned Lou. "What do I do? What do I do?"

"You answer," we all said at the same time, as if we had rehearsed this for days.

He clicked the mouse and the screen filled up with the image of a woman who looked to be about my mom's age. She wore a bright colored scarf tied loosely around her close-cropped hair. She was wearing a matching loose-fitting dress. One look at her and there was no mistake that this was Lou's mom. Next to her stood a girl about thirteen or fourteen dressed in a hot pink Nike t-shirt and cut-off jeans. She wore her hair in cornrows. She looked like Lou's younger twin.

When the woman saw Lou she burst into tears. She began repeating Lou's Ethiopian name over and over again, "Grace. Grace. Grace."

"Mama. Mama. Mama," Lou repeated back to her.

The teenage girl smiled, but her eyes looked afraid.

The woman began to speak, but none of us could understand her. The girl began to translate.

"Mama says, I love you. I love you. Are you okay? Are you safe?"

"You speak English?" Lou asked, although it was pretty obvious that she did.

"Yes, I spent time in the orphanage and they taught us English there."

"They do," Lou said nodding. "I remember."

"Please tell her I'm okay."

The girl translated and the woman brought her hands up to her face and began to cry again.

"Tell her I love her and I've missed her."

Again the girl translated. The woman held her hand over her face and nodded as her sobs increased.

"What's your name?" asked Lou.

"I'm Hana."

"Do you remember me?"

The girl looked embarrassed. "No, but our mother told me all about you."

"Are you guys okay?"

"Yes, we are now. I had to go to the orphanage for a while. Papa sent me when he lost his job. Mama said he was afraid there wasn't enough food and he thought the orphanage would give us both better lives. He didn't know we would be adopted; he just thought we would be going to America to go to school and then we'd be back. About two months later he went away to find work and never came back. When he didn't come back Mama came and got me."

Lou nodded, unable to speak.

The woman pulled her hands away from her face. She swung her hand back and forth in front of the camera and said something.

"Mama wants to know if this is your family," said Hana.

"No. I mean sort of. These aren't the people who adopted me, but they're like my family." Lou introduced each of us, referring to me as his best friend and to Dylan as his boyfriend, which made jealously surge through me. I knew he had to do that. He had to be Grace, the long-lost daughter with a nice American boyfriend. It still stung.

Everyone said their hellos and nice to meet yous. Lou's mom smiled big and waved.

She spoke again.

Hana translated. "She says you are all very beautiful. She says she would like to meet you one day. She says thank you for taking care of her daughter. She says Grace, can you come to see us?"

"Yes, yes. I want to come. I want to be with all of you. I want to hug you," said Lou.

Hana translated and then asked, "Is it nice in America?"

"It is nice, but it's complicated. Some things aren't nice. It can be dangerous. What's it like there?" Lou asked.

"It's hard here. We are very poor and there isn't enough food, but we get by," said Hana.

Lou nodded. "I want to come see you and see our home."

Lou's mom didn't take her eyes off of Lou. She spoke again.

"She asking what we were saying," said Hana before translating for their mom.

The woman nodded and smiled. "My Grace," she said in English.

"Do you, or I guess I mean, do we have any other brothers or sisters?" asked Lou.

Hana translated and then answered. "We had an older brother Kofi. He died when I was eight."

"Will you ask our mom who took me to the orphanage?"

Hana translated.

The woman began to cry. It took a while before she began to speak and she spoke for a long time. Hana translated.

"She says that our father's brother took you. She said she had gone to the market with me and when she came home you were gone. She ran three miles towards the orphanage to try to find you. She caught up with our uncle and begged him to let you go, but he said our father had demanded it. He said there wasn't enough food and you would be safer there. She did not want you to go. She says she lost half of her heart that day."

"Tell her I remember. I remember her running after us and I remember she told me she loved me." Lou's voice shook.

Hana translated and Nyla reached her hand up towards the screen as if to touch Lou. Lou began to sob and the woman's sobs matched his. Lou reached his hand up as if to touch his mom's hand.

I realized I was crying too. I glanced around to see that Dylan, Henry, Mom, Alice, and Sam also had tears running down their cheeks.

"She looks like you," said Henry.

Lou looked at him and smiled through his tears. "We do look alike."

A man stepped in behind Lou's mom. He said something in Amharic.

"He says we have two minutes," said Hana.

"What? No." Lou sounded frantic. "Please can we have more time?"

Hana turned to the man and repeated Lou's plea.

"He says time is up."

The woman began to cry.

"Oh Mama. Mama . . ." Lou burst into tears.

Hana began to cry. She put her hand on her sobbing mother's shoulder.

"I love you, sister," said Hana.

"I love you too, Hana."

The woman began to speak rapidly.

Hana waited until she was finished and then spoke. "Mother says she loves you. She says when you were a baby she called you her little papaya and that she never gave up on you. She said she knew she would see you again. She says she never wanted to give you up. She wants you to come to us."

Lou was sobbing hard now. "I will come see you. I will. Please tell her that I never gave up on her either. Tell her I still have my doll. Tell her I never let them take my doll from me. Tell her she is my mother and I love her. And I love you, Hana. I love you."

"Bye bye," said the woman.

"Wait," said Lou. "Do you have an address or some way I can get a package to you?"

Hana translated to her mother as she scribbled something on a piece of paper. She held the paper to the screen.

"Do you all have a pen?" asked Lou.

"I'll take a picture of it," said Mom, pulling out her phone.

She snapped a photo and then said to Lou. "Sweetie, why don't you take a screenshot of this so you have a photo of the three of you together?"

"Oh course. Yeah. Thank you, Jane."

The man said something in a gruff voice.

"Tell him just one more minute," said Lou as he frantically fumbled with the computer keyboard.

Dylan leaned over. "I g-got it. Sit b-b-back and smile," he said.

Lou leaned back in the chair and smiled at his long-lost family.

"Tell her we are taking photos," Lou said to Hana.

Hana translated and the woman began to smooth her dress and adjust her scarf. She and Hana smiled at Lou and Lou smiled back. They all had tears streaming down their smiling faces. Dylan clicked away, taking photos.

The man barked at them.

Lou, Hana, and the woman all began speaking at once, saying their goodbyes and I love yous. "Tell her I'll arrange to call again," said Lou just as the skype call ended.

Lou fell forward onto the table sobbing. Mom came around between Dylan and Lou and pulled Lou to her. Lou buried his face in her neck and clung to her as if he were drowning.

"It's okay. It's okay. It's going to be okay," she whispered into his ear as she ran her hands up and down his back. "Shhh now. Shhhh it's okay. You found them. It's going to be okay."

Gracie stirred awake and Alice quietly picked her up. "Henry, will you come help me with Gracie," she said, heading into the living room.

Henry seemed grateful for an excuse to leave the room and ran after her.

Mom let go of Lou. "I'm going to make us something to eat. Would you kids mind going out to the garden and picking some raspberries? Sam, will you lend me a hand?"

Mom was trying to add some distraction. I knew her too well.

Lou wiped his eyes and he, Dylan, and I went out back to Mom's little garden. The heat had taken its toll on the lettuce, peas, and spinach, but the tomatoes, berries, beans, kale, and pumpkins had gone crazy. The season was just about over. I grabbed the yellow plastic harvest bucket off the hook on the fence post and waded into the lush green. Lou followed me in, as Dylan settled in on the cinder block wall that ran along one side of the garden. Dylan was allergic to pretty much every plant in existence and he still had his walking cast.

Lou was quiet as he popped cherry tomatoes into his mouth.

"Are you okay?" I asked as I began to fill the basket with ripe berries.

He nodded, but the tears started up again.

"You sure?"

"Yeah. It's just that seeing my mom has released all of these memories that I didn't even know I had. My brain is sort of spinning right now. And I can't stop worrying about how I will ever be able to stay in contact. Like they live across the world. Ethiopia is a mess and trying to get them here seems pretty much impossible with how things are for immigrants. There's no hope that they could ever live here and I'm not a citizen of Ethiopia, so I don't think I could live there."

I tried to keep my face steady. Would Lou really go back to Ethiopia for good? Just days ago he had promised me he wouldn't.

He picked another tomato. Silence hung in the heavy humid air. I searched for the right words, but before I could find them he spoke again.

"I couldn't live in Ethiopia anyway. I mean, I'm queer. I'd have to spend the rest of my life pretending to be someone I'm not and..."

He looked up at me and held my eyes. "And I could never leave you or Gracie. Or even Dragon Boy." He turned and smiled at Dylan.

Dylan smiled back, but Dylan's eyes were fighting back tears. "Y-y-you all are my f-f-family too," said Dylan.

"I'll find a way to get them here. I will. I can't live there."

Relief washed over me. Guilt was quick to follow, but more than anything I was relieved. I guess that makes me selfish, but isn't being in love selfish? If I told Lou I might move far away I would want him to be upset; maybe I would even want him to try to stop me. I tossed a few more berries into the basket and called it good.

"Let's go back inside," I said. "It's too hot out here and I'm sure the queen needs to eat by now." I didn't know what to say to Lou, so I went with Mom's methods and decided on distraction as the best bet. I set the basket of berries next to Dylan on the half wall and Lou and I made out way through the rickety gate.

"The Three Must Be Queerdos together forever," said Lou.

"Amen," said Dyl.

"All for one and one for all," I said, and I meant it.

Chapter 30

I lay on my bed, feeling the cool night air seep in through the open window. I was so glad that fall was finally winning its battle against summer. It was still unseasonably warm for early October. The air finally had a crispness to it and the nights were definitely cool. Instead of turning colors, the leaves had just turned brown and shriveled up. I craved rain.

The shorter days and cooler weather always dampened my mood. Partly it was all the back to school talk that started in early September. I hadn't been to school in years, but the dread of the first day back to school was so tied to the crisp autumn days that I would probably be fifty and still feel the creeping apprehension and sadness. It was a part of me. And on top of that, the bleakness of the Pacific Northwest winter with its endless rain and dark days made me want to crawl in bed and stay there until spring.

Maybe I had Seasonal Affective Disorder. Mom said SAD was just a normal human reaction to the changing of the seasons. She said we were supposed to be in sync with the cycles of nature and those of us who lived in areas with distinct seasons were supposed to turn inward when the dark days hit. Maybe she was right. Maybe she wasn't. Either way I hated this time of year.

This year brought more reasons to dread fall. It was fast approaching the one-year anniversary of Gray's death. I was trying to prepare myself for how I would handle that day, but something told me there was no preparing for it. At my last session with Anna we had talked about the upcoming anniversary and she had told me that it was important to just let myself feel whatever it was I felt.

There was something else, something that caused terror to slowly seep into my guts like melting ice. Lou was leaving for Ethiopia in just two days. He was on his way over and I was trying hard to savor our last couple of days together rather than dwell on my fears. I guess I hadn't expected him to leave so soon after the call with his family, but he had booked a flight the very next day. Janice and Doug had actually paid for it.

There was a knock on my door before the door opened.

"Can I come in?" Lou asked.

Gracie turned her head when she heard Lou's voice and when she saw him her face erupted in a smile and her legs exploded in happy kicks.

Lou's smile matched Gracie's. "Gracie, I love you so much," he said as he picked her up out of her swing and kissed her face. She cooed in reply. She was making so many cute babbling sounds now—ma ma ma and ba ba ba and coos and squeals. It blew my mind that she was already such a little human. It was wild and it was exciting, but it also filled me with anxiety. I felt like it was going too fast. It's like if you're a parent you can never relax because if you do your kid will leap ahead and when you open your eyes again you will realize you missed all sorts of things.

I remembered the day Mom and I had watched Juno. I had been so angry at her that day. I had hated her for all the ways she let me down. She had come into my room and apologized. I remember her words so clearly. "I kept thinking that tomorrow I would spend time with you. Tomorrow things would be better. Tomorrow I would sign you up for gymnastics and swimming and summer camp. Tomorrow I would start a family game night and have lazy nights watching movies with you.

And then one day . . . one day I realized that there had been hundreds of tomorrows and somehow you had grown up and I had never done any of the things I had planned to do with you."

I needed to do everything I could to remember that, when it comes to motherhood, there is no tomorrow, there is only today and I needed to do my best to always stay in today.

I watched Lou with Gracie. There was no doubt that he loved her and in her own tiny baby way she loved him. She was always so happy to see him. Whenever Lou was here Gracie followed him everywhere with her eyes. And nobody could make her squeal in delight like Lou. I swallowed hard. My eyes stung and I had to look away to keep the tears locked inside.

Lou looked from Gracie to me. "Are you okay?" he asked.

I nodded.

"Are you sure? You don't look okay." He balanced Gracie on his hip and walked the four steps to the bed where I sat. He put his arm around me. I leaned my head on his shoulder and felt my breath go shallow as he ran his hand through my hair.

"Promise me you'll be safe?" I managed to say.

He leaned his head on mine. "Of course, I'll be safe. I have a family who needs me," he said.

"We need you too," I said as tears began to slide from my eyes.

He pulled back and looked into my eyes, "I was talking about you, goofball. You and Gracie."

My face crumpled, and I fell into him. I buried my face in his chest and wrapped my arms around him. He held me and Gracie. "Shhh Banjo. Please try not to worry. I love you both so much. I have to do this. You know that. I promise you that I am coming home and when I get home I will be a better partner to you and a better parent to Gracie. I promise. I'm going to get a job when I get back. I want to work for a year and then think about school. Maybe we could get a place together, or maybe your mom would let me move in here?" He was speaking fast in that super hyper way that happens when he's feeling nervous or worked up.

I nodded but didn't move my face from his chest.

"Is that okay? Like, I'm not overstepping, am I?"

I shook my head. Words felt dangerous to me right now.

"Banjo, can I ask you something?"

"Yes," I managed to say.

"Do you think, I mean you can say no and that would be totally okay, but do you think that since Gracie doesn't have another parent on her birth certificate that maybe ..." His voice trailed off.

My stomach fell to my knees. I wanted him to finish what he was saying and I didn't want him to finish what he was saying. I sat up and faced him.

"Never mind. It was a dumb idea. I'm sorry."

"No, finish. Please?" I concentrated on my breath. In. Out. In. Out.

"Well, I mean Gray is Gracie's parent. No doubt. For sure. And I think she should know all about Gray. Like they are a part of her, but I was thinking that maybe I could like adopt her. You know, like a second parent adoption sort of thing?" His words were deliberate, yet flying out of his mouth.

"I was just thinking that maybe it would be a good thing for her, and for me, and for you, but it's totally okay if you think it's a dumb idea. For reals, it's okay to say no."

I smiled and swallowed the enormous lump in my throat.

"I'd like that, Bapa. I'd like that a lot."

Now it was his turn for tears.

"I love her so much. I always will, no matter what. I know what it's like to be adopted and not wanted. I will always want her. I promise on my life. And I know that she needs to know all about Gray; they were her first parent. Nobody understands that more than I do, so I would never be like jealous or try to make her love me more than Gray." Words were exploding from his mouth.

"I know," was all I could say as I fell back onto him and wrapped my arms around him and Gracie. I needed Lou and I suddenly understood just how much he needed us. He needed us to come back to. Gracie and I were his home.

He held me for a long time, but then Gracie began to fuss and then let out a giant fart.

"Oh man, she just exploded," said Lou, lifting Gracie up and away from him. A dark brownish-yellow stain spread up the back of her body suit and poo oozed out the legs.

"How can someone so tiny make something so disgusting?" Lou asked as he laid her on the changing pad on the floor while he went to get the diaper bag off my dresser.

He knelt on the floor and began to clean her up. As I watched him change her, love pounded through me. Then tiny needles of guilt began to poke at me. I tried to imagine Gray here changing her instead of Lou, but I couldn't do it. I couldn't bring the image to my mind. Instead I forced myself to remember what Anna said: loving Lou did not diminish my love for Gray and it didn't erase Gray. I deserved to be happy and Gracie deserved to be loved by Lou.

"It's going to be so hard not to talk about you and Gracie when I'm gone," Lou said as he scraped the poop off of Gracie's little butt. "I guess I could download Telegram. I think that's mostly what they use there. It probably makes more sense than trying to text. You need to download it too."

"Okay, let's do that tonight. But please don't talk about me. Please, Lou. You can't take chances with people finding out that you're queer."

"Don't worry, I won't. It will be hard to not talk about you all though. I mean not talk about you like you're my people." He fastened the clean diaper and then wrestled Gracie into a clean sleeper.

"What time do we have to be at the airport?" I asked.

"My flight leaves at nine thirty, so I guess no later than seven, or maybe earlier," he said.

"Nine thirty in the morning?"

"No, at night. There are only late-night departures. It's a twenty-six-hour flight with a short layover in D.C. I'm not sure how in the hell I'm going to survive being on a plane for that long all alone."

"Damn, twenty-six-hours?"

"Yeah, I fly into Addis Ababa and then the next day the searcher will take me to my family. I don't even know how far away that is or how long it will take," he said. "I'm so nervous. I wish I wasn't going alone."

"Me too. He's going to meet you at the airport though, right? The searcher guy, I mean."

"Yeah. His name is Yacob and he seems pretty nice. Neela said he was a good guy. I'm so glad I met her."

"You got lucky," I said.

"I owe it to you and Gracie. If I hadn't met you, I never would have met Neela."

Part of me was happy to hear that and part of me wasn't. If he hadn't been there that day then maybe he wouldn't be leaving in two days. I'm a selfish jerk, but sometimes it's hard not to be a selfish jerk when you love someone.

We sat in silence for a while.

"Hey, I need to buy some presents for my mom and my sister. Want to go with me? Target is open until ten."

"What time is it?" I asked.

He pulled his phone out of his pocket. "Just after eight. We have time. I have to find a few more girls' clothes too. Like I can't go dressed like this," he said looking down at his button down shirt and men's cargo shorts.

He set Gracie in her swing.

I smiled. "Sure, I'll go. I'm stoked to watch you try on dresses," I said, winking.

He pushed me down on the bed. "Take that back," he said, laughing.

"What if I don't?"

"Well, then I'll have to kiss you until you do."

"Okay," I said as his mouth met mine.

"You know," I said, "you're totally kissing me with poop hands."

He laughed. "Who would have thought I'd ever kiss a girl with poop on my hands?"

"Hey, do you want to stay over on the night before you fly out?"

He sat up. "Really?"

I felt my face go red. "Yeah. I'd like that." I couldn't look at him.

His smile was so huge I thought it might break his face. "Hells to the yes I would like to spend the night. Will your mom be cool with it?"

"It's not like you can get me pregnant." I was feeling unusually bold.

"I could try," he said, wiggling his eyebrows in the way he does.

I smacked him with my pillow.

"Whatever. Anyway, my mom has Alice over all the time, so it's only fair. She can't really say no. I may have to state my case, but she'll say yes. She always does."

The thought of a night alone with Lou upped my anxiety by about eight hundred percent and my excitement by about nine hundred and eighty-four percent. Not a bad ratio I suppose.

Chapter 31

Lou arrived around 3:00 with his backpack slung over one shoulder and dragging his bulging suitcase behind him.

"It's really real," he said.

"How were Janice and Doug today? Were they cool?"

"Yeah, it's weird. Janice cried and hugged me and even told me she loved me. I don't completely get it. Doug was Doug. I mean he was nice and all, but he's like a lump of wet tofu with no real personality of his own. They weren't drunk, so there's that.

"Janice though. I don't know. Maybe things will change after this. I almost felt sorry for her. She told me to charge everything to the credit card and even told me to buy my mom and sister anything they might need. Maybe she's just happy that there's a possibility that she can be rid of me." He hesitated. "But it didn't seem that way. I dunno. It was weird. Maybe my adoption was just as hard on her as it was on me. Today made me want to try harder to be friends with her or, I don't know, maybe even have her be my other mom. Is that crazy?"

"No," I said. "That makes sense. I mean she is the mom you've known the longest. My dad is a huge jerk and abandoned us completely, but I still want to know him. I still even miss him sometimes. Parents are weird."

"Are we weird parents," he asked shyly.

"Definitely, but good weird. Right?"

He nodded.

"What do you want to do today?" I asked.

"I was hoping you wouldn't mind going shopping with me again. I've been doing some research and it looks like those little satellite communicators that hikers use might be a good way for me to stay in contact with my family once I'm back here. Cell phones just aren't a good option. Way too expensive. And there's no internet in their village. These little communicators let you send and receive text messages and they only cost like thirty dollars a month for the plan. So I need to go to REI."

"I love that store. I can check out camping gear because as soon as Gracie is old enough, I want to take her camping in the mountains and the desert and on the coast and everywhere," I said.

We were being so awkward and formal with each other. I realized that he was just as nervous about us spending the night together as I was. This calmed me. I gathered up the diaper bag and Gracie, while Lou grabbed her car seat.

"You're serious about this camping with Gracie thing," he said, as he led the way down the hall and through the living room.

"I am. I want her to have all the experiences that Gray didn't get, ya know? Like Gray's mom used to promise that one day they would leave Florida and Gray's abusive asshole dad. She would settle Gray in at night by describing the Pacific Northwest and how they would one day wander the woods and see snow on the mountains and watch the stars at night. She was never able to make it happen. I want Gracie to have that. Plus, some of my best early childhood memories are of camping with mom, Sam, and James."

Suddenly a thought came to me.

"Can you take her out to the car? I'll be right back," I said, handing Gracie over.

I ran back to my room, pulled out Gray's shoe box. Gray had worked two shitty, low-wage jobs and lived on ramen to save this box of money. They were saving in case they ever decided to go on hormones or transition, and also as a safety net. They had spent time homeless and never wanted that to happen again. The day they died I had gone through their apartment gathering up their things, and Rags of course. This box of money had sat untouched since that day, other than the one time Lou and I had counted the money. Up until this moment it had felt disrespectful to Gray to spend their money.

I counted out two hundred and fifty dollars. I would take some of Gray's hard-earned money to give their daughter something they never got. I swallowed hard. "Don't worry Gray, I'll make sure Gracie has everything you never had," I whispered as I stuffed the bills into my pocket.

We got back from REI with a Garmin satellite messenger—which Lou spent over an hour trying to figure out how to activate—and a fancy backpack that could carry Gracie and hiking gear. The pack was more than two hundred and fifty dollars, but Lou financed the rest for me.

Mom, Sam, and Henry were just getting ready to leave when we got back.

"Thanks for letting me stay over, Jane," said Lou.

"Oh sweetie, don't thank me. You're welcome here anytime."

She turned to me. "I hope you don't mind that I marinated some steaks for you. They're ready to cook whenever you two get hungry." She took Gracie from me. She had agreed to give us the house to ourselves for a little while. Like a date night. I kissed Gracie and then watched my family load into the car and drive away. Lou and I were now all alone in the house.

"What do you want to do?" asked Lou.

I shrugged. "Dinner?"

"Sure."

I busied myself shucking corn, chopping vegetables for salad, toasting bread, and frying up the steak while Lou sat on the counter making small talk. You could cut the tension with a knife. As I brushed past him to put a dish in the sink he caught my arm and pulled me to him. He was still planted on the counter, so I had to look up at him. He bent down and kissed me. Heat flooded through me, landing particularly hard right between my legs. I willed my boobs to not do their Old Faithful impersonation.

We pulled apart when the smoke alarm began to shriek.

"Shit," I said. The steaks weren't burned, but there was smoke pouring from the pan and I think any hope of a tender medium-rare was out the window.

"You're smokin' hot," said Lou, pretending to shoot me with his finger.

"You know what? You were born to be a dad because you are like the biggest dork ever. You need to buy yourself some white tube socks and slip-on hiking shoes so you look that part."

"What. Ever."

After dinner we snuggled on the couch and watched the first couple episodes of Stranger Things, stopping the show every so often to make out. Around nine, Mom and my family returned home with Alice in tow. I fed Gracie, and after watching another episode with the entire family, I passed the baby off to Mom again and we went to my room. Lou brought his computer, so we propped some pillows up against the wall and sat on my bed with the computer on Lou's lap for another episode. We didn't speak. I barely noticed what was happening on the screen because my mind was bouncing with desire. My heart beat so loud in my ears I could hardly hear what was happening on the show. Having Lou in my bed for the night, and Gracie gone, unleashed so many feelings that I had tried to shove aside since Gray died, as well as a whole pile of feelings that I had never felt before.

This is what being in love feels like, I thought.

No, that's not right.

I had been in love with Gray and not felt this. This is what spending real time with someone you're in love with feels like. This is what it feels like to get to know someone as a partner and not just a friend. This is what it feels like to know that no matter what, the person you are in love with will be there for you. This is what it feels like to make a choice to raise a child together. This is what trust feels like. Trust and lust, I thought. Not a bad combination.

We could hear the muffled voices of Mom, Alice, Sam, and Henry in the other room. We could also hear Gracie start up her fussing and that started up the tingle in my chest.

"I know this is super romantic, but do you mind if I do a quick pump? If I don't you may have to dig out your rain gear."

"Pump away, my lady," he said.

The life of a teenage mom.

I had thought ahead and had all the stuff stashed in my room so I wouldn't have to go out and mess around with it. I sat down in the rocking chair, suited up with a cup on each boob, hit the switch, and tried to pretend I wasn't more than a little uncomfortable.

After I drained the kid feeders, and stashed the milk in the fridge—being careful not to let Gracie hear or see me—I climbed back onto the bed next to Lou. I grabbed my phone off the nightstand and glanced at the time. It was already eleven-thirty. This time tomorrow night Lou would be in the air on his way across the world.

I decided to be brave.

I took the laptop off of his lap and laid it to the side and then I climbed on top of him. I think he was more shocked than I was. I pressed my body against his and softly kissed him on the forehead and then each cheek. I nibbled on his right ear. He wrapped his arms around me and turned his mouth to meet mine. My body exploded. It was like every nerve had gone electric. I pressed into him and he arched his back slightly to press against me.

"Is this okay?" I asked.

He smiled, "More than okay."

"Just a second," I whispered. I leaned over and plugged in my blue twinkle lights, and then turned off my bedside lamp. I scooched back into position on top of him and smiled. I was blown away by my bravery, but I tried not to think about it too much. I'm way too skilled at ruining the moment with overthinking. Instead I let my body lead the way.

It led the way until Lou decided to take over. He rolled us over so that he was on top of me. "Can I take off your shirt?" he asked.

I nodded.

He gently pulled off my shirt. I was thankful that I had pumped my boobs, and also changed out of the gross, milk-stained nursing bra. My tattered sports bra might not be Victoria Secret material, but compared to the alternative it wasn't so bad.

He pulled off his own shirt revealing a thin binder wrapped around his chest.

"You do remember that I've never done this before, right?" he said.

"I remember," I said. It was hard to believe that confident, kind, intelligent, and wildly handsome Lou had less experience than I did. "I'm not exactly a pro. I've only done this once," I said.

We began kissing again. My skin against his felt amazing. I wanted to stay this way forever just lying here feeling my belly against his. Little memories of feeling my belly against Gray's were trying to seep into my brain, but I refused to let them in. Each time a foggy memory of Gray began to sharpen I refocused on the feel of Lou's body against mine, the feel of his lips against mine, the soft touch of his fingers as they worked their way down my body. My body stayed just one step ahead of my brain.

As Lou's fingers reached the top of my shorts he stopped. "Are you okay? I mean is this okay? Can I?"

I nodded and he tugged off my shorts. I was glad I was wearing my fancy tomboyX rainbow boxer briefs that Mom had ordered for me off the internet. When he saw them he smiled. "You're so cute," he said.

"Is it okay if I um take mine off?" he asked. This boy was well-schooled in consent and it was hot.

Again, I nodded.

He rolled off of me and pulled off his basketball shorts. He got tangled up in them and we both laughed at the awkwardness of this whole thing. He pulled them off without looking at me. Under his shorts he wore loose, orange paisley boxers. They sat low under his soft, round belly and the orange of boxers made his brown skin glow.

"You're beautiful," I whispered.

He climbed back on top of me. His legs were over mine and he wrapped his ankles around my ankles. His lips found mine again and our bodies ground into each other. Neither of us made any moves to remove our underwear. We ground against each other and as we did I felt heat build between my legs. I adjusted myself slightly until it felt like I had positioned my clit against his. I put my hands on his hips and held him against me. My eyes were closed and I let myself float along on the pure sensations of my body.

"Is this still okay?" he gasped. "I feel like, like it won't . . . it won't be long for me."

"Me too. Don't stop," I whispered into his neck and then began to kiss and lightly bite his neck, just under his jaw.

I felt his bare feet press hard against the tops of mine. Tiny sounds escaped his mouth and his breath came out in jagged gasps. Feeling his body begin to stiffen against mine caused waves of pleasure to crash through me. My own body stiffened against his as I lost all control as the waves ricocheted through me. I felt his body relax on top of me, but I couldn't stop the waves that were crashing. He wrapped his arms around me and held me until they subsided.

"Wow," he said.

I couldn't speak. I opened my eyes to see him smiling down at me. He kissed me and I noticed that he was crying.

"Why are you crying?" I asked.

"I don't even know." He laughed. "Why are you crying?" he asked.

"I don't even know," I said through my laughter.

"Maybe crying is just what we do," he said.

We wrapped our arms around each other and rolled over so we were side by side. I'm safe, I thought and that's the last thing I remember before drifting off to sleep in Lou's arms.

Chapter 32

woke up with my face just inches from Lou's. He still had his arms wrapped around me and was quietly snoring. I lay there watching him sleep until the pain in my breasts told me it was way past feeding time. I slid out of Lou's arms and somehow managed to keep from waking him.

I got dressed, pulled open the door as quietly as I could, and tiptoed down the hall to find the breast pump. I had left it in the kitchen last night. I hoped that mom had washed the parts for me so that it was all ready to go. Instead, I found Mom in the kitchen preparing a bottle for Gracie. She looked ragged, like she had barely slept all night. She was in a pair of old sweats and her threadbare Big Dyke tank top. Alice sat at the table sipping coffee, holding baby Gracie, and looking just as wiped out as Mom.

"Morning," said Alice.

"Morning. Thanks for watching her," I said.

Mom turned around. "Oh Banjo, did we wake you?"

"No, my boobs said it was way past feeding time. I can feed her." When Gracie heard my voice she instantly began looking for me. When she saw me she squealed and began her gurgling and cooing noises, then instantly switched to hungry fussing.

Alice handed her over to me. I settled down in the chair across the table from Alice. "Hey stinky toes, did you have fun with Grams and

Alice?" I asked Gracie. She ignored me as she frantically latched on and began slurping away. The relief I felt as she began to drain my boob was instantaneous. Mom handed me a cup of coffee. I thanked her and took a sip.

I tried to avoid eye contact with Mom and Alice. They had to know what happened last night. I mean they aren't stupid. Mom works for a pro-choice reproductive clinic and Alice is an obstetrician, not to mention that they're both teen moms.

"Is Lou still asleep?" asked Mom.

"Yeah."

"Okay, let him sleep. He has a long night ahead of him. When he wakes up, I'll make us a good breakfast," said Mom.

"Your Mom and I were talking, and we'd be happy to watch Gracie for you today if you'd like," said Alice.

"Yeah, maybe for an hour or two, but I also know Lou wants to spend time with her before he goes."

"He's a good boy," said Alice.

Mom smiled and nodded.

My face flushed. "Yeah."

We sat in silence for a while. Mom busied herself washing dishes and Alice scrolled on her phone while she drank her coffee. I sat watching my baby. Every now and then she would take a break from eating to give me a shy smile, and then she'd resume her eating. She finally finished up and I gave her back to Alice. Gracie watched me intently from the safety of Alice's lap. "If it's okay I'm going to go back to bed for a bit."

"Of course, dear," said Alice, lifting Gracie to her shoulder.

I returned to my room and slipped back under the covers. I pushed my back against Lou's chest so that he was spooning me.

"Hey," he said, kissing the back of my neck and wrapping his arms around me. His voice was heavy with sleep.

"We can sleep a little longer. Mom and Alice said they'd keep Gracie, and then Mom is going to make us breakfast."

He kissed my neck again. "I love you," he said.

My stomach knotted. "I love you too."

We slept for another hour and then wandered out for breakfast. While Mom and Alice scrambled eggs, flipped pancakes, and broiled slices of uncured, free-range turkey bacon, Lou sat with Gracie on his lap soaking up his last hours with her. Mom quizzed Lou as she poured pancake batter into the pan.

"Now you have an empty water bottle?"

"Yes."

"Your driver's license and passport are somewhere safe?"

"Yes."

"Money? Cell phone? Liquids are in the right containers? Phone charger and plug-in adapter?"

"I got it, Jane. Pinky swear," he said. I could tell he liked her concern.

"Have you talked to Janice or Doug yet today?" asked Alice.

"Not yet. I was thinking I might swing by and see them for a few minutes today. Or maybe I'll just text them."

"Maybe you should just call," said Alice. "Leave on a good note and then when you get back you can begin the repair work."

Lou nodded.

Henry and Rags came in from outside and Henry climbed onto Lou's lap next to Gracie as if it were the most natural thing in the world. He leaned his head on Lou's chest and played with Gracie's hand. Lou looked totally at home balancing two kids on his lap.

"Me and Rags are going to miss you," said Henry.

"I'm going to miss you too, Buddy. And Rags. But I'll be back before you know it and I'm going to bring you back the coolest present ever."

"What are you going to bring me?" he asked, looking up at Lou.

"I have no idea. I'll just know it when I see it and it will be the raddest present that any kid ever got from Ethiopia."

Henry wrapped his skinny arms around Lou again. "I love you."

"I love you too, kid." Lou looked like he might cry.

"Lou?"

"Yeah bud?"

"Can you bring me some Ethiopian money? Like maybe some coins?"

"You got it."

Henry smiled.

We spent the day watching T.V., taking Gracie and Rags for a walk, packing and repacking Lou's bag, and snuggling on my bed. With each passing hour my anxiety grew just a little bit more until I was a jagged mess.

Dylan showed up at five, just in time for dinner.

"I-I'm so excited for you," he said, biting into his chicken taco. "I w-w-wish I could have made it work to come a-a-along."

"It's okay, Dyl. I understand."

We all sat in silence. The only sound was of crunching taco shells and of Rags slurping on her feet.

I kept glancing at the clock on the stove. It read 5:48. The minutes continued to slide by. I couldn't believe it was happening.

After dinner Sam and Alice cleared the table and began putting things away as the rest of us just sat looking at each other. Nobody quite knew what to do or say.

"We should get on the road soon," said Mom.

Lou nodded.

I felt my legs begin to shake.

Lou, Dylan, and I went down the hall to my bedroom to gather up Lou's luggage. He unzipped his suitcase and went through everything one last time. Then he opened up the pockets of his backpack and made sure everything was in order. Doll Doll was shoved into his pack. She would be his only traveling companion. He touched the top of her matted head and then zipped the pack and attached a small yellow carabiner to secure the zipper.

Lou had chosen a pair of blue track pants with yellow and orange stripes down the sides, a yellow unisex t-shirt, and yellow Chuck Tailors for the trip. His look was very androgynous.

"I don't want to do this," he said, looking up at me and Dylan.

"Yes y-y-you do," said Dylan.

I couldn't speak. My words had sunk like rocks to the pit of my stomach and vanished. I bit my lower lip.

Lou's eyes met mine. He smiled and then lifted his pack to his shoulder. Dylan took his suitcase and then the three of us just stood looking at each other.

"Kids, it's time," Mom called from down the hall.

We filed out of my room into the living room where Henry, Sam, and Alice took turns saying their goodbyes. Lou got down on his knees and gave Rags a hug and then a kiss on the top of her smelly head, and then we loaded into the car. Dylan in the front with Mom, and Lou, Gracie, and I in back. The ride to the airport was quiet. Lou and I held hands over the top of Gracie's car seat which was buckled into the middle seat. Lou spent most of the ride making faces at her. She smiled and cooed at him as tears slid down his cheeks.

A half hour later Mom pulled up to the fifteen-minute drop off in the departure area of the airport. She parked the car along the curb, leaving it running, and we all got out. Lou leaned back into the car to kiss Gracie all over her fuzzy head. "I love you so much, little bean."

He held her hand for a moment and then straightened up and joined the rest of us on the curb.

"I remember not so long ago when we could have all come with you right to the gate," said Mom.

"I wish you could now," said Lou. "Sitting all alone for two hours sounds really scary."

Mom pulled Lou into a hug. "You're very brave. I'm proud of you," she said, kissing his cheek. She held him for a minute and then climbed back in the car, leaving Dylan, Lou, and me alone on the curb.

The three of us bowed our heads together and wrapped our arms around each other's shoulders like a teeny football team huddling before the big play.

"Man, can you believe how far the three of us have come?" asked Lou.

We were all crying.

"The two of you changed my life. I never thought this day would come and I don't know if it would have if I hadn't met you all. I love you guys so much," he said.

"I-I-I love you all t-t-too," said Dylan.

I was silent.

We untangled ourselves. Lou and Dylan stood looking at each other. For a minute I thought they might shake hands in some dumb dude-bro move, but I should have known better. As if on cue the two of them fell together, burying their faces in each other's necks. Dylan ran his hand over Lou's head as if he was a small child needing reassurance. Finally, they pulled apart, bumped fists, and Dylan returned to the car.

Still I was silent. The lump in my throat had grown into a mountain. I began to feel like I couldn't breathe.

"I'm coming back," Lou said. "I promise. I love you and Gracie more than you can ever know."

I nodded. I wanted to say, I love you too. I wanted to say, I love you in a way that I didn't know was possible. I wanted to say, you and Gracie are my world and I don't think I could live without you. I didn't say any of those things. I just collapsed into his arms and held on as if my life depended on it, because at that moment it did.

Lou's mouth found mine and he kissed me deep. I didn't care if Mom was watching. I didn't care who was watching.

"I need to go," he whispered.

I bit my lip so hard I was afraid it would split.

I forced words out of my mouth. "I love you so much. Please be safe. And check in with me at least once a day. Promise me?"

"I promise you," he said.

"One more thing," I said reaching into my pocket and pulling out a wad of Gray's money. "I want you to convert this to birr and give it to your mom. Or buy her a house or something."

"Dude, no—"

I cut him off. "Don't argue with me. Gray worked hard for this money to make their life better. Too late for that." I let out a small laugh without meaning to. "Make your family's life better. It's not even that much really."

He nodded, stuffed the money in his pocket, and then he kissed me one more time, adjusted his backpack, grabbed the handle of his suitcase, and headed towards the doors of the airport. I reached up and touched the smooth elephant necklace and then I yelled, "Lou, wait!"

He turned around and I ran to him unclipping the chain from around my neck and clipping it onto his. "You might need this more than I do right now," I said. "Anna says it helps with grief and elephants are all about moms and this will help you remember me and..."

He put his finger to my lips to silence me. "I love you," he said. He kissed me one last and final time and then turned and vanished through the sliding door.

I climbed into the backseat, buckled my seatbelt, kissed Gracie's sweet smiling face, and then turned and leaned my head against the passenger door window. The cool glass felt good against my cheek. Dylan plugged Mom's audio cord into his phone and brought up a playlist.

He turned around to look at me. "This playlist is called friendship. I made it for today but I was so anxious that I forgot to play it for Lou," he said as Mom pulled the car away from the curb and headed towards the freeway.

I didn't look at him or acknowledge him. He turned back around.

"That's really sweet of you, Dylan," said Mom.

They made small talk in the front while I stared out the window completely unable to focus on their conversation or the music playing in the background. The tears had dried up, but the empty pit in my stomach remained. I reached for my necklace and then withdrew my hand, remembering that it was gone with Lou.

Suddenly Mom turned up the music. It was that cheesy song from the '70s, "Thank You for Being a Friend." Mom and Dyl started singing along together. Dylan turned around to sing the chorus to me. I couldn't help but smile and that sort of pissed me off. I was invested in my sadness and here he was trying to drag me out. He turned back around as he and Mom continued to belt out that song. Dylan never stuttered when he sang.

I stared out at the passing scenery, determined to keep myself insulated from any lightness. My partner was about to fly off across the world and I was in no mood to be happy.

The song finished up.

"Can you guys turn it down, please?" I asked, not hiding my irritation.

I saw Mom glance at Dylan as she reached for the volume, but she barely turned it down a notch.

"We Are Going to be Friends" by the White Stripes came on next and the jerks in the front seat started up their ridiculous duet again. Gracie seemed to be enjoying the whole thing. She sat in her car seat bouncing her arms and legs and cooing away, as if she was joining in. Everyone in the car seemed to be dead set against me and my sadness. The song ended and before I could say anything Bruno Mars's "Count On Me" came on. My stomach clenched. Why did he have to put Bruno Mars on this playlist?

The two idiots in the front sang along, completely oblivious to my sadness. I dug my fingernails into my palms. The emptiness and anxiety inside me felt like it was about to swallow me whole. What I wouldn't do for a nice sharp razor blade, I thought.

And then suddenly Dylan was turned back around, shoving Mom's phone in my face. There was Lou sitting in one of those airport chairs totally belting out Bruno at the top of his lungs. Dylan had Facetimed Lou. I could see people around him smiling and frowning.

"You all are nuts," I yelled over the music and their cracking voices.

Lou grinned, put his hand on his heart, stared into my eyes through the phone. "I'll be there . . ." he harmonized with Mom and Dylan.

I rolled my eyes, but the smile couldn't be contained. "Okay, you all win," I yelled and let go of my determination to feel like crap. I joined in, making their trio into a quartet. "Hand me that," I said as I took the phone from Dylan and pointed it at Gracie's face. Her little face froze in confusion and then erupted in a smile and her legs began to kick wildly at the sight of Lou's phone face.

I handed the phone back to Dylan so he could hold it up to give Lou the best view of all of us.

The song ended and Mom turned the volume down.

"I love you guys," Lou said, laughing. "Like you all are the best."

"We love you too. Fly safe," said Mom.

"Bye," said Dylan.

"Hand me the phone," I said.

Dylan handed the phone back to me. I held the phone up close. "Bye. I love you," I said quietly. This time I was smiling rather than crying.

"Love you too. See you soon. Kiss Gracie for me."

We all yelled one more goodbye and hung up.

"That was like the ending of some cheesy teenage movie," I said.

"Our life is like some cheesy teenage movie crossed with an MTV reality show," said Mom.

Just then, as if the universe had been listening, the sky opened up with the first real rain storm of the season. Drops the size of dimes pelted the windshield as thunder rumbled the sky and lightning flashed off in the distance. Mom turned the wipers up to high and dropped her speed. I had brief moment of panic worrying that lightening might strike Lou's plane, but it vanished almost as quickly as it came. He wouldn't depart for another hour and they wouldn't fly into an electrical storm.

"I have a s-s-song for this," said Dyl.

"I'm afraid," I said.

The car exploded in the twinkling sound of "Vampire Weekend's A-Punk."

"Seriously Dylan, you always find a way to squeeze in a little Vampire, don't you?"

"I do," he said, as we drove into the next scene of my cheesy teenage movie life.

photo by Lisa Moody

NINA PACKEBUSH is a queer-identified, grown-up teen mama. She is the author of two YA novels, *Girls Like Me*, winner of the 2018 Golden Crown Literary Award for YA, finalist of LAMBDA Literary Award for YA, finalist of Washington State Book Award for YA, and its sequel, *Three Queerdos and a Baby*. She loves her dogs, hiking, digging in the dirt, and making comic zines about empowered snails. Nina lives in the Pacific Northwest with her partner, a collection of kids, and a pack of wayward pets.

ALSO FROM YESYES BOOKS

I'm So Fine: A List of Famous Men & What I Had On by Khadijah Queen

If the Future Is a Fetish by Sarah Sgro

Gilt by Raena Shirali

Say It Hurts by Lisa Summe

Boat Burned by Kelly Grace Thomas

Helen Or My Hunger by Gale Marie Thompson

As She Appears by Shelley Wong

RECENT CHAPBOOK COLLECTIONS

Vinyl 45s

Inside My Electric City by Caylin Capra-Thomas

Exit Pastoral by Aidan Forster

Of Darkness and Tumbling by Mónica Gomery

The Porch (As Sanctuary) by Jae Nichelle

Juned by Jenn Marie Nunes

Unmonstrous by John Allen Taylor

Preparing the Body by Norma Liliana Valdez

Giantess by Emily Vizzo

Blue Note Editions

Kissing Caskets by Mahogany L. Browne

One Above One Below: Positions & Lamentations by Gala Mukomolova

Companion Series

Inadequate Grave by Brandon Courtney

The Rest of the Body by Jay Deshpande